# HARVEST THE WIND

Also by Toni Morgan

*Echoes from a Falling Bridge*
*Lotus Blossom Unfurling*
*Queenie's Place*
*Two-Hearted Crossing*
*Patrimony*

# *HARVEST*
## THE WIND

A Novel By

# TONI MORGAN

Adelaide Books
New York / Lisbon
2018

# Harvest the Wind

a novel

by Toni Morgan



Published by Adelaide Books, New York / Lisbon
adelaidebooks.org

Editor-in-Chief
Stevan V. Nikolic



For any information, please address Adelaide Books
at info@adelaidebooks.org
or write to:
Adelaide Books
244 Fifth Ave. Suite D27
New York, NY, 10001

ISBN13:  978-1-7320742-0-0
ISBN10:  1-7320742-0-8

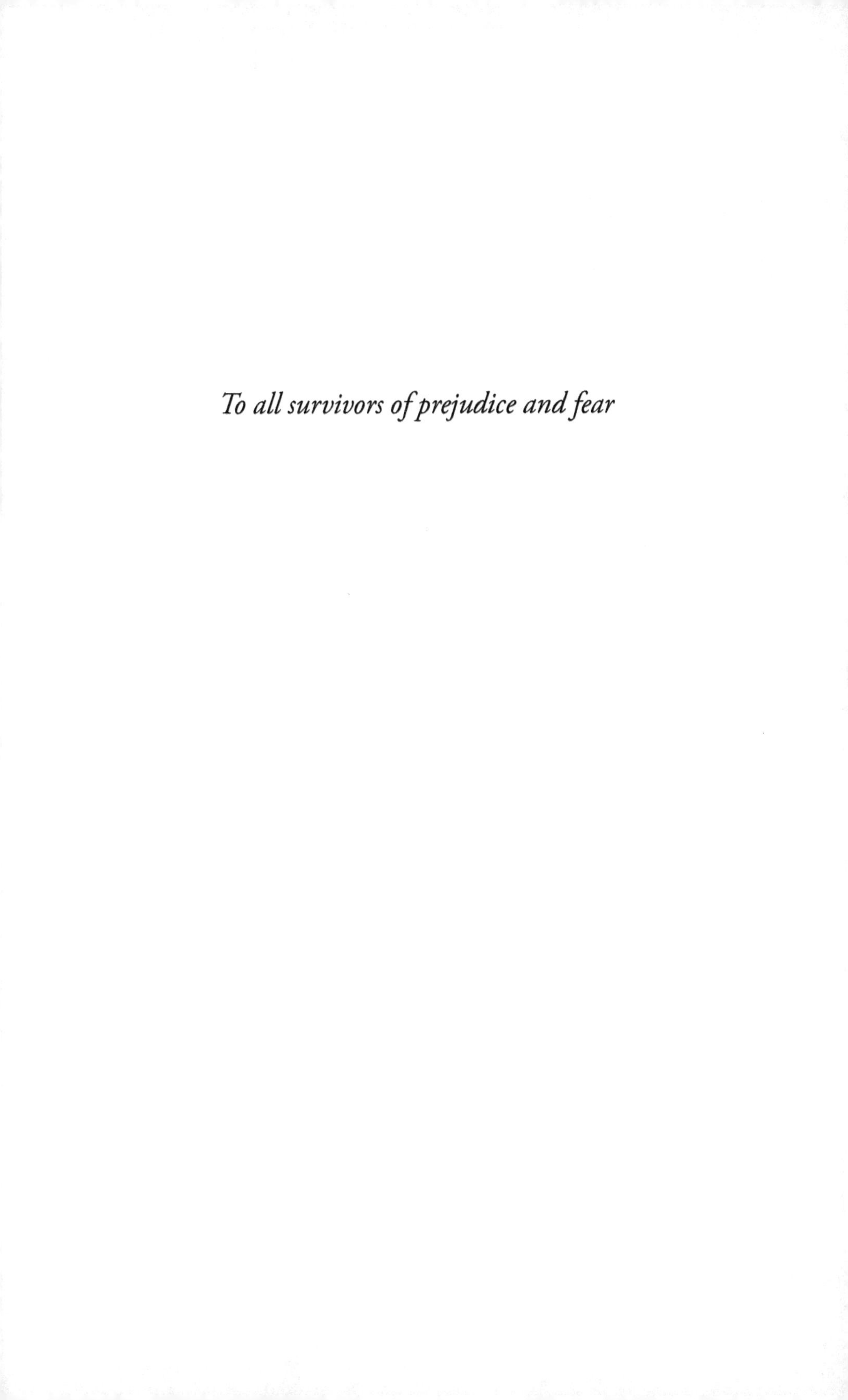

*To all survivors of prejudice and fear*

# *Acknowledgements*

Although I grew up on the West Coast, and at some level must have known about the internment camps, it wasn't until moving to Idaho and reading about an annual pilgrimage to the site by Minidoka survivors that I became intrigued. Further, I was amazed to realize that the fields I saw from my living room windows had once been worked by Japanese-American internees and German and Italian POWs. I was surrounded by WWII history. As a history major, it was too much to resist.

My thanks to the folks at Jerome County Historical Museum—reading their collection of *The Minidoka Irrigator* issues was excessively helpful in understanding everyday activities and concerns of those imprisoned at Camp Minidoka from 1942 to 1945. Thanks, too, to Friends of Minidoka, an organization dedicated to keeping Camp Minidoka, a national historical site, a profound experience for visitors. My thanks also go to Oregon Nikkei Legacy Center and Oregon Nikkei Endowment, which are dedicated to sharing the experiences of Issei and Nisei during WWII. Finally, I am thankful to all those who've spoken out about their experiences in the camps and after.

If I have gotten anything wrong in this novel, it is on me.

*Toni Morgan*

# Contents

# BOOK ONE

*The War Years*
*1941 - 1945*

# 1
# VIRGINIA

My father was a mean and bitter man. I think my mother may have died just to get away from him. As soon as I turned seventeen, I escaped, too, leaving him and Idaho behind as though the hounds of hell nipped at my heels. And yet, ten years later, here I was, about to put myself within his grasp once again.

Marc, the only one of us kids still on the farm, sounded skeptical when I called to say I wanted to come home. I persisted. "You need someone to cook and clean for the two of you." I didn't tell him about being pregnant. I hadn't told anyone, especially not Tucker, the baby's father.

The bus pulled up to the sidewalk outside the depot in Jerome. I stood and reached for my small traveling case on the shelf above the seat, along with the tin soldier that I bought when Tucker and I were in Mexico.

I peered out the window, searching for Marc. Please, God, let it be him meeting me, not Dad. Unable to spot either of them, I straightened and edged along the aisle with the other passengers. The bus driver stood at the bottom of the steep steps and reached up his hand to help me down.

Only nine o'clock in the morning and heat waves already rose from the concrete. Through-passengers hustled toward the depot to buy a cold drink or use the rest room before returning to the bus. I could almost see them wilting like day-old violets in the hot sun.

My shoulders sagged with relief when I saw my brother heading toward me, walking with his customary rolling gait. He'd broken his leg jumping out of the hay loft when we were young and it hadn't healed right.

Good looks ran in our family—Marc no exception. Tall and slender, his sun-lightened blond hair provided a sharp contrast to his tanned face, where fine lines had formed around his dark blue eyes. With only ten months between us in age, we were often mistaken for twins when we were growing up. The strong resemblance remained, although I was diligent in caring for my skin; I searched in the mirror every night for signs of wrinkles.

"I thought you might not be here," I said after we greeted one another and he'd made a brief comment on my *doll.* "Afraid you'd send Dad."

"I considered it—don't understand why you wanted to come home, when you always hated him and the farm so much." Eyebrows raised in question, his eyes bored into mine.

Heart thumping, I turned away. The bus driver passed down suitcases from where they were secured to the roof. "That one's mine," I said, before Marc could question me further.

He led the way to the truck, my big blue suitcase swinging weightlessly from his hand. "You can eat breakfast when we get home."

"So how is Dad," I asked a while later, even though I really didn't want to know.

"Getting old. Still mean as hell. Nothing's going to change that."

I stared out the truck's side window. I could only imagine.

My father, an Italian immigrant, came to Idaho with other immigrants—French, German, Polish—to work on the Minidoka Dam, the first in a series of dams along the upper Snake River.

My mother was seventeen when they met. "And the shyest girl in Jerome. With my pale skin, nearly white hair and washed out blue eyes—I couldn't believe such a good-looking fellow wanted an ugly duckling like me. The other girls in town were so jealous." She'd given an embarrassed little laugh when she told me that.

After a brief courtship, they married and homesteaded forty acres—even though neither of them knew anything about farming. I can only imagine how hardscrabble it was back then—it was bad enough when us kids were young.

To supplement the family's meager income, Dad often took work as a laborer with the Northside Canal Company, and twice he worked on new dams, one in northern Idaho, the other in Wyoming. When he worked on those projects, he stayed away for months. Leo, Marc, and I—mostly Leo and Marc—managed everything from plowing the fields in the spring to harvesting them in the fall.

Leo was thirteen the first summer Dad left and put him in charge. Marc, eleven, objected, claiming he could manage the horses better than Leo. "He's scared of them."

Dad told him to shut up and do what he was told.

All the while Dad was gone, Leo and Marc argued about who should be in charge, never more than during haying season when they fought over the hay derrick, a gigantic, top-heavy contraption used for stacking the hay. Six horses were needed to move it.

"Slow 'em down, you're gonna make the thing tip over," Leo repeatedly cautioned, even though his dire predictions never occurred; Marc really was better with the horses.

But no matter how hard we worked, how hard we tried, Dad always found fault when he got home.

"You shoulda taken better care of the horses. Look where old Floyd's side is rubbed raw, the hair gone. Why didn't you put a rag or something under the harness?"

Marc hung his head.

Dad cuffed his ear then turned his anger on Leo. "How many times did I tell you to keep those damned ditches cleared of weeds? No wonder we only got half the potatoes as last year." He took a swipe at Leo, too, knocking him sideways, into a fencepost.

My hands clenched, my stomach in a knot, I waited to be told where I had fallen short. It wasn't long in coming.

"Didn't I tell you to help your brothers?" Dad pointed to a jump rope tied at my waist. "Appears like you were doing more playing than working." I expected a cuff, but he only sneered and turned away. "Can't trust any of you."

My mother got the worst of his ire. I put the pillow over my head that night when he started going at her, his voice loud and raw. "You let those kids get away with doing nothing all summer, while I worked day and night to put food on the table for you bunch of ingrates." He may have been drinking. Sometimes he did.

The next morning, I cried when I spotted the side of Mom's face puffed up and bruised from where he'd hit her. She hushed me and said I shouldn't worry. "Go on out and do your chores, Virginia. It'll soon be time to leave for school."

Mom was gone now, and me supposed to be an adult. Still, I stared out the truck window, steeling myself for meeting my father again.

I frowned and pointed to a complex of long, low buildings in the distance, nearly obscured by roiling clouds of dust. "What's all that?"

"Camp Minidoka," Marc said. "The place is filling with Japs from Seattle and Portland."

"Do you mean they're from Japan? What were they doing in Seattle and Portland?"

"Most of them say they were born there. But the government rounded them up—all those on the West Coast. Claim they can't be trusted not to have spies among them."

Marc glanced at the dust-enshrouded buildings then returned his attention to the road.

"This isn't the only place, either. There are a couple of what they call 'internment camps' in California, one in Wyoming, another in Arkansas or Alabama, I can't remember which. One or two in Arizona, too—I'm surprised you haven't heard about them."

He took another quick look at the distant camp.

"Been a big boon to the economy around here—they say any guy who can hold a hammer can get a job."

I continued to stare until I could no longer make out anything of the camp except the cloud of dust hovering over it.

When Marc turned into our lane, it didn't surprise me to see weeds in the fields and the irrigation ditches caved in or blocked by more weeds. The place had always looked rundown, but with only Marc and our father to attend to things, it appeared to be in even worse shape than I remembered.

The house looked the same, too—paint flaked and peeling, the screen around the porch and on the door sagging, the patch of lawn in front of the house dried up for lack of water, and the rose bushes Mom planted around it grown out of control, their roots choked with weeds, their creamy white petals dead or dying. An old truck and several pieces of rusted farm equipment, unused for years, their parts periodically cannibalized for newer models, sat beneath a cottonwood tree.

When Marc pulled to a stop, I sat a minute, unable to move. Then, shoulders rigid and a stone that felt about the size of a cantaloupe in the pit of my stomach, I climbed down from the truck's high seat.

Marc grabbed my suitcase from the back. "I guess you'll want your old bedroom. It'll be all yours now Irene's gone. Some boxes and old newspapers are in it, but you can shift them out easy enough."

Our sister, Irene, married straight out of high school. Right away she and Bob moved to Portland, no doubt at Irene's insistence. Bob enlisted in the Army right after Pearl Harbor, but Irene stayed on in Portland, working in the shipyards. I'd been tempted to join her. Before discovering I was pregnant, that is.

Marc and I went in through the kitchen door. Memories rushed at me as I gazed around at the cluttered countertops, the sink filled with dishes and bowls, a pan of crusted something on the stove, and the cupboard doors, some half-ajar, all covered with fingerprints. I forced a smile.

Marc set my suitcase down. "I've got work to do. See you later."

"You're not going to eat breakfast first?"

"Already ate."

"Wait a minute." I panicked. "What about Dad? Where is he?"

"In here." The shout came from the front room.

He sat in the over-stuffed maroon chair next to the window. One glance at his caved in chest and his scrawny legs and arms told me that at least he no longer presented a physical threat.

He stared at me, unsmiling. "So, you're back."

I stiffened. I hadn't expected a warm welcome—that would have been beyond my father's capability. But maybe a sign, even a little one, to suggest he'd missed me? Without answering, I retreated to the kitchen.

For several minutes, I gazed out the open window at a turkey vulture floating high over the hay field. I thought about how scared, but at the same time how good I'd felt, standing up to Tucker, standing up for me. I could do the same here. I didn't need to let Dad's sour disposition affect me. And I wouldn't let small minds, Dad's included, hurt my unborn child.

The loud *kok-cack* of a pheasant startled me out of my reverie. With my tin soldier under one arm, I picked up my suitcases and carried them up the stairs to my old bedroom.

# 2
# KEIKO

The rattle-trap bus we boarded in Eden, Idaho—that name had to be someone's sick idea of a joke—fell into line behind a long line of rattle-trap buses taking us to Camp Minidoka, located somewhere in the desert wasteland visible through the bus windows. From my seat near the front, I leaned forward and stared at the cloud of dust towering like a giant colossus above the desolate landscape. We headed straight toward it. Frightened murmurs sprang up around me. I gave Mama what I hoped was a reassuring smile, but it probably fell short. I was as nervous as the rest—when I wasn't busy being angry at President Roosevelt for making us leave our home in Portland's Japan-Chinatown.

The driver appeared unconcerned as we drew closer and then into the immense cloud. Though early afternoon, it felt like night closing in. Grit seeped into the bus despite the closed windows and door. The air grew thick with dust and we all coughed, but still the bus clattered on.

Finally, it halted. Through the dust-filled air and the dust-covered window, I made out a small stone building. If not for the sweltering heat and the air being brown instead of white, we could have been in one of Portland's dense fogs. The bus-driver opened the door and another armed soldier stepped in. Without closing the door, the driver slowly pulled forward, up to a long tarpaper-covered building.

"This here is the Reception Center," the soldier said, his voice both raspy and lazy. "Inside they'll tell y'all which barracks yer gonna live in."

"What about our things?" My mother laid her hand on my arm, warning me to hush. I wouldn't be quieted. After enduring the foul misery of the Portland Assembly Center all spring and summer, the Center nothing more than a stock yard where we slept in animal stalls, they'd brought us to this godforsaken place. I shook off my mother's hand. "Where are they? Where are our suitcases?"

His expression making it clear a mere girl didn't intimidate him, the guard stepped from the bus without answering. Everyone else shuffled forward. Shaking with impotence, I followed. My brother gave me a commiserating smile.

Once off the bus, my eyes began to water and I quickly tried to cover my mouth and nose. The banging of hammers, shouting voices and the rumble of heavy construction equipment swirled in the air along with the dust.

"This way," the guard said, nudging people toward the door of the building. We were behaving more sheep-like than ever. I gave an angry toss of my head as I passed the man.

Inside, pandemonium reigned. Men sat behind a row of tables lining the walls. Cardboard signs with letters on them hung on the wall behind each table. My father pointed to the T-Z sign. "We need to go to that far one," he said, raising his voice to be heard above the din. A long line snaked in front of the table. "Your brother and I will go, Keiko. You stay with your mother." He smiled at Mama and told her to sit on a bench shoved up against a wall.

Another soldier, this one unarmed but with silver bars on his shoulders and a whistle in his hand, came into the room through a door at one end. He blew the whistle, and the talking and questioning immediately stopped. "If you'll all keep quiet this will go quicker," he said.

People shuffled from foot-to-foot, but no one said a word.

"After each head of family registers, you are to proceed to the laundry building, located directly behind this one." He pointed to a door in the back of the room. "There, everyone will be given a physical examination. Each family has been assigned a place to live—there will be four to six families per barracks depending on the size of the family. Trucks will arrive shortly with your things."

Lips tight together, I nodded, only slightly mollified.

"As soon as you get your housing assignment, along with a map, you can sort out what you've brought and then find your quarters. Dinner will be in your assigned dining hall at five o'clock. You'll hear the whistle telling you when to go. Project Director Stafford welcomes you to Camp Minidoka." He finished, and another man repeated everything in Japanese.

"Mama, did you understand? It's going to be like the Portland Assembly Center. We won't have a place of our own here, either, or our own place to eat. We'll be with other families all the time."

My mother, sitting on the bench and leaning her back against the wall, closed her eyes.

Like a pot of rice set on the back burner, my resentment simmered. It's all so unjust, I thought for the hundredth, no, thousandth time. We were loyal Americans. I wanted to scream my frustration, but screaming wouldn't change things and would shame my parents. Still, I struggled to remain quiet.

An hour passed before my father reached the front of the line and registered our family. We then each endured a doctor's brief examination and were ushered out of the laundry building, into a cloud of dust, to collect our suitcases.

"Look, they've dumped it all into a hodge-podge," I said when we got to the place where everyone's bags were piled. "How are we supposed to find ours in that mountain of suitcases and boxes? It's covered in dust and grit, too."

"Daughter, be still," my father said. "Your words are unbecoming. We'll find our things. I believe the suitcase with the yellow string on the handle is one of Tomoyuki's. Check the number on it, Tommy," he told my brother.

Like us, our possessions were tagged with our family number. No longer the Ugawa family, we were now 1796327. I pressed my lips together to keep my angry words locked inside.

Following a search for all our luggage, complicated by several other families rummaging through the heap, I gripped a suitcase in each hand, another tucked under my arm. Along with his own suitcases, Tommy carried a duffle-bag over his shoulder containing necessities and family treasures, including diplomas, childhood pictures and pictures of grandparents along with a vase my mother prized and some bird books and books of poetry my father declared he couldn't live without. My mother had added a few yards of muslin, scissors, needles, and spools of thread to the bag 'just in case,' plus a tea kettle, cups, and supply of tea. The final thing to go in, the bed linen we'd been instructed to bring.

Tommy nearly staggered under the duffle-bag's weight, but leaning forward, he managed to carry the bulky bag. My father carried his suitcase in one hand and with the other aided my mother as we walked through the rows of tarpaper -covered barracks with dozens of other families, also struggling with their luggage and their few possessions—a parade of the dispossessed.

Like a thousand tiny needles, windblown dust and sand peppered my skin, and with my hands and arms full of suitcases, I couldn't wipe the tears once again streaming from my eyes.

My father stopped and set down his suitcase. He took the papers from his pocket, holding them tight so they wouldn't be torn from his hands by the wind. "I believe this is our place," he said after glancing at the pages and gesturing with his head to the number painted on the side of the barracks.

Other than the number, our building looked no different from the others. Once inside the structure, our footsteps echoed on the bare wood floor. I stared open-mouthed. Our portion of the hundred-foot long building, partitioned to accommodate five families, offered a space of about twelve feet by eighteen feet. One bare light-bulb hung on a cord from the middle of the ceiling. No insulation existed between the exposed two-by-fours holding up the walls. Gaps glared between the board siding. Visible cracks surrounded the windows, too. Dust poured through them like smoke and lay on every surface.

After one glance around the space, empty but for a black pot-bellied stove against one wall and four iron cots with metal springs, shoved into a corner next to four thin, rolled-up mattresses and a pile of blankets and pillows, my mother gave a low moan and slumped against my father.

"Keiko, show your brother how to make up our beds," my father said. He ran his hand through his hair. "I'm going to find your mother something to drink."

I sorted through the bedding on the floor and pulled our sheets from the duffle bag. My father, his face drawn tight, led my mother to a spot near a window and helped her ease down to the floor.

"Wait," I said. "Here's a pillow to sit on."

"Come give me a hand," said Tommy and threw a sheet at me.

I inspected the cot he worked on. "Sixteen and you still can't make a bed properly."

"Shut up."

I pulled everything off the cot. "You have to get the bottom sheet tight or it will be a mess to sleep on."

Tommy smirked. "Go ahead. Be my guest."

"You're not getting off so easy. You can make that one up."

"Stop quibbling," Papa said, his eyebrows knotted in a frown. "Have some consideration for your mother." I mentally winced, unused to the harshness in his tone. Tommy looked as sheepish as I felt. Papa nodded and stepped out of the door, shutting it tight behind him.

When all four cots were made to my satisfaction, I organized our suitcases, setting them against the wall, next to the appropriate bed.  I didn't take anything else out of the duffle-bag since I had nowhere to put it. Although good-sized, the only closet held no shelves, nor did it have a door.

Papa returned with a cup of water and after a brief rest on a cot, my mother seemed to revive.  When the whistle blew, she said she felt well enough to go to dinner with the family.  We followed a line of people to the dining hall. Dust still filled the air.

Even when the wind didn't blow fifty-miles-an-hour, we had no respite from the dust, not while the construction of new barracks continued unabated.  Each day brought more families, some from as far away as Alaska.

Despite the continuous building, we had no hot water in either the laundry or the communal showers. Even the cold water ran sporadically.  And since the sewer system had yet to be constructed, we were again forced to brave the stench of outhouses, just as we'd done at the Portland Assembly Center.

At least in our quarters we'd found a way to achieve a modicum of privacy. Tommy and I strung ropes across the room and draped blankets from them, giving our parents and each of us separate spaces.

"What will we do when winter arrives and we need the blankets on our beds?" Tommy asked.

I shrugged. "I guess we'll cross that bridge when we come to it."

Several internees were carpenters. The authorities provided a shop with basic tools, and before long, the men began making and delivering furniture. My father chortled in pleasure with the bookcase and the small table we received. The bookcase gave him a place to store his books and the table a place to write letters and compose his poetry.

Then a grinning Tommy came in proudly carrying an armload of boards. "People are fighting over them, but there are plenty to go around. The guy in charge said we should take whatever we needed." Together, we put up shelves in the closet and a shelf near the stove for family pictures and my mother's celadon vase.

I was pleased to discover a well-thumbed Sears, Roebuck catalogue making the rounds of internees. To help our small space become even more homelike, I ordered enough material to make curtains for the two small windows and to replace the blankets separating our beds.

They were adequate, but not nearly as well-made as my mother would have produced, if she'd only been well enough to sew. Because of the dust, every time she tried to do anything, she ended up gasping for breath.

The curtains were finished just in time. The blankets they replaced were needed on our beds, since night temperatures had started to dip into the thirties. Tommy and I took turns fetching buckets of coal from a huge pile at one end of our barracks block. Even with a fire in the black, pot-bellied stove and wearing two pairs of socks, I often woke with nearly numb feet. I could see my breath, too. But by noon, the heat returned. We dressed in layers and it seemed we were constantly putting sweaters or jackets on or taking them off.

We'd been at Camp Minidoka ten weeks. My mother's constant wheezing grew worse, and like many, she was plagued by difficult to stop nosebleeds. One morning before breakfast, my father confided his concerns. "I am worried about your mother's deteriorating health. She needs to visit a doctor."

"I've been urging her to go," I said. "But each time I suggest it she refuses. Yesterday, I asked her again. She said she didn't want to waste the doctor's time."

"I will speak with her."

The next afternoon, the nurse at the hospital ushered us into Dr. Toma's office. Dr. Toma had graduated from Harvard Medical School and did his residency in a hospital in New York City before returning to the West Coast to practice. He was well-respected in the camp. For several minutes, he listened intently to my mother's lungs and heart. Finally, he straightened. "She has asthma," he said as I helped my mother sit up once again. "Her lungs are struggling with the cold and the dryness."

"She didn't suffer from asthma in Portland." I patted my mother's hand, hoping to reassure her. "She caught colds easily though, and they often went into her chest."

Dr. Toma spoke in a solemn voice, lecturing me. "Portland is west of the Cascades and at sea level. It's warmer and damper. Here we are inland and at 4000 feet. It's an entirely different climate. The lack of moisture, plus all the dust in the air, isn't good for your mother. I'll write a prescription for something to help—my nurse will get it for you." He turned to Mama. "You need to wear a mask over your mouth and nose to filter out the dust, Mrs. Ugawa. And keep inside as much as possible."

He didn't add what I already knew. Mama's struggle to breathe strained an already weak heart.

Then, like someone turned a switch, the daytime heat disappeared and rain started—hard, day and night rain—turning our confined world even more desolate. For weeks, the rain beat down on the roof, until the noise seemed to fill every nook and cranny of my brain. And though it washed the dust from the air, an instant relief for my mother, the rain turned the walkways between the rows of barracks into ankle-deep, muddy quagmires.

My parents mostly remained inside, my father reading or writing, my mother resting on her cot, while Tommy and I attended our new school—him a junior, me a senior. But when my mother wished to bathe or use the latrine, Tommy carried her on his back, the same when we went to the dining hall to eat. I assisted our father. Mud got tracked everywhere because there were no entry spaces in any of the buildings where we could remove our shoes or scrape the mud off them.

As abruptly as it began, the rains stopped and the weather turned bitter cold, the air once again dry. The wind never ceased. Several times a day Tommy and I filled the stove with so much coal the chimney glowed red. Despite the stove's warmth, the simmering kettle of water on top adding moisture to the air, plus frequent visits to Dr. Toma, my mother's asthma returned worse than before. A high whine, like a trapped insect, accompanied every breath she took.

One Saturday, fully dressed, she lay on her cot under several blankets. Her eyes were closed, but I sensed she was awake. From the other side of the thin partition separating our quarters from our neighbor's, came the young, piping voices of two children playing at jacks or pick-up sticks.

"Would you like a cup of tea, Mama?"

"No thank you, Kei-chan," my mother said, using my childhood name, something she'd been doing more of late.

My father sat at the small table, working on a poem. "Here you are, Papa." I set a cup of tea next to his elbow. Deep in thought, he didn't appear to notice.

"I believe I'll go and see Suki and Margaret," I said.

Neither of them responded, so I donned my coat, made bulky by the two sweaters I wore beneath it. Even with the multiple layers, once outside I shivered in the freezing wind.

I slipped many times on the footprint-pocked mud, now frozen and crusted with snow, before I reached the recreation hall. People looked my direction when I struggled to get the door closed, frowning as the blast of cold air reached them. Two pot-bellied stoves, one at each end, inadequately heated the large space. After stomping snow from my shoes, I went to join my friends.

I spotted Tommy at the opposite end of the room, playing a board game with several other boys. At another table, men played cards, drank tea, and talked. At yet another, several women sat knitting or sewing and sharing stories.

I slipped out of my coat and draped it over the back of the chair. "Has everyone finished their homework?"

"Don't be a nag," Margaret said. She shivered and pulled her coat tighter. Margaret constantly complained of being cold. She also hated school.

Suki smiled and leaned toward her. "You can look over my paper if you like. It's due tomorrow, so you'd better get busy."

Both of Suki's parents died from influenza when she was six. For years, she'd shuttled between three sets of aunts, uncles, and cousins. At Minidoka, she lived with the family of her father's youngest sister, who often called on Suki to care for her children, ages two, three and five. Suki once told me she thought the children were the reason her aunt and uncle took her in. That was the only time I heard her voice criticism of anyone. She quickly amended her words by saying how much she enjoyed her little cousins and appreciated her aunt and uncle's generosity.

"Okay, okay," Margaret said. "After dinner, I promise." We all knew it unlikely our fun-loving, procrastinating friend had even started the paper we'd been assigned to write. She snapped her fingers to an imaginary tune. "I wish we had some music, a juke box or something. I'd love to dance right now."

"Get me a piano and I'll play you some jitterbug," I said. I loved playing fast-paced popular songs, even though my piano teacher had disapproved. I feigned a laugh, staring at my dry, chapped hands. Only the year before I'd taken such pride in them, rubbing in lotion every night, cream into the cuticles, buffing my nails—they were a stranger's hands now and I doubted I could play anything with them.

Margaret distracted me from self-pitying thoughts. "I hear they're going to build basketball and tennis courts for us next summer."

"I love to play basketball," said Suki, agreeable as usual.

"Let's hope they supply the basketballs and tennis balls to go with them," said Kazuko. She drummed her fingers on the table and appeared bored, a pose she often affected.

"And racquets," I added. I didn't care much for sports, but it would be good to have tennis and basketball courts to play on—anything to take our minds off our surroundings—even if I made a fool of myself doing it.

The Ito family moved into our barracks. Tommy soon made friends with Mako Ito, even though Mako was a year older and a senior, like me.

The Itos had a daughter, too.

"She went to Japan to live with Mr. Ito's sister for three years. You know how some Issei send their kids back to the old country," Tommy said, holding the door open for me with his foot.

"Oh yes. We girls must learn how to become proper wives." I carefully held the heaping bucket of coal away from my coat. Tommy carried another bucketful.

My brother ignored the sarcasm in my words. "Nobuko, that's her name, lived there for a little more than two years when Mr. Ito wrote and told her she had to come home. She was on her way when Pearl Harbor happened. They haven't heard from her since. They don't know if her ship got sunk or turned back. She might be in a prisoner-of-war camp right now," he added, wide-eyed, the small scar caused by a missed baseball standing out on his chin.

I stared at him. "That's terrible. No wonder Mrs. Ito always has such a sad expression on her face. They must be sick with worry. Poor Mako." As I said the words, I realized how lucky our family was—at least we were together. I slipped out of my coat and gave Tommy a hug. He allowed it for a moment before pulling away and ducking his head, preventing me from seeing the expression in his eyes.

My girlfriends went gaga over the handsome Mako Ito. They made the flimsiest excuses to come to our barracks. "I wonder if I can borrow one of your hair-ribbons," they asked me, or "When is the next history assignment due?" Silly things I'm sure he saw through, if he was there and not off somewhere with Tommy, Billy Hara, and the rest of the boys they hung out with.

Personally, I found it difficult to be infatuated with someone with whom I practically shared living quarters. I did notice he made a point to always say goodbye or goodnight to me when he left our quarters. He was very polite.

# 3
# *VIRGINIA*

I should have told Marc about being pregnant. I should have told him when I called to say I wanted to come home. But I figured he'd tell me to stay in Phoenix. I should have told him and Dad when I got here, but again took the coward's way and kept silent. Even wearing the baggy shirts I'd found in Leo's closet, I knew my pregnancy couldn't stay hidden much longer. Even so, I kept stalling, afraid when I told them they'd throw me out on my ear.

My time for stalling ran out on an especially bitter December afternoon. I stood on a kitchen chair, reaching to put a painted tin star on top of a tree I'd gotten from a tiny lot in Eden the day before, when Marc walked into the room. Leo's old shirt had pulled up, revealing the growing bulge rising above my pelvis.

Marc stared at me. "When did you plan to tell us, when you went into labor?"

I climbed off the chair, the star still in my hand. "I guess," I said with a sheepish grimace I hoped resembled a smile. "If I thought I could get away with it."

Marc didn't fall for my sorry attempt at humor. "Who's the father?"

"No one you'd know."

"Have you told Dad?"

I shook my head.

"When will you?"

I shrugged. "When my water breaks and I start yelling?"

"What are you two talking about?" Neither of us had heard Dad come out of his bedroom. His eyes darted from Marc to me. I clenched my hand and the points of the tin star stabbed into my fingers. Marc and I answered together.

"She's pregnant."

"I'm pregnant."

Dad's head jerked back as though he'd been struck. He stared at me with narrowed eyes, his mouth a grim slash across his face. "How far gone are you?"

"Four and a half months." Thump, thump, thump— the blood pulsed in my throat. I was twenty-six-years-old, but I felt like a teenager.

"I knew when you ran off like you did nothing good would come of it. At least Irene got married first. Who's the father? A soldier? Or some other fly-by-night you met in a bar?"

Naturally he'd think the worst. "Neither, but you don't need to know his name. I'm done with him."

"What are you planning to tell folks—our neighbors, our friends?"

He exaggerated. We had no close neighbors and few friends. "I thought I would say my husband is a pilot, his plane shot down."

"Well, I guess you're good enough at lying, you might pull it off. Just don't be asking me to back you up."

Marc said nothing until our father returned to his bedroom. "I need to go to Jerome for a part," he said, heading toward the door.

"Wait. I'll go with you." He kept walking. I put the star on the chair and ran to get my jacket. The fun of decorating the tree had flown. At least neither of them said anything about throwing me out.

Marc drove the truck in silence. We were nearly to the highway before he spoke. "I'll go after him if you want. Make him pay for what he's done."

I swallowed and put my hand on his forearm, more touched by his words than I could express. "Don't bother," I finally managed. "He isn't worth your time or effort."

The silence became companionable after that, each of us thinking our own thoughts, until we reached the outskirts of Jerome.

Jerome, the sign outside town said, was founded in 1907 by officials of the Twin Falls-Northside Land and Water Company. Faded red Christmas bows flapped against lamp posts as we drove down East Main to Lincoln.

Marc pulled up in front of the cafe next to the old Northside Inn, once the pride of Jerome, but now rundown and mostly vacant. "Let's get lunch. I'm hungry and you need to remember you're eating for two now."

After our burgers and French fries, Marc dropped me off at the grocery store. I needed a few things I hadn't found in Eden the day before. "I'll pick you up in a half-hour," he said before heading off to get the part he needed.

I recognized a few of the other shoppers and nodded to them as we pushed our carts down the aisles. Christmas only a week away, a festive mood filled the store—along with exasperation because of the bare spots on many shelves, spots an assortment of items filled only a short time before.

The empty spaces put me in mind of all the young men, including my brothers, Leo and Paul, who would be absent from their spots around the tree on Christmas morning, and later whose chairs at dinner tables would remain vacant, some forever.

In a somber mood, I paid for the items in my cart. The cashier tried to cheer me. "A warm wind is coming our way I hear. Guess we're gonna get us a Chinook for Christmas."

I took the change he held out and stuffed it into my pocket. "Being warmer would be nice, especially for all those folks out at that Japanese internment place."

"Yeah, well, you ask me, they got life pretty easy."

"Doesn't look so easy to me," I said. I gathered my things and left, but I felt his eyes following me all the way to the door.

On the way home, I could see Marc mulling something over. "What's on your mind?"

"Some talk at Gordon's." Gordon's was the local farm and feed store where most farming information got gathered and redistributed by Milton Gordon, grandson of the original owner.

"What?"

"Remember how I told you the government said farmers needed to solve their own labor shortage problems?"

"Uh-huh." He'd mentioned it several times in fact, worried how he'd manage come summer. The Twin Falls newspaper was full of talk about impending labor shortages, too. With so many Magic Valley boys gone to war or to work in factories or shipyards, most farmers expected to be short-handed. The paper urged high school students and community groups to volunteer. I remained skeptical how well that suggestion would work.

"Well," Marc continued. "Next spring, they say they're going to let some of the Japs at the camp work in the fields."

I frowned, instantly concerned. "Isn't that dangerous? What if some of them really are spies, maybe even worse?"

Marc shrugged. "The authorities will have sorted all that out. I'm sure they've gotten rid of any troublemakers. Help would be a godsend. With Paul and Leo gone and Dad next to worthless in the fields, I can't get all the work done alone. I could use three of them just clearing the ditches."

"I can help." He didn't answer, but looked pointedly at my stomach. "Well, after the baby's born," I said. "I don't want someone around who might murder us in our sleep."

February brought more snow, and I felt myself grow fatter by the day. To conserve fuel, we kept trips to Jerome at a minimum, but every few weeks one of us or both Marc and I needed to go in. Each time, I stared in the direction of the internment camp, wondering what the people did to pass the time and whether they managed to stay warm. This time of year, with the shortened daylight hours, the temperatures rarely rose above the teens. I thought about having a baby in the conditions people said existed in the hastily built barracks. They had a hospital, run by a white doctor and head nurse. Who knew, though, if the Japanese doctors and nurses were trained.

My own confinement would be in a hospital in Twin Falls, the town where my doctor practiced. I'd seen him twice and each time he assured me everything appeared fine. I'd given him the story I told Dad, about my husband being a pilot and being shot down. The doctor was all compassion. I felt only a twinge of guilt at my lie, which I'd come halfway to believing.

The life I'd led in Phoenix, the dancing, the drinking until two in the morning then going to work the next day, still half-drunk, coming home and doing the same the following night, seemed never-ending. I'd been thrilled and excited at first, flattered that so many men, including several Army pilots, wanted to take me out on the town. Then a co-worker introduced me to Tucker. Tucker swept me off my feet with his phony charm and seemingly endless supply of money and important friends, like Jack and Kay. The charm began to wear off even before we went to Mexico. By San Ignacio, I'd had enough.

Now I found I could easily cast aside our time together, the circumstances of him being my baby's father, nothing more than a biological accident. I wanted no part of him, or whatever he might offer in the way of financial support. I would find a way to get through this and raise the child myself. The first challenge would be figuring out how to pay the hospital bill. My mother used to say, 'Heaven will provide,' but I doubted God was on my side. I couldn't remember a time I thought He was.

"Penny for them," Marc said.

I sighed. "They're not even worth a penny."

We were headed into Jerome once again. Marc needed to stop by Farmers and Merchants Bank. I went along for the ride. In the distance, Camp Minidoka's guard towers and buildings were easily visible now the constant construction had ended. "What do you suppose they do all day?"

"The Japs?" Marc shrugged. "Who knows?"

"Well they must do something. Otherwise they'd go stark-raving mad."

"I suppose they read, make things. The kids go to school."

"Wait, kids are in that place? Who teaches them?"

"Virginia, close to nine-thousand people live in those barracks. They're not all farmers, fishermen and nursemaids. They have doctors and lawyers among them, and yes, even school teachers. It's like a city, and a hell of a lot bigger one than Jerome. They're probably a hell of a lot better educated, too."

I stared at the rows and rows of snow-covered barracks, trying to imagine educated people living in them. And children.

"Have you heard anything more about getting some to come and work for us in the spring?" I asked.

Marc glanced over at me and grinned before returning his eyes to the highway. "I thought you wanted no part of them. I thought you were scared about getting murdered in your sleep." He swerved to avoid a pothole.

I brushed his teasing aside. "Well, have you?"

"We need to apply. An association of some sort is form-ing. They'll inspect us and the farm. Assuming we get the help, I guess we'll have to make sure they don't run off."

"You mean we have to guard them? How in the world are we supposed to guard them with only the two of us?" We both knew Dad would be no help.

Marc shrugged his shoulders once again. "I'm not sure. We'll need to figure that out somehow. I'd sure like to have the place really productive, maybe for the first time ever."

Ironic, too, if it happened with the help of people many considered enemies. I left that thought unspoken.

I didn't only mean physically when I said Dad would be no help. Since returning to Idaho, I hadn't heard him utter a kind word to or about anyone. Japan, the Japanese, and Camp Minidoka were prime targets for his ire, especially Camp Minidoka. "They don't do a damn thing but sit on their asses, because everything is provided for them at taxpayers' expense. Governor Clark had the right idea when he said to send them all back to Japan, then sink the island."

Dad and Idaho's former governor weren't the only ones who viewed the residents of Camp Minidoka with suspicion and contempt. "If they'd done nothing wrong, the government wouldn't have put them there," seemed to be the common sentiment in and around Jerome and Eden. I didn't know for sure how I felt, but the grimness of Camp Minidoka held my attention. Unlike Dad, I doubted they pampered anyone out there.

The Twin Falls newspaper reported the people in the camp would plant crops in the spring. The place took in some thirty-thousand acres, though much of it, like our property, filled with lava outcroppings, in other words, unsuited to planting. The article stated that with irrigation, enough food would be grown to feed the people at Camp Minidoka and at some of the other camps. Irrigation being key. A part of the Northside canal system ran past the camp, so, per the newspaper, ditches could easily be dug to bring water to the proposed crops. I paused at the 'easily' bit. Obviously, whoever wrote the article had never dug ditches in Idaho's rocky soil for a living.

A man with the Agricultural Adjustment Administration came by the farm one afternoon. He and Marc talked while I served them coffee. I'd frowned at the near-empty coffee tin when I made it, wondering if I'd be able to find more on the stores thinning shelves.

"Food for Defense," the man said, words we'd often heard or seen. They were constantly on the radio, in the newspaper, on billboards. "Farmers all over the country. Everyone's asked to raise more food. Wheat, corn, even sugar beets—no need to depend on foreign cane sugar." He readjusted the fingerprint-smeared glasses on his nose. "So how much more do you think you can produce here?"

Marc stirred cream into his coffee before answering the man's question. "Well, a good bit depends on how much help I can get."

"How much do you need?" The man looked like he might have been an accountant or worked in a bank. I felt sure he'd never spent any time on a farm.

Marc glanced at me. "Our two brothers are overseas. One is in Europe, the other in the Pacific. Our father can't help much and as you can see, Virginia will be a mother soon. I'm going to need people to help with the irrigation ditches, cultivation and weeding and eventually the harvest.

I'd say at least five—more if I can get them, especially when we harvest."

The man wrote something in his notebook then stood and thanked Marc for the information. He ducked his head to me, his pale cheeks suddenly flushing. "Thank you for the coffee."

"I think I made my point when I told him how shorthanded we are with both Paul and Leo overseas fighting," Marc said after the man left and I'd filled the dishpan with soapy water. "I'm pretty sure we'll get as much help as we need from the Camp."

"They'll be working crops there, too, if the newspaper is right. All the other farms in the area will need help as well. Do you think there'll be enough laborers to go around?"

"We'd better hope so."

I handed him a coffee cup to dry. "Assuming you're right, where are we going to put them?"

"We'll clean out the old prove-up cabin."

The prove-up cabin was more a shack than a cabin. Dad built it when he and Mom first homesteaded the property, before they built the house. For years, the place had been used to store who knew what all. Junk mostly. I didn't look forward to the job of cleaning it, especially now that my belly had grown so round.

"We'll get started tomorrow. Before you get so fat you can't bend over."

I gave him a fake scowl. "Very funny."

We began right after breakfast the next morning, another brilliant blue day with the temperature near freezing.

Underneath my jacket, hat, and gloves, I soon worked up a sweat. I carried a box of dusty canning jars to the house when Dad came out the kitchen door.

"What are you and Marc doing with the prove-up?"

"Cleaning it out."

"For what?"

"You'll need to ask Marc." I chided myself for cowardice as I moved past him and went inside with the jars. When I came back out a couple of minutes later, the two were in an intense argument.

Dad's face flushed red. "I'm not having a bunch of goddam Japs living here."

"Leo and Paul are gone. Virginia won't be able to help much longer. You can't. And the government wants us to produce more than we've ever produced before. So, tell me, Dad, what do you want me to do?"

Dad then went off on a tirade against Leo and Paul. "Traitors to their own family, that's what they are. Instead of volunteering like they did, they shoulda stayed here where they're needed. Irene, too. Why doesn't she come home now her husband's gone off to fight?"

Marc, as angry as I'd ever seen him, leaned into Dad's red face, his own blotchy, the cords in his neck protruding. "She's doing her own bit. I'm damned proud of her, and so should you be. I'm proud of Paul and Leo, too. I envy them. You think I don't want to be with Leo, kicking the shit out of the Krauts? Or with Paul, wherever he is in the Pacific? If you think I don't, you're crazy as hell. But this needs doing, too, and by damn if I need the help of those Jap internees to do it, I'll get their help, you damned cantankerous old goat." His voice had risen to a shout by the time he finished.

Without uttering another word, Dad stomped back in the house and slammed the door, while Marc stomped toward the prove-up. "Don't just stand there," he growled at me over his shoulder.

The junk piled nearly to the ceiling, we'd cleaned about a quarter of the way in when we discovered a box of dynamite. Wispy gray threads fell from the wooden box through the gaps in the widely-spaced floorboards to the dirt below.

I scowled. "The thing looks like it's growing hair."

Marc had calmed down by then. "It's old. No telling how stable it is. Give me a hand, and let's get it out of here." We gingerly picked up the heavy box and crab-walked it outside then carefully slid it into the back of the truck. "I'll drive out to a lava outcropping and blow it up. Why don't you go in and fix lunch? While you're at it, make sure Dad hasn't died of a heart attack or something."

As I cut sandwiches for the three of us, a huge boom shook the house. The window panes and the dishes in the cupboard rattled. A cupboard door swung open. Heart pounding, I ran outside when Marc drove up a few minutes later. "Are you okay? That explosion shook the whole house." My voice came out higher pitched than normal.

Marc gave an embarrassed grin. "My ears are still ringing." He followed me back to the kitchen and poured himself a glass of milk then gulped it down.

I didn't say anything, waiting for him to explain.

"I set the box on a pile of dry twigs and lit them. Then I ran like hell to the truck and peeled out. When I looked in the rearview mirror, though, it didn't seem like the fire had caught. I was about to turn around and go back when the thing blew." His hand shook as he set the empty glass on the counter. "Stuff flew in every direction, up, down and sideways—like being in mammoth wind and hail storm at the same time. A big chunk of lava nearly hit the truck—landed not more than ten feet in front of me. Scared the hell out of me."

I shuddered, picturing the whole thing in my mind. "Dad came running, shouting 'what the hell'…. I told him the Japanese were attacking."

"Oh, God, you didn't."

I gave a sheepish grin. "Not really. If I did, he probably would have gotten his shotgun out and started shooting before he knew it was you."

We looked at each other and began to laugh, harder than normal, then both of us stopped.

"Shit," Marc said.

An understatement, I thought.

After lunch, we returned to cleaning out the prove-up.

# 4
# KEIKO

Something woke me. The scratching sound of windblown tumbleweed rubbing against the outside wall of the barracks? Sparks, a lump of coal shifting and settling in the stove? One of the little girls in the next apartment, coughing or talking in her sleep? I lifted my head, alert but puzzled. Then it hit me. Silence…my mother's heavy breathing…gone. I sprang from my bed. "Mama!"

I threw back the curtain separating us and couldn't move. My father sat on the edge of my mother's cot, holding her hand. Silent tears washed his cheeks. He raised his eyes to mine and slowly shook his head.

Tommy appeared at my elbow, rubbing sleep from his eyes.

"She's gone," I said. "Mama's gone."

We were Christians, but like many *Issei*, my father still clung to the traditions of his childhood—the Shinto belief of spirituality in the natural world and the Buddhist traditions of stoicism, obligation, and patience. What happened in the days following my mother's death were a combination of all three.

We held her funeral at night, a custom begun years before to accommodate those who worked during the day. On a table holding a vase of flowers and a photo of my mother as a young woman, many left scrip or money, another well-established custom. The room smelled of incense. Papa, Tommy, and I stood inside the door, shaking hands, and greeting each person as they entered the reception hall, dutifully listening to their condolences and their stories of similar family tragedies.

Papa tried to remain strong, but when not speaking with someone, he wore a pained expression and seemed to stare into nothingness. Tommy and I were just as distraught. Tommy couldn't settle anywhere and jumped at every sound. I couldn't speak without my voice breaking or tears threatening.

Reverend Greene led the service. Reverend Greene had followed his flock of Japanese-American Methodists from Seattle, and now lived in Twin Falls with his young family. My father sat still and upright, his hands resting in his lap, appearing intent, listening to every word Reverend Greene uttered. I clutched a handkerchief in my hand and tried not to cry. The words, no doubt meant to heal, were meaningless to me. Tommy sat beside me, his body rigid. I'm not sure he listened to Reverend Greene's service, either. Afterward, someone served food, but I didn't want to eat. I thought I'd never be hungry again.

The following day dawned cold and wet. A few people gathered in the small graveyard; my mother wasn't the first to pass at Camp Minidoka, though most were cremated and their ashes placed in urns and kept by the families. My mother had been terrified of fire and made Papa promise she would be buried instead. Reverend Greene again said words, but I didn't listen.

A plain wooden cross carved with one of Papa's poems marked Mama's grave. The poem had been one of her favorites.

> *Flowers bloom*
> *She treads among them*
> *Their fragrance*
> *Lifting her spirit aloft*
> *Heavenward*
> *To God*

As the cold and dreary weeks followed one after another, winter and my mourning merged, melding into one, intending to go on forever. Then, almost overnight, the snow began to melt, drip-by-drip, from the barracks' roofs, once again turning the walkways between them into muddy bogs. Our first spring at Camp Minidoka had arrived.

On a cold but sunny day, Papa and I walked along the barbed wire fence separating us from the rest of the world. Patches of green sprouted in the fields beyond. Although empty of water, along the banks of the canal emerald green cattail spears poked out of the ground.

A small rabbit hopped along the fence ahead of us then froze as a large bird flew over, its shadow crossing over the ground in front of the rabbit. Papa's eyes followed the bird for several moments before he spoke. "A red-tailed hawk. She and her mate have a nest in that cottonwood next to the canal." He pointed to a tree where, half-way up, I spotted a large bundle of sticks wedged in the crotch of two limbs.

When the bird and its shadow were gone, the rabbit darted to a sage brush and hid beneath the twisted branches. The red-tail made another searching sweep.

"I miss the many songbirds from home. How your mother loved them, especially the swallows." His eyes went soft with memory. "She said they were the happiest of birds, swooping through the air, taking pleasure in the joy of flight."

I looped my arm through his. "Every morning she made sure to fill the feeder outside our kitchen window."

Papa nodded. "The birds would be plentiful and noisy right now, the beginning of mating season." He stopped talking for a moment and we strolled on. "It's also interesting to observe the many birds of prey in these skies, hunting for mice, baby rabbits—like the one now hiding under the sage bush—and even snakes."

I pretended to shudder when he mentioned snakes. I envied his interest in birds and poetry. He missed Mama. Naturally he missed her more even than I did. Still, I thought he could be content or nearly so anywhere, whereas I continued to grow more restless and resentful. My mother's death was yet another thing to be held against the authorities who brought us to this godforsaken place and seemed intent on keeping us here. I wanted to yell and stomp my feet, throw my head back and howl like a dog. Most of all, I wanted to scream my indignation at someone.

Scream at whom, though? The camp administrator? He'd give a false smile and do nothing. The government? So nebulous and far away, it would be like fighting smoke and cobwebs.

I took a shaky breath. We walked along the fence for a while longer then turned onto the path leading past the administration buildings, eventually taking us to some dormant vegetable gardens.

"You will be graduating in May," Papa said, breaking into my brooding thoughts. "Have you an idea what you'll do when summer comes?"

I frowned. I wouldn't be preparing to enter university next fall on a music scholarship, so what does he think I'll do, take up knitting or bird watching, write a novel, move to New York City. "I have no idea," I said.

He ignored the bitterness I'd made no attempt to keep from my voice. "They say it is possible to get permission to leave camp and go to college in the Midwest or in the eastern part of the country. They tell me some of your friends are planning to apply."

"Papa, you know we don't have the money for that. I would need a scholarship." A representative of an organization claiming to be dedicated to the education of Japanese-American women had come to our school. She said her organization would help match up students and colleges. Despite what Papa had been told, getting the necessary papers to leave would be difficult, let alone finding a school offering a music scholarship to a Japanese-American, especially one who hadn't played the piano in nearly a year.

"Your old music teacher might be willing to help," my father said, appearing to read my thoughts.

"Maybe." Mrs. Bevins wrote me several times while we were still in the Assembly Center in Portland and twice after we arrived in Idaho, but none since before Christmas. I feared she'd forgotten me. I stared at the path. Tears pricked my eyes.

"You should write her again and ask. In the meantime, I'm told local farmers need help in their fields. Internees are encouraged to volunteer. Perhaps you'd like to do that?" He said the words as though asking a question, but they sounded more like a command, or at the least a very strong suggestion.

I stopped walking. Shock drove away my self-pity. "Work in the fields for one of these illiterate farmers? Papa, you must be joking."

I rubbed my fingers together and thought how they used to play a concerto or a ragtime tune, never stumbling as they rippled over the keys. The idea of those same fingers hoeing or pulling weeds horrified me.

"I think working on a farm would be a good opportunity for you. You need to get away from this place—meeting a few 'illiterate farmers' would be good for you, too. You tend to pre-judge people by what they do for a living."

"What about you and Tommy? Who would look after you?"

Papa didn't fall for my poor attempt to shift the reason for my reluctance to the two of them. "I expect Tommy will find work as well. You know they are planning to grow crops here at Camp Minidoka. He might find work right here."

My father hadn't spent all his time with his head in the clouds, writing. He'd been busy making plans for my brother and me.

"I don't like the idea of you being on your own so much of the time, Papa. Who will fix your tea the way you like and remind you to eat?" He frequently got lost in his reading or writing and often didn't notice the whistle calling us to meals.

He turned to me, his head cocked to one side, a slight smile on his lips, reminding me of when I was a little girl and said something that amused him. "I believe I can manage, Keiko. As, I'm sure, can Tommy."

We turned onto another path, this one leading to the poultry area. I scuffed my shoe against a rock and thought again of my brother, seventeen now. Since January, when the Secretary of War announced a reversal of the army's policy about Nisei men being unacceptable for military service because of their ancestry, army recruiters came regularly to our high school, encouraging boys to sign up as soon as they graduated. Mako Ito already spoke of joining and I feared Tommy might do the same when he turned eighteen.

Right now, though, his mind remained full of baseball. Several teams were being organized and Tommy, in his glory, right in the middle of it. Papa was right; given a choice, this summer at least, my brother would remain here at the camp.

That night I dreamed of the time I played Rachmaninoff's Piano Concerto No. 2 in a recital. The dress I wore, pale yellow and of the lightest material. Mama had made the dress for me, her stitches in the rolled hem so small they were nearly invisible. Waiting backstage, my hands shook, as they always did before I played in public. The moment I took my seat on the piano bench, lowered my head and took a deep breath, my nervousness fled. I lifted my hands and for a fraction of a second held them poised above the keys before I brought them crashing down to begin the fast opening of the concerto.

I still brimmed with exhilaration when I woke in the morning, but long before I opened my eyes, I became aware of the lumps in the thin mattress on my narrow cot in my small space at one end of Barracks 31, Block 14 of Camp Minidoka Internment Center. My exhilaration drained away, replaced by angry frustration. Another day in a hostile environment. Another day without my mother.

Suki attempted to draw me out after breakfast. Everyone gone from the dining hall, we were alone except for the storekeeper restocking some shelves in the back room. Cleaning the kitchen after the morning meal was our daily chore.

"I believe we'll have an interesting time in school today, don't you?" Suki said, drying a dish, and adding it to the stack. We were scheduled to dissect a frog in biology class— someone had caught some frogs near the canal and our biology teacher used chloroform on them. The whole idea made my stomach roll over, but Suki liked science. She claimed she wanted to become a nurse.

What else might be considered interesting, I didn't know. Mostly we'd be doing reviews in preparation for end-of-year testing, and working with the younger children. Since they didn't have enough qualified teachers at Minidoka, some of us seniors spent part of each day helping in the primary grades, listening to children read or working with them on art projects or their spelling words, whatever their teachers required.

"Maybe," I said, but went no further. I scrubbed at some dried oatmeal stuck to the side of a pot. When the cooked-on oatmeal wouldn't come off, I filled the pot with water and set it aside to soak.

Suki tried again. "I understand Mako Ito plans to volunteer for the army."

"Yes," I said and reached for another pot. "Though why, I have no idea."

I'd talked with him about his plans several times in the past weeks. Mako tried repeatedly to convince me I was wrong to feel resentful.

"I'm an American," he'd said just the night before, pacing back and forth in our small living area. "I want to defend my country." He kept his voice lowered because my father had retreated behind his curtain, retiring for the night.

"After how we've been treated? Yes, we're Americans. I know that. But what our country has done to us is wrong. German and Italian Americans haven't been rounded up and put in concentration camps—and that's what these so-called internment camps are." My voice may have started out lowered, but soon escalated. "We aren't dissenters or protesters. We aren't a hotbed of spies. Even J. Edgar Hoover has admitted as much."

I, too, stood and began to pace.

"The only reason they've put us here is because of our yellow skin and 'slanted' eyes. It's pure racism." Adamant and heart pounding, flushed with the fervor of my argument, I gave Mako no opportunity to convince me of an error in my thinking. "They're even talking about Nisei being in a special unit—that's segregation. Why would you go along with that? Why would anyone?" I flung up my hands for emphasis, then flopped down in my chair once more.

Unlike me, Mako kept his voice only slightly above a whisper. "Because it's a brilliant idea. If Japanese-Americans are spread out in the army, our efforts will be diffused." He resumed pacing then stopped again and turned to me. "If we are together, though, in one unit, and we prove ourselves, our service will bring honor and recognition to all Nisei."

I shook my head, refusing to be convinced. Partially because I was right, but underneath my arguments, I realized I didn't want Mako to leave Camp Minidoka. I didn't want to think of him going off to fight in Europe or anywhere else. The realization nearly took my breath away. But I couldn't tell him that. Eventually he said goodnight, before returning to his family's space at the opposite end of our barracks. Tommy looked at me and shook his head then he, too, went to bed.

At the memory, my eyes smarted with unshed tears. I blinked them away and washed the last dish before handing it to Suki.

She said nothing. I sighed and emptied the dishpan. I finished wiping down the counter and told her I'd see her later, then went back to our barracks to prepare for school.

The weeks passed. I thought often about my mother. Not as she'd been in recent years. Even before we came to Camp Minidoka, beginning about the time I entered high school, she'd lost some of her zest for living, becoming frailer with each passing year. I thought instead of how she'd once been. I remembered running to her the moment school let out to tell her about my day. She'd listened to my prattle with rapt attention and absolute interest.

Every winter she took Tommy and me to the Meier and Frank department store's Christmas windows. We'd gaze at the windows on Morrison then weave our way through the crowds to the windows on Sixth. Like us, Mama would watch the fancily-dressed wooden figures gliding on their narrow tracks—across what looked like an ice-covered pond, or inside a Victorian house, dipping and twirling, appearing to decorate a Christmas tree. The scenes were magical. Mama's eyes, like ours, sparkled with merriment and wonder, her cheeks bloomed.

In the spring and summer, while Papa remained bent over his writing or translating, worked at the University Club, or tutored one of his students, Mama took Tommy and me on picnics along the Willamette River or outings to the museum or to the big library on 10th, where books filled shelves that stretched to the ceiling.

Later, when her health began to fail, she loved to listen to me play the piano while she sewed or embroidered. She especially liked Chopin nocturnes and the dreamy music of Brahms and Shubert. But her toe tapped when I played a lively Strauss waltz or a popular dance tune.

No matter what, though, even when sick, Mama never missed the opportunity to vote. Because Papa was an Issei, an alien, when they married, the government stripped my mother of citizenship. Congress eventually restored citizenship and the right to vote to all who'd been affected by their unscrupulous law, but it took them ten years to do it. Mama took her restored rights seriously. Long before election time, she studied the issues and the slate of candidates and listened to their speeches. Well informed prior to going to the polling place, she proudly cast her ballot.

That was the woman I missed, not the shadow-woman she became, the woman who gasped and struggled to breathe. For that woman, death must have come as a release, allowing her to cast off her weak and traitorous body. Somewhere her spirit now soared, happy in its freedom from restraint. That thought alone kept me from giving in to sorrow.

Over two-hundred students took part in our high school graduation ceremony near the end of May, including Margaret, which surprised her friends much more than her. No one knew how she accomplished such a feat. Her homework assignments were always late and slapdash, when they were done at all. But she easily passed her year-end examinations and graduated, I'm sure to the relief of her parents. "I always do well on exams," she said. "I just don't like homework. It's boring." We all nodded, as though we understood. In truth, it quite amazed me to discover it possible to procrastinate or brush aside one's assigned duties and still succeed.

Mako, true to his word, volunteered for the Army as soon as school let out. I refused to go see him off. Instead, I went for a walk. When I changed my mind, I rushed toward the spot where the Army bus waited to collect him and the other volunteers, but I was too late. The bus had already closed its door.

I stood with sisters, brothers, mothers, girlfriends, and wives and watched the bus lumber away. At the gate, it paused for a moment before turning onto the road. The driver shifted gears and the bus slowly picked up speed.

# 5

# *KEIKO*

To keep from thinking about Mako, about missing Mama, about where we were, I reluctantly decided to follow Papa's dictate, couched as a suggestion. I dutifully put my name up to work for a local farmer and after a brief interview, they assigned me to a farm about fifteen miles from camp. The irony of their Italian name, Franconi, didn't escape me.

The wife showed me to the room where I would sleep. She struggled to climb the stairs. Pregnant, she would soon be confined. "You'll stay here," she said. "The men will sleep in the prove-up."

I had no idea what she meant by prove-up, other than the three teen-aged boys and the older man, John Sato, who'd accompanied me to this place, wouldn't be staying in the house. The woman opened the door to a small room no more than ten feet square, a palace compared to my curtained-off barracks space.

"This is my brother Leo's room" she said. "He's in the Army now." I nodded and entered while she remained by the door. I set my suitcase on the bed. "Come downstairs when you've put your things away—I've cleared out the top two drawers of the bureau—and I'll show you around the kitchen."

When she left, I went over to the window and discovered the room overlooked the front yard. Bordering a ragged patch of grass were rose bushes, most of them nearly choked by weeds. Only when I leaned closer to the window did I notice a small cleared section next to the house. Some rusted and strange-looking equipment I didn't recognize and an old truck, its hood up, were parked under a tree. Beyond were the fields. Already, John Sato and the three teen-aged boys were being led out to them. They carried hoes and shovels in their hands, even the man leading them. I opened my suitcase and put my things into the empty drawers then retraced my steps to the kitchen.

"You're a tiny thing," the woman said in her low, musical voice. Not only pregnant, she towered above me by four or five inches. Her wavy blonde hair tied back in a pony -tail, wisps fell around her face. I thought her very pretty by Caucasian standards. Oval face, straight and narrow nose. Her eyes were an astonishing navy-blue.

"I'll need to get a step-stool so that you can reach things on the shelves," she said.

"I'm to work in the house, not the fields?"

"Most of the time. I'm not going to be able to fix meals for all these people much longer. You can call me Virginia, by the way. What's your name?"

"I'm to cook?" I struggled to keep the panic from my voice. Though my mother had tried, I had limited cooking skills. Tommy would say none. I had no idea how to prepare the kinds of meals I would be expected to produce.

She smiled. "Help keep the house up, too, and the yard whenever we can manage. At times, though, like harvest, we all work in the fields."

My temples pounded as her words sank in. I finally nodded. "My name is Keiko Ugawa."

I set a plate of sandwiches in front of the old man, who never looked at me without hatred pouring out of his eyes. The sandwiches were made with potted meat. I'd trimmed the crust and cut the sandwiches into triangles, as my mother used to do.

He stared at the sandwiches, his lower lip protruding. "What's this?"

I couldn't keep my chin from lifting a fraction. "She said you like sandwiches."

"Huh. Is that what you call these piss-ant things?"

"That's enough, Dad," the woman said. I couldn't feel comfortable calling her Virginia. "Let's go, Keiko. They're coming back from the field now. Dad can look out for himself." The old man always ate alone and inside. Meals were served on a picnic table at the side of the house. "Don't mind my father," she said when we were outside. "He's more hot air than anything else."

A lunatic more likely, I thought.

After a week, the husband, Marc, said the ditches already showed improvement. The woman explained to me that the main canal, which came off the Snake River, wove for miles through what was once nothing but sage brush, tumbleweed, and lava outcroppings. Ditches and sub-ditches ran off the main canal, she said, offering a specific amount of water to each farmer based on the number of acres under cultivation. A ditch bordered the Franconi property. With wooden 'dams', they could block or release water into their fields. Weeds and cave-ins prevented the water from flowing evenly between the rows. An ingenious system, but not new. I remembered studying in school how the early Egyptians did much the same with the Nile River.

While I made the customary sandwiches, the woman fixed a salad of potatoes to go with them and filled a bowl with the applesauce she'd made several days before. I found the applesauce almost sickeningly sweet. I later smiled to myself seeing my two former schoolmates picking at both after the two platters of sandwiches were eaten. Neither of them said much, only muttered under their breaths to one another. I knew John Sato only by sight. He lived in one of the barracks of unmarried men and looked to be close in age to the woman and her husband. He was the only one to eat either the potato salad or the applesauce.

"They've barely touched a thing other than the sandwiches," the woman said after the men left and we carried the lunch things back inside. "It's been like that all week. I'd think they'd be starving after working all morning out in the sun."

"We're still not used to this kind of food, even though it's mostly all we get in the camp dining hall, too."

"What do you mean 'this kind of food'? What's wrong with it?" She put the empty plates into the metal dishpan and sprinkled soap powder over them then turned on the water.

"Nothing, it's just not what we're used to, what we'd prefer."

She swished the water in the pan and appeared a little miffed at the suggestion she couldn't prepare an edible meal.

Her curiosity got the better of her though. "What kind of food would you *prefer?*"

I pretended to ignore her stress on the word prefer. "Rice balls are good for lunch. And pickled ginger, some fish maybe, if it's fresh." I inwardly shuddered, thinking of the strong-smelling canned tuna sometimes served to us in the dining hall. "My mother often fixed us picnic lunches with rice balls and vegetables. And fried tofu stuffed with sweetened rice for dessert."

"Can all that rice be good for you?"

I stood at the table and spooned uneaten applesauce back into the jar. At the thought of my mother, tears came unbidden to my eyes. I brushed them away with the back of my arm. "We have rice for all our meals in some form or another—plain and steamed, wrapped around bits of fish and vegetables or pickled ginger, sweetened, fried. It is very versatile."

"I guess I'll need to add rice to my shopping list." Her tone had lightened.

That afternoon we took a break from housework and pulled more weeds from around the rose bushes. I smiled to see her struggle to get to a kneeling position.

Waving off my offer to help, she told me her mother had planted the bushes years before. "They've been neglected since her death."

I didn't tell her my own mother had recently died, but for the first time I felt some kinship with the woman.

A loud yell awakened me. A short time later, a knock sounded on my door. Moonlight shone in through the window. I pulled a sheet around my nightgown and went to the door, opening it a crack.

"The baby is coming," the husband said. "She wants you."

I pulled back, my eyes blinking in alarm. "I don't know anything about having babies." I gripped the door knob. "She said she was going to a hospital in Twin Falls, that everything was arranged."

"It's too late. Hurry and get some clothes on."

"But I don't know what to do." My voice shook.

"Neither do I, but at least you're a woman." He hurried away and clumped down the stairs. I stared after him for a moment then dressed and went to find her.

She lay on her side, her knees drawn up. Her nightgown and the sheet beneath her were wet and streaked with blood and feces. "Oh God," she gasped. "I didn't know it would hurt like this." She tensed as another pain gripped her.

I reached out to brush hair away from her sweating forehead. My hand trembled. "I think the pain wouldn't be so bad if you tried to relax instead of fighting it," I said, though where such a notion came from, I don't know.

"I've brought hot water and towels." The husband entered the room with a steaming pot in his hands and towels tucked under his elbow. He kept his eyes averted from the woman on the bed.

"What for?" I asked.

"I've heard that's what's needed."

Obviously, none of us knew anything about childbirth, not even the woman. I glanced around the room, surprised she had no reference books on the subject. I vowed when I became pregnant, assuming I did someday, I would read everything I could about it. I stared at the man, his hands hanging at his sides. He looked utterly helpless. Surely, he must have birthed calves or piglets. They were farmers. Farmers knew about such things. At least they were supposed to.

The woman licked her dry lips.

"She needs a glass of water," I said.

He quickly turned and left, appearing eager to have something to do. He brought the water and I held the glass to his wife's lips. Greedy with thirst, she emptied it. He left again, saying he would get more.

I turned back to the woman as another pain swept her. The water came back up. I used the towel to mop it, but she was too intent on her pain to notice. "It's coming," she gasped when the spasm had passed. "Look and tell me what you see."

I reluctantly lifted the hem of her nightgown. I didn't want to look. Everything was swollen and smeared with mucous and blood. At first, I didn't know what I was seeing. Then I made out a smooth crown. "I think I see the head."

She cried out when another pain tore at her and the baby's head pushed out a little farther.

"It is coming," I said.

She cried out again and the baby's head completely emerged, then the shoulders. The rest of the body slithered out in a puddle of blood and pulsing cord. I stared, unsure what to do next.

"What is it?"

"A girl, I think."

She pushed to her elbows. "Let me see her."

I started to pick up the baby, but pulled my hands back when she let out a wail. "The cord is attached to her still. What are we supposed to do with the cord?"

"Cut and tie it with thread." She smiled at me. Her face glowed with sweat and something else. "At least I know that much. Mom's sewing basket is over on the dresser. I was going to sew some buttons back on one of Marc's shirts."

A brightly-colored tin soldier stood on the dresser next to the sewing basket. I got the scissors and thread and returned to the bed. "Where is your husband? He should be doing this."

"You mean Marc?" She laughed. "He isn't my husband. He's my brother."

"Oh." I took a closer survey of the bedroom. It contained a second bed, but I saw for the first time the room clearly belonged to a woman. I wanted to ask where her husband was, but didn't. Most likely overseas in the Army, where Mako would be after he finished training. I'd written to him. I wondered if he'd write back.

"I'll tie and you cut." When we finished, she lay back against the pillow. I cleaned up the baby with the cooled water and another towel then put the baby on the woman's chest. Without warning, she tensed once more. "My God! There must be another one."

Instead of another baby, it was what I later learned was called the placenta or afterbirth.

I emptied a dresser drawer, set it on the floor and lined it with more towels. "I'll put the baby in here so we can get you cleaned up."

I called downstairs for more hot water, but the house remained silent, neither her brother nor her father answering. I took the pot down to the kitchen and filled it. On the way back to her room, I got soap from the lavatory. She told me where to find the sheets and I got them, too, along with a clean nightgown from her dresser. Together, we managed to clean her and change the stained bedding.

Just as dawn turned the room rosy gold, she murmured her thanks and closed her eyes. Before she fell into sleep, she opened them again. "You need to call me Virginia," she said. "Please."

# 6
# *VIRGINIA*

I hadn't expected we'd get a girl. In the beginning, she kept her eyes blank and her mouth unsmiling, hiding her thoughts and emotions. Although she appeared too small to cause us any harm, beneath that frozen surface, I sensed anger. Her anger worried me. She didn't want to be with us. Still, despite her anger and distrust, I had to admit she was tidy and clean and worked hard. I don't believe the kitchen ever sparkled so, even when my mother was alive. I told her as much, but she only stared at the ground and said it was nothing. I felt like a slave owner.

After Bella was born, holding her in my arms, feeding her or simply resting as Keiko quietly went about preparing most of the meals as best she could, sweeping and dusting and making beds, I wondered how I would ever have managed the night of my daughter's birth without her. Marc certainly proved himself no help.

I purposely waited to tell him I was in labor. The pains had been coming all day, mild at first but steadily growing stronger. He questioned me at lunchtime, but I told him nothing was wrong, only a twinge. I shouldn't have put him and Keiko through all that, but without money to pay the hospital bill, I believed I had no choice. How foolish. When

I think about what might have happened if something had gone wrong…well, I would be forever indebted.

With Bella's birth, Dad had a new topic to rant about. Instead of going on about Paul and Leo deserting us, the easy life the people at Camp Minidoka had at taxpayer expense, rationing, and a host of other things he considered designed to make his life miserable, it now centered on whores and bastards living under his roof.

My blood boiled whenever he said that about Bella. How could he call an innocent baby such a terrible thing? "What's wrong with you? She's your granddaughter." I renewed my vow to find some way to protect my daughter from my father's vicious tongue.

Several times Keiko tried to insert herself between Dad and me, but her efforts, sadly, did little except bring his hateful words down on her head instead of mine. I appreciated that she never asked about Bella's father. One day I would tell her—as a cautionary tale if for no other reason.

To my relief, and no doubt Keiko's too, Dad mostly kept to himself. When at home, he sat on the porch and whittled, retreated to his room, or worked on his truck. The ancient vehicle was subject to frequent breakdowns, but at least working on it kept him out of our hair. When it ran and he had fuel, he sometimes drove off to visit one of his cronies.

Shortly after breakfast one morning, leaving Dad with his head stuck beneath the truck's hood, Keiko and I went into Jerome for groceries and to pick a part up from Gordon's Farm and Feed for Marc, my first excursion since Bella's birth.

"Shall we stop at Camp Minidoka and check on your father? We have time and enough fuel." We'd prepared everything for lunch before we left and the meal only needed to be carried outside to the picnic table. I remained more curious than ever about the camp.

Keiko eyes lit up. "Thank you. I'd like that."

As we drove down the road that led toward the gate, the sheer size of the place and the number of barracks, block after block of them, astonished me. Keiko must have guessed my thoughts. "It's nearly two miles from one end of the complex to the other," she said in a voice unmarked by emotion.

A young, armed soldier held up his hand and I stopped. "This is government property, ma'am. No trespassing."

"We've come to visit her father." I nodded to Keiko.

After several questions and answers, he took my name, Keiko's, and Keiko's father's name before he let us through his gate.

"With that angelic face and those innocent blue eyes, he looks like he should still be home and in school," I said when we drove away.

"I couldn't say," Keiko said. Her voice sounded bitter and I gave her a puzzled frown, but she stared straight ahead. "You'll need to park over by that fence." With no shade, we made sure both truck windows were rolled all the way down. Even so, the seats would be burning hot when we got back. A young male kestrel with a coppery red chest perched on a strand of the barbed wire fence. He flew off when we shut the truck doors.

Keiko led the way past a display of large boulders, earthen mounds, and several black locust saplings. She nodded at what was obviously a work in progress. "An *Issei,* an immigrant like my father, designed this garden. Volunteers are doing the work."

"It's like a condensed landscape," I said. Even incomplete, the garden appealed to me.

Lined with lava rocks, the path we followed had been raked and tended. No paper or weeds littered it. I stared up at a guard tower as we passed beneath it.

Keiko's gaze followed mine. Her mouth turned down. "The barbed-wire fences and the towers were erected several months after we got here—even though they couldn't cite one incident of someone trying to escape. People became so angry, some cut the wires and went out into the desert in an act of defiance." She lifted her chin toward the guard tower. "They say they put them up to protect us, but if that's the case, why are their guns pointed inward?"

Only then did I take in the two rifle barrels poking from the box at the top of the tower. My eyes widened and a prickling had the hair on my arms standing on end.

"Have they ever shot anyone?"

Keiko shook her head, but as we walked on, I had the peculiar feeling that a target hung on my back.

The feeling continued even as we walked between the rows of tarpaper-covered barracks where children were playing. The children appeared indifferent to the guard towers, the barbed wire, and the dirt. In a patch of shade, five little boys, their dark eyes gleaming, were engaged in a loud game of marbles. Two little girls played with their dolls, a miniscule tea set and a board used as a makeshift table. The children being unfazed by their surroundings only added to my shock.

Some teenagers sat on a rough concrete step, gossiping and laughing. One of the girls waved to Keiko as we passed. Keiko, still holding Bella, waved back.

"What are those colorful things the girls have in their hair?" I asked, glad for something to say.

Keiko glanced over her shoulder at the group. "Just something we make in our spare time. Crepe-paper flowers. This is our barracks."

Many of the barracks we'd passed had small gardens in front of them. Some held mainly flowers and shrubs while others were strictly for vegetables like carrots, radishes, cabbage. Still others were a combination of the two. Edged by the ubiquitous lava rocks, each was a stark contrast to the building it bordered. The garden in front of Keiko's barracks was more like the garden near the gate. It even included a small pond.

"Is this one yours?"

Keiko nodded. "My father built it in memory of my mother. Tommy and I found the rocks in the desert."

Keiko had only recently confided her mother's death. She couldn't keep the anger from her voice when she told of the dust in camp causing her mother to struggle for breath. I understood her frustration at being unable to help. I'd experienced the same feelings when my mother got sick and later died. But Keiko hadn't wanted my sympathy when she told me of her mother's death, nor did she want it now.

She opened the door to the barracks and we went inside. I nearly gasped at the crushing heat in the narrow hallway. Keiko quickly opened the door to their apartment, where I found the heat marginally less intense. She called out. "Papa?" No one answered. "He must be out bird-watching or visiting a friend."

The door behind us opened. I turned as a thin, distinguished-looking man with gray hair and eyes that glinted like obsidian entered. He carried a small bucket and sponge. A towel was draped over his arm.

"Papa!" I took Bella from her arms so that Keiko could greet her father, expecting her to give him a hug. She bowed instead. "This is my father," she said when she straightened. Though they hadn't hugged or even touched, her voice filled with pride when she introduced him. "Papa, this is Virginia."

"How do you do, Mr. Ugawa?" I held out my hand. He paused for a fraction of a second, then took it and dipped his head in a slight bow.

He offered me a seat in one of the room's four chairs. "Thank you," I said.

"Keiko-san," he said, turning to his daughter. "Go to the dining hall and get some hot water to make tea for our guest."

"I'll be right back," Keiko assured me. "The dining hall isn't far." I wondered if she thought I was afraid of being alone with her father.

Mr. Ugawa sat. "Your baby is young."

"Five weeks tomorrow." I would have told him how much his daughter had helped with her birth, but didn't know if she'd want me to. "Her name is Bella."

"Ah, yes. Beautiful." His eyebrows went up. "Your family is Italian?"

"My father is. Like you, he came to the United States in his youth. My mother was Swedish, but born here—in

Jerome, actually." I babbled. "Keiko tells me you're a translator. Do you speak Italian as well as English and Japanese?"

"Only a little." He held up his fingers to indicate how small.

I gazed around the room, searching for something else to say. Muslin curtains hung to the floor from a rope stretched across the room. I assumed they separated the family's sleeping quarters. In addition to the chairs, this portion held a small table with writing material, an overflowing bookcase, a black pot-bellied stove, and a shelf holding pictures along with a beautiful green vase. Newspaper had been stuffed into a large crack beneath the window. Unfortunately, the dust still passed through. A light film covered everything.

Following the direction of my eyes, Mr. Ugawa gave a rueful smile. "We're still not used to all the dust here. I've tried to take over Keiko's battle with it, but so far I've not succeeded."

Keiko returned with a steaming tea kettle in hand. Mr. Ugawa opened a square tin with a picture of cherry blossoms and a snow-covered mountain on the side. He scooped out tea leaves and sprinkled them in the bottom of a clay pot then poured in the steaming water. As the tea steeped, Keiko explained that in the winter, when they kept a fire in the pot -bellied stove, water remained always ready for tea. "It's too hot for the stove now, so they keep water simmering for us in the dining hall."

Hot was right. I'd taken the light blanket from around Bella and loosened her nightie. I wanted to loosen my own clothes. Still, I was surprised to find that I enjoyed the tea's mild flavor. I even began to feel a bit cooler as we drank.

Mr. Ugawa appeared to enjoy his tea as well, cupping his hands around the bowl and slurping loudly. Keiko queried him about her brother, Tommy.

"He complains the work is hard and the temperature is often intolerable, but he likes to be useful. Working here at the camp has another benefit, of course, allowing him to play baseball in the evenings and on the weekends."

Keiko chuckled. "My brother would rather play baseball than eat. I don't believe he misses his violin for a moment."

"His violin? What happened to it?"

Keiko studied her teacup, appearing uncomfortable at my question. "We had to sell it," she said. "Along with my piano."

Mr. Ugawa explained. "We were only allowed to bring what we were able to carry."

"What about your furniture, your dishes?" I once again took in the bareness of the room. "What about all the other things a family collects?"

Keiko stared out the window, the corners of her mouth drawn down once more. "Sold as well. Some were able to put their things in storage, but most people, like us, sold everything."

I somehow felt responsible. "I'm sorry."

When we finished our tea, Keiko excused herself. "I want to say hello to Mr. and Mrs. Ito before we leave. I promised Mako I'd check in on them."

On our way to the truck, I told Keiko I needed to use the restroom.

"It's in that building," she said, nodding to one on our right. "You will have no privacy."

I grimaced and shrugged. "Must be all the tea I drank."

"I'll wait outside with Bella."

I went into the building to find several other women and girls. Two women were taking showers, their naked backs turned to the others, their clothes carefully folded on a bench pushed against the wall. At the sinks, a couple of teenaged girls stood gossiping and fixing their hair. A mother held her young toddler over a toilet—one in a row of toilets, several already in use. With no partitions or doors, just a large open room, I sensed I was to be the object of all their eyes. But no. Each woman, girl and even the toddler acted as if I was invisible. I forced myself to walk to an available toilet, my footsteps echoing on the concrete floor, pull up my skirt and squat. I don't believe I've ever been so self-conscious. I washed my hands in the sink, but found no towels to dry them.

Keiko examined my flushed face when I emerged, but said nothing, merely handed Bella to me. Two boys ran past us, their laughter trailing behind them.

As predicted, the truck felt like an oven. I started the engine and drove back to the gate, nodding to the guard as we went through. Once back on the highway and picking up speed, the inside of the truck cooled off a bit. I tried to forget the restroom.

"Did you notice how my father hesitated before shaking hands with you?" Keiko asked. I nodded. "Most *Issei* men are the same," she said. "In Japan, men and women shaking hands is considered taboo, immoral even. Or at least that was so when they were growing up."

"Good grief."

Keiko giggled. The unexpected sound of her amusement made be smile. "I know," she said. "Very old-fashioned."

"Do you suppose it's changed?"

"I doubt it." In an unusually talkative mood, she went on to tell me about the daughter of the family she'd gone to see. "They've been trying to contact her through the Red Cross, but so far, they've had no word. Mrs. Ito fears her ship got sunk."

"Why did she stay in Japan for two years? That's a long time for a visit." Thinking fleetingly of my own experience in Mexico, of how anything might have happened to me after I made Tucker, Jack and Kay leave me in San Ignacio, I mentally shook my head at the unexpected consequences of the decisions we make.

"Her parents sent her to live with her aunt and uncle for a time, three years, in fact, so that she could learn the customs of our ancestors, and to learn how to be a 'proper wife.' She took classes in all sorts of things."

"Like what?" A rabbit hopped half-way across the road in front of us. I slowed down to avoid hitting it. The rabbit paused then darted madly back to the safety of the ditch.

"Poor little bunny."

"They're everywhere in this part of the country. Farmers hate them." I smiled when she frowned. "What kind of classes did the Ito's daughter take?"

"Cooking, flower arranging, tea ceremony, dance, probably learning to play an instrument like the *koto* or *samisen*. It's not unusual. Many parents send second- and even third-generation daughters back to the 'home country' as they call it."

"And boys?" I asked, thoroughly intrigued with this custom. "Do they go?"

"Oh yes. To learn *kendo* and martial arts, things like that."

"What about you, Keiko? Did your parents plan to send you and your brother when the time came?"

An empty farm truck passed us in a rush of wind and noise, spitting out gravel and dust in its wake.

"No." She sounded adamant. "We have no family in Japan, plus my father says our future lies ahead of us, not in the past. Besides all that, I have no intention of becoming a 'proper' Japanese wife, bowing and scraping to a man like our old neighbor, Mrs. Tanaka does her odious husband. Or rather did, before he got sent to Fort Missoula."

"You mean you don't intend to marry? What about this Mako Ito—you seem quite fond of him." I'd handed her a letter with his name and return address on it the week before and noticed the softness in her voice when she'd earlier said his name.

"I didn't say that." She buried her face in Bella's blanket, but not quickly enough to hide the red flags flying in her cheeks. The movement didn't disturb Bella, who slept soundly now she had a full stomach. I'd fed her before we'd left the camp. Keiko and her father had been kind enough to give me some privacy by taking a walk.

We both were silent for a while. As I drove I thought more about the Camp. The rows and rows of barracks were like soldiers lined up in formation. And yet, with the gardens, they'd been made distinctive and unique. I realized the internees' acts of defiance, like cutting the barbed wire and collecting items for their gardens, as Tommy and Keiko had done, was both an assertion of who they were as individuals and a statement of their cultural heritage.

We entered Jerome and I slowed the truck. Several people on the sidewalk stared at us as we drove by. The same in the grocery store. They stared as much at Bella and me as at Keiko. I wondered why their eyes were so cold. I'd grown up around here, gone to school with some of them. I frowned, thinking of my father. For my part, I'd continued to put out the story my husband had been shot down and was presumed dead. I could even detect the prick of tears in my eyes telling it. Too bad it wasn't true. No telling what Dad might have said, though.

I lifted my chin and stared back, refusing to let the small minds that had once driven me away from doing so again. I'd leave here if, or when, I decided to do so. Holding my precious daughter in one arm and pushing the cart down the grocery aisle with the other, I pointed out to Keiko what we needed, including a twenty-pound bag of rice. "I haven't forgotten," I said as she hoisted the bag into the cart. "You'll need to show me how to cook it properly, though."

At the check-out stand, the cashier, the same man who'd once made the comment about people at Camp Minidoka having things easy, rang up everything without a word to either of us. My back was as stiff as a plank of wood by the time he finished. I glared at him as I handed him the money to pay for our things. He didn't even flinch, merely scooped up the money and turned his back on me.

Keiko was silent on the drive back to the farm, while I inwardly fumed. These were the people Bella would grow up around. I didn't want her harmed by their narrow-minded thinking, but what could I do to protect her?

I thought again about the man who was her father. I often wondered why I'd agreed to go to Mexico with Tucker, Jack, and Kay. When Tucker first mentioned it, he'd seemed indifferent whether I went or not, but Kay had made it sound like a lark.

The sparsely furnished room Tucker and I were offered in the little town of San Ignacio appealed me. A bright magenta blanket covered the double bed. Intertwining roses and vines on the wooden headboard, delicate but crudely carved, made me think of the unknown, unskilled artist who'd carved them. Did he ever wonder about the people who would sleep in his bed? As though in blessing, a gold-painted crucifix hung on the wall above it.

Across from the bed was the room's single window with a carved and painted chest below. On it, I propped the tin soldier I'd bought in Mexico City.

"Why in hell do you drag that thing to our room every night?"

I stepped back to admire my handiwork. "He makes me smile." I turned to survey the room and once again enjoyed its simplicity. No rug softened the wide-planked wood floor, no curtains hung at the window.

Tucker hadn't appeared to notice. "I spotted a cantina across the road. Let's get a drink."

I shook my head. "I want to take a bath and wash my hair."

"You can do that later.  Now I want a drink."

Resisting the urge to argue, I followed him out of our room and down the narrow flight of stairs.  A door at the bottom led outside.

"I want you to be nicer to Jack."

I stopped mid-step. "Be nicer to Jack? What is that supposed to mean?  How am I not nice to Jack?"

Tucker didn't pause or look back. "You know how you can be.  He likes you.  I can tell by the way he watches you."

"So what?" I hurried to catch up with him as he shoved open the door.  "Lots of men like me. Besides, I am nice to Jack."

"Well, be nicer.  I need his money."

"What are you asking me to do, Tucker?"

"Nothing.  Forget it." He took my elbow and started to walk across the road to the cantina.

I pulled my arm away. "How can I forget something you just said?"

He didn't answer.

Inside the cantina, Jack and Kay sat at a table near the bar.  Two glasses of tequila, a plate of sliced lemons and a dish of peppers stood on the table between them. Kay's heightened coloring told me they'd been arguing.

Jack glanced up and waved. "The tequila isn't bad," he said when we reached their table.

A brown-skinned woman with coarse gray hair, braided and hanging over her shoulders, came to take our order.  She wore a gathered skirt of black cotton with an embroidered white blouse falling off one shoulder, her dusty feet thrust into leather sandals. She didn't smile, but stood silent, waiting. In rapid Spanish, Tucker ordered a beer for himself and a glass of tequila for me.

My gaze traveled around the room. A single bulb, dangling on a short, black cord at the center of the low-ceiling, cast a weak light that didn't reach into the corners. Along with the smells of beer and cigarette smoke, the air was ripe with cooking odors.

Two men sat at a nearby table, a bottle of beer and a glass in front of each. Between them stubbed out cigarettes overflowed an ashtray. One man wore a dark suit. His thin black tie hung loose at the collar of his white shirt, but otherwise he appeared tidy, as though someone who cared about his appearance tended him. His companion was thin and dark, with pockmarked skin drawn tight over his narrow face. His dark eyes stared out from under thick bushy brows. Unlike Tucker's, my Spanish wasn't good enough to make out what they said, but the thin one drew lines in some beer spilled on the table and in between jabbed his finger at the man in the suit.

The waitress brought our drinks. Between sips of the tequila, enjoying the sharp taste on my tongue and the spreading warmth in my belly, I tried to make conversation with Kay. She answered my questions with one or two words, lighting one cigarette from the end of another.

After the third, she leaned back and folded her arms across her chest. "Well, y'all will find out soon enough. I'm pregnant."

"Oh, for Christ's sake, Kay. Do you need to blab every-thing?" Jack scowled and took a large swallow of his tequila.

"Well, I think our friends should know I'm knocked up, sugar." She turned to me, her eyes glittering. "Aren't you thrilled for me, honey? Do you suppose it'll be a boy or a girl? I'd love to have a little girl. But then a little boy would be nice, too—I just know he'd grow up as good-lookin' n' sweet as his daddy." She lit another cigarette then stubbed it out and started to cry.

"Shut-up, Kay," said Jack. "Goddammit, can't we finish this trip and think about our problem later? Where's the waitress? Let's get something to eat."

"I don't want anything to eat. Besides, it's my problem, not yours. You already have a wife and son." Kay downed the rest of her tequila in one gulp before pushing back from the table. She got up and walked unsteadily to the bar where she loudly ordered another drink. From experience, I knew there was no point in arguing with her or trying to get her to go back to our rooms with me. She would stay until the bar closed.

Jack ignored her. He pulled the map out of his pocket and spread it across the table, the plate of lemon slices and the dish of peppers pushing up the worn and creased paper in the middle like small mountains. "The problem will be water," he said.

"This is the eastern edge of the three parcels, right?" Tucker tapped a spot on the map with his finger. "And the river is here, the closest point. That's what, three miles. It won't take long to ditch three miles."

Jack's expression remained doubtful. "Who's going to do the work? Think about what we drove through today. There are no people. The place is empty."

Tucker brushed aside Jack's concerns. "We'll bring them in from Leon and Guanajuato. Plenty of people in those places want work. They can throw up some shacks to live in. In a year or two we'll be producing tons of cotton. And with next-to-nothing in labor costs, it'll be ten times cheaper than anything grown in the States. The government will buy everything we can produce."

Tucker procured things for the Army, and the Army needed cotton for uniforms. Tucker's purpose for coming here was to show Jack the cotton-growing potential of Mexico's central and western regions. Jack frowned, still unconvinced, but Tucker went on talking about the plan and the route the four of us would take the next morning.

Kay remained at the bar. I returned to watching the two men at the other table and wondered if they'd get into a fistfight. The pockmarked man seemed calmer though. The man in the suit got to his feet and said goodnight. As he turned to leave he nodded to me. "Buenos noches, Senora."

I drank the last of my tequila, then stood and told Tucker I was ready to go back to the room. "I still want to get a bath and wash my hair tonight."

Tucker's eyes traveled from me to the man in the suit, nearing the door, then back to me, one eyebrow raised. "Lowering your standards, aren't you, Virginia?"

Not deigning to answer, I walked away, my back stiff.

I lay under the magenta blanket later that night, after my bath, and thought about Tucker. When he wanted to be, like when we first started going out, he was the most charming man I'd ever met. At some point, he'd stopped showing me that side. What drove him to say such hurtful things? I'd never tried to keep secret that I'd been with other men before we met—I was twenty-five by then—but I wasn't a tramp.  So why did he treat me like one? More important, why did I let him?

I pushed Tucker from my mind and thought about Kay instead.  I felt certain Jack would try to make her get an abortion. Even though they were illegal, abortions weren't a problem when you had the money and knew the right people. I had little doubt that's what they'd been arguing about.   I frowned, wondering if Kay would do what Jack wanted.

I punched up the pillow. The bedsprings protested as I rolled onto my side.  Somewhere far off, a dog barked.

I awoke with a start and no idea of the time. Footsteps sounded on the stairs.  Someone tripped and fell against the wall.

"Shit."

Tucker's voice.

"Shhh."

Jack or Kay, I couldn't tell.

The door to our room opened and Tucker entered.  He stood still for a minute. Over his heavy breathing, two sets of footsteps traveled down the hall, then a second door opened and clicked closed.

Tucker crossed the room and dropped down on the end of the bed; I drew my feet back just in time.  Shoes dropped to the floor, first one and then the other.  I pretended to be asleep.  Tucker muttered under his breath as he struggled to get out of his trousers and shirt.  He climbed into bed and pulled me to him.  His arms and face were cold from the night air and his breath smelled of beer and tequila.  I turned my head and tried to move away. He jerked me to him again and thrust his hips against me. His erect penis poked my thigh. He thrust at me again and his forehead cracked me on the cheek bringing a stinging pain and tears to my eyes.

"Quit, Tucker. I'm not in the mood."

"What's the matter? Your little Mexican bandito wear you out?"

"I mean it, Tucker. You're drunk. I'm tired. We've had a long day. Let's get some sleep."

"*I mean it, Tucker,*" he mimicked.

His hot breath smelled foul. I pushed away from him one more time.

"Come here, dammit. I didn't bring you along to tell me you're not in the mood. I'm in the mood and that'll have to be enough." He grabbed my arms and rolled on top of me.

When he finished, I slipped off the bed and searched along the floor for my nightgown. I tied the torn straps together and slipped it over my head then rolled the already snoring Tucker over. I wrapped myself in the magenta blanket.

Tucker ignored me the next morning as he repacked the small suitcase he'd brought in from the car the night before. After a while he left the room.

I followed a few minutes later. Jack glanced at me, but said nothing, returning his attention to his coffee. Tucker sat across from him. Neither man looked happy.

A hammered silver coffeepot, several earthenware mugs, and a tray of rolls along with a pot of butter, were on a table near a passageway coming from the back of the hotel. I filled a mug with steaming coffee then crossed the room to sit down on a chair Jack dragged over from another table.

"Where's Kay?"

"Still upstairs," Jack said. "She'll be down pretty soon."

"Where's your bag?" said Tucker. "Aren't you packed yet? We want to pay the bill and get out of here."

"I'm not going."

Tucker frowned. "What do you mean, you're not going?'

"What I said. I'm not going with you. I'm staying here."

Kay came in wearing dark glasses and carrying her overnight case. "You can't stay here," she said.

"She's not staying here," said Tucker. "Now go get your things together, Virginia, and stop playing games."

"I'm not playing games, Tucker."

Kay stared at the end of her cigarette then tapped the ash onto the floor. I felt Jack's eyes on me.

"How are you going to get back to Phoenix then? We're not coming back here for you," Tucker said.

"I'll find something." I felt reasonably certain busses passed through San Ignacio to somewhere I could get transportation north.

"You're crazy. I'm serious. Are you coming with us or not?"

"I'm not." I hoped no one would notice my hands trembling.

"Suit yourself." Tucker stood, pushed his chair back and walked away. Kay didn't glance at me, but stood and followed Tucker.

"My God, Virginia," Jack said after they'd left. "Are you out of your mind? Whatever Tucker's done can't be this bad. You're cutting your damn nose off to spite your face."

"Maybe, but I'm still not going."

He leaned toward me. "Tucker's right. You are crazy. There's no telling what might happen to you down here. Your Spanish is no better than mine, the American Embassy is miles away and a war is going on, for Christ's sake. Or did you forget that?" He straightened. A wet spot spread across his shirt from some spilled coffee.

"Europe is a long way from Mexico and so is the South Pacific," I said then jumped at the sound of the car horn blasting out Tucker's impatience. I took a deep breath to slow down my racing heart. "I'll be okay."

Jack asked me one more time to change my mind. I still refused. He gave an exasperated sigh and got to his feet. I stood, too.

"Do you have enough money to get home?"

"Yes," I lied.

"Here's some extra, in case." He handed me several large folded bills then turned and went to join Tucker and Kay.

*Wait, I've changed my mind.* The words hovered on my lips, but I didn't say them. Instead, when the door closed behind Jack, I fled up the stairs. Once in the room I picked up the tin soldier and looked out the window. Only the dust-covered rear window and the extra fuel cans strapped to the bumper were visible as the station wagon passed a church and disappeared around a corner. I looked down. At the side of the road, near where we'd parked the night before, lay my big blue suitcase.

Crowded with people, poultry, assorted boxes and luggage, the bus I finally managed to catch in Leon broke down countless times before arriving in the small town at the Mexico-Arizona border. I said good-bye to several well-wishers. The driver left his bus, along with all his passengers, and walked me to the crossing point. Dusty and disheveled, lugging my two suitcases and the tin soldier, I crossed the bridge into Arizona with just enough money for a bus ticket back to Phoenix.

I pushed Tucker and Mexico from my mind. I couldn't change what had happened, nor did I want to, not with Bella the result. I looked over at her, still asleep in Keiko's arms. I reached out and stroked her warm cheek.

When we got back to the house, Marc stood in the yard talking to two men I didn't recognize.

"They didn't tell me," he said later, when I asked him what they'd wanted. "Just asked if I was satisfied with how the field workers were doing and if we planned to grow sugar beets next year."

"Where were they from?"

Keiko and I were putting the groceries away. I stooped to slide several cans of condensed milk onto a shelf in a lower cupboard while Keiko dealt with the rice and a large bag of flour.

The minute we walked into the stifling kitchen, I'd flipped on the oscillating fan on the rear counter. The heavy air barely moved, even with the windows opened wide. At least the house wasn't as hot as the Ugawa's apartment had been.

Marc, leaning against the counter next to the sink, took the last bite of an apple he'd been munching on. He straightened and dropped the apple core in the garbage. "Some sugar company," he said. "I'm going back to work. See you at dinner."

The heat wave continued into the following week. Wednesday night, a huge windstorm blew through, breaking several big branches off the cottonwood tree and causing a major power line to go down near Twin Falls. The power interruption apparently caused all sorts of havoc in town, but the dropped temperature was a welcome relief.

To commemorate the cooler weather and Bella being all of six weeks old, I put her on a blanket outside and took several pictures. "I think she may have been smiling in that last one," I said.

Without looking at me, Keiko asked if I would take a picture of her, too. "We aren't allowed cameras in the camp."

She was a beautiful young woman with smooth, almond-colored skin and black eyebrows that tilted upward, like wings, above her equally black eyes. The more I came to know her, the more those eyes revealed. I posed her sitting on the porch step, her chin on her hand, looking pensive. "I suppose you'll be sending this to Mako," I said and snapped the photo. She blushed and nodded.

I pretty much forgot about the men from the sugar company and soon the hay was ready to be cut. Marc used the horses whenever he could to conserve fuel, but he used the tractor to mow, claiming the mower was a horse-killer because it vibrates so much. Every night after dinner, he went out to the machine shed and re-sharpened the mower blades for the following day.

On a warm evening, while Keiko did the dinner dishes and cleaned the kitchen, I wandered out to join him. "Remember when we were kids and Dad did this?"

Marc struggled to get the blades off the mower. They came loose and he carried them over to the grinding wheel. "So that we could watch the sparks flying everywhere. Oh yeah, I remember—and I remember Dad yelling at us when we tried to catch them—claiming we were in his way and to get out."

"They were like fireflies."

When Marc started the grinding wheel and held a blade to it, I thought of fireflies again, a roomful of them.

With Idaho's arid climate, the hay didn't need long to dry once it was mowed and raked. In just a few days, it was ready to stack. Marc brought all six horses from the pasture to move the hay derrick out to the field. It was the same one we'd used as kids. On long railroad-tie skids, it was tall, heavy, and extremely awkward.

The teen-aged boys from the camp, likely city boys, were nervous of the horses. They stood well back while Marc and John Sato harnessed them and backed them up to the derrick. The horses snorted and stomped their huge feet. The boys moved back even farther.

"The boom makes the derrick top-heavy, so watch it doesn't tip over on you," Marc said. The boys' eyes widened.

Even with all six horses pulling, getting the derrick out to the hayfield proved slow work. Marc walked to one side, holding the horses' reins. He glanced over his shoulder every couple of minutes to make sure the derrick, on its skids, remained steady. John Sato and the boys followed well behind. I returned to my chores.

The hayfield was close to the house. Keiko frequently stopped her work to check on the men's progress.

I didn't need to watch. Haying season was part of every summer, part of growing up in the country, part of my childhood. I could picture everything. Once the derrick was in position next to the already formed foundation of the stack, Marc would unharness the horses and lower the heavy boom. Using pitchforks, two or three would fork the loose hay into the boom's large net, spread on the ground.

When the net filled, they'd hoist the boom, swing it over the stack and release the hay. The other two, probably John Sato and one of the teen-aged boys, would be stationed on top of the stack to spread the released hay. Over and over, the net would be filled and hoisted until the forty-foot long stack reached about fourteen feet tall and just as wide.

With no escape from the blazing sun, haying was hot, sweaty work. I twitched, remembering bits of hay clinging to my sticky bared skin.

Keiko and I had everything ready and set out on the picnic table when they broke for lunch. I carried Bella outside and spread a blanket for her to lie on while we ate. Keiko had been right. Rice balls and vegetables were delicious, especially when dipped in a little soy sauce and hot mustard. We'd also made sandwiches and cut up a watermelon. Earlier in the summer, we'd resurrected my mother's garden. The watermelon was one of the season's first.

Bella waved her fists and made cooing sounds as I ate. John Sato squatted down beside her. I tensed, instantly alert, but he only smiled and said something in Japanese to one of the boys before standing and getting another slice of watermelon. He nodded to me as he passed. "Very pretty baby—she takes after her mother."

My cheeks reddened and I tried to cover my discomfort by coughing.

From the very first time I'd seen him, the day he and Keiko and the boys had come to the farm, I'd often found myself studying John Sato, listening to his calm, deep voice. He was about my height and slim, but with wide shoulders and a triangle-shaped face that came to a firm point at his chin. The fold of his eyelids, slightly more pronounced than Keiko's, intrigued me. I wondered what his skin felt like, so golden.

Marc stood. "Let's go."

The air that afternoon was yellow with heat, the mountains on the horizon barely visible through the haze. A few flies buzzed lazily, banging into the window screens. I fed Bella. Just as I put her down for her nap, tempted to take one myself, I heard a frantic yell. I instantly thought of the derrick. The yell came again. Heart pounding, I rushed down the stairs, meeting Keiko at the bottom. Dad nearly bolted from his bedroom. We all pushed through the door and onto the porch to see John Sato running toward us.

"What's happened?" I shouted.

John was out of breath by the time he reached us. "The derrick," he gasped. "It tipped. Your brother is hurt."

"Oh, my God! How bad?"

"I don't know. The boom knocked him out. He's still unconscious."

My heart pounded even harder. "Dad, get your truck. Keiko, stay with Bella." Dad drove. I bounced nearly to the ceiling as we hit a bump. I twisted around to make sure John Sato hadn't been thrown out of the back then quickly faced forward again. "There they are."

The boys were trying to control the horses, but they were clearly frightened of the animals. The equally frightened horses plunged and whinnied. They were still hitched to the fallen derrick, their twisted harnesses entangled with the derrick's skids. I hopped out of the truck and rushed to Marc's side.

He'd regained consciousness. With his left shoulder pinned beneath the boom, his face was screwed tight as a fist. He fought to keep from crying out every time the horses reared, the derrick jerked and the boom ground into his shoulder. John and Dad ran to take control of the horses.

Kneeling, I gently brushed dirt from the lump on my brother's forehead. His face and lips were as pale as the sandy dirt beneath him. I worked to keep the panic from my voice. "It won't be long. They'll get the horses untangled and we'll get this thing off you." Marc nodded but said nothing. Dad and John took several minutes to calm the animals and get their harnesses straightened. It seemed like hours.

John looped a thick rope over the boom and Dad urged the horses forward. Slowly, the boom began to lift. When it reached about ten inches from the ground, with the help of one of the boys I pulled Marc free. He roared, his mouth forming an 'O' with a white ring around his lips, and flung his good arm across his eyes.

My father left the horses to John and came over to stand next to us. He stared down at Marc. "Looks like you'll be out of commission for a while."

The doctor held the x-rays to the light, one at a time, studying each intently before setting it aside. He turned to Marc, sitting on the examining table, cradling his left arm with his right, his face still ashen. "You're lucky nothing's broken. Man last summer wasn't so fortunate. In a wheelchair now—damned derrick broke his back."

Marc clamped down on his lower lip while the doctor strapped up his injured shoulder.

"Every few hours, take a couple of aspirin for the pain."

With that final instruction, the doctor sent us home.

My hands wouldn't stop shaking.

The next morning, Marc rose early, nagging everyone to get a move on. He barely gave anyone time to eat the breakfast Keiko and I prepared. Beyond his arm being strapped, only the pallor of his cheeks and the dark rings below his eyes showed he suffered any discomfort. If he'd spent a sleepless night, he didn't admit to it.

When the horses were harnessed, I used an empty oil drum to climb aboard the broad, dusty back of one of the horses. "Give me Bella."

Keiko scowled her displeasure at this idea, but John

Sato took Bella from her and handed up my daughter. Like a parade, we set off for the hayfield.

The derrick lay in the dirt like a slain giant.

I lowered Bella so that Keiko could reach her then swung my leg over the horse's back, slid part way down and jumped to the ground. I dusted brown horsehair from the seat of my blue jeans then took Bella and balanced her on my hip.

"We'll need to drag the derrick away from the hay stack so that we can maneuver around both sides," John said.

Marc directed him to connect two ropes to the derrick's skids then told the boys to be prepared to push.

"Okay, Dad, get the horses moving. Slowly, slowly, now." The derrick began to move. "That's it. Good. John, make sure the rope on the top skid doesn't slip."

Moving, but at a sluggish pace, the behemoth came clear of the hay stack.

"Okay, now you can loop the ropes around the top of the derrick. Dad, bring the horses around to this side." Cradling his arm, his back held rigidly straight, Marc moved out of the way of the horses so Dad could reposition the team.

When all was ready, Dad got the horses moving forward again and the derrick began to rise. Suddenly the lower skid slipped forward and the horses backed, unable to hold the weight. The derrick slammed back to the ground. The boys jumped even though they were nowhere near.

Marc yelled at Dad to have a care with the horses, stomping and plunging in their harnesses. "We don't need them all lathered up or getting spooked."

Dad scowled at him.

John looped another rope, this one to the boom.  When the third rope was secured, Dad started moving the horses forward again.

"Steady," Marc shouted.

The derrick rose slowly, the top arcing through the air. Then it seemed to hang, balanced on one railroad-tie skid, before the second skid came down with a great thud, sending up a cloud of dust. The boys hoorayed and slapped one another on the back.

While Dad and John unharnessed the horses, Keiko and I returned to the house with Bella, demanding to be fed.

The men, Marc included, though what kind of help he provided with his arm strapped up I couldn't say, finished stacking the hay then strung a barbed wire fence around it. When winter came, Marc would go out each morning and throw hay over the fence for the horses and the cattle.

# 7
# *KEIKO*

Digging and bagging potatoes was the hardest thing I'd ever done. Everyone had to pitch in. I often found myself working next to the old man. At least he kept his venomous tongue between his teeth. He probably lacked the energy to say anything derogatory to me. A good thing, because after a few hours of digging potatoes, I had no energy to defend myself.

Finally, the last heavy bag was hauled to the cellar—a musty tomb-like earthen structure identical to many dotting the countryside—the hay stacked, the beans picked and the garden put to bed. Harvest was over and summer with it. We said goodbye to Virginia and Marc, who still favored his shoulder, and a school bus delivered us back to the camp.

John Sato and I headed to our separate barracks. "Will you be returning to the farm in the spring?" I asked.

John stooped and picked up a piece of torn paper from the path. He straightened. "I don't know. Now Japanese-Americans are no longer considered unfit for the military, we're supposed to register with Selective Service. I'll probably be drafted."

"What will you do? Will you sign up? If you do, Virginia will miss you."

He gave me a sideways look, frowning. "I'm not sure."

"Seriously?" Unlike Mako, who'd enthusiastically enlisted in the Army, a few refused to sign a questionnaire about fighting anywhere they were sent, and about renouncing allegiance to Japan's emperor—this even though they were American citizens and had never sworn service to the Emperor in the first place. These men said they needed to be released from the camps before they would sign up. "If I were a man, I wouldn't have signed their questionnaire," I said. "And I wouldn't join the Army, either."

John appeared to consider my words. I waited for him to say something, but he didn't, merely nodded. After a moment, he headed toward his barracks. I watched him go then headed toward my own.

Eager as I was to be with Papa and Tommy again, I was acutely conscious my mother wouldn't greet me at the door and admonish me to put my things away. Whenever I thought of Mama, of her absence, I felt a hollow ache inside me.

★

In the weeks following my return to camp, I couldn't help but be aware the camp had become more organized. The schools were now fully staffed with white as well as Japanese-American teachers. The hospital, though under a white Head Physician and a white Head Nurse, was staffed by Japanese-American doctors and nurses. In addition, a resident-run cooperative store had been established. Also, a cinema, barber and beauty shops, and radio and watch repair shops. There was a canteen serving sodas, too. The canteen even had a jukebox.

Papa was proud of what had been achieved, much by older Issei, like him. "This place is like a small city. We have all we need here now."

I thought it truly impressive what had been created from almost nothing, but I couldn't endorse my father's opinion Camp Minidoka now had everything we required. Far from it; without our freedom, the rest was meaningless, or nearly so.

I did discover something thrilling in the recreation hall: an old upright piano, a donation from the First Congregational Church in Twin Falls. Out of tune when delivered, the instrument was quickly put right by a resident who'd been a piano tuner before the war started. Some of Camp Minidoka's residents played smaller instruments, like the trumpet and even the saxophone. Thinking their instruments more important than clothes, they'd managed to bring them along. Within a short time, we had a band. Every other Friday and Saturday night would find us playing together.

Kazuko and Myoko could always be counted on to support our efforts along with Suki, if she wasn't caring for her young cousins. Margaret, however, had been fortunate enough to receive acceptance to a women's college in Connecticut. Her departure from Camp Minidoka left us all stunned.

Kazuko dropped her usual air of indifference. "It's so unfair. Margaret, of all people—I'm glad for her, but I'm so jealous. How did she do it?"

Myoko, another friend, shrugged. "Maybe something can be said for ignoring assignments."

I took a sip of my Coke, savoring its flavor. Until returning from the farm, I hadn't had one since leaving Portland and Japantown. I'd forgotten how the bubbles stung the roof of my mouth. "I think her mother is pen pals with someone connected with the school, but you can't deny Margaret is very smart."

Kazuko swirled her Coke with her straw. "You're right. As I said, I'm just jealous she's the one who got out of here and I'm still waiting."

I understood her perfectly. I was jealous too. I didn't want to go back east to school, though, as more young women internees were being allowed to do. Both Kazuko and Myoko had applied and hoped they'd soon get a letter telling them an eastern or mid-western school had accepted them. I wanted to go to a school in Portland. I'd dreamt about doing so for years, ever since I was ten and my music teacher first brought up the possibility. My parents encouraged me in my dream.

I wondered how much Portland might have changed. From my bedroom window, I used to watch the headlights of cars streaming down off Council Crest, the beams of light poking between evergreen trees as the cars followed the twisting road down the steep hillside. From the rooftop of our building, where Tommy and I frequently went to discuss events of the day or share our plans and dreams, in addition to the cars coming down from Council Crest, we could see Mount Hood and Mount St. Helens and sometimes the late afternoon sunlight flashing off the Columbia River.

No matter we'd lived in Japan-Chinatown, I thought of Portland as my place in the world, the city of my birth and where I'd spent the first seventeen years of my life. Though I'd begun to appreciate the desert's beauty, the wildflowers in the spring and year 'round the mountains off in the distance, I didn't think I'd ever belong anywhere but Portland, Oregon. On the other hand, I felt as though Portland had relinquished me without a fight, given me up as not worthy of a protest.

I started as a hand took my elbow. I whirled around to see who had come up behind me. My eyes widened and my heart gave a little hiccup. Mako smiled and held out his arms. I caught myself before falling into them. Resplendent in his uniform, he was more handsome than ever.

He grinned. "Want to dance?"

We didn't talk while we danced to the fast-paced song, and when the song ended I lowered my eyes, suddenly shy. "My break is over." Three of us played piano for the band, each with a different style. We took turns, but I could easily have delayed for at least one more song. Mako let go my hand, reluctantly I told myself later, and I retook my place on the piano bench. Later, I saw him dancing with Myoko and then with a girl I hadn't seen before. My lips pressed flat and a burning sensation I'd never felt before grew in my chest.

When the evening ended and the lights were turned out, Mako once again appeared at my side. "I'll walk back to the barracks with you."

I don't know why I'd become so shy around him. For a year, we'd practically lived in one another's pockets. "Okay." I opened the door and a gust of wind nearly tore it from my hand. Once outside, Mako helped get the door shut again.

The cold wind, which had started up in the afternoon, blew with renewed gusto. Anything loose went flying. Mako and I leaned into it, lowering our heads to keep the driving sand and dust from our eyes. He took my elbow as dried up tumbleweed blew, rolled, and bounced past us, joining piles of tumbleweeds and other debris at the base of each barracks. Talking was impossible. The wind tore the words from our mouths, carrying them off into the desert night.

I was grateful to be wearing a man's heavy coat. The feminine coat I'd carefully packed and brought from Portland was no match for Idaho's winter. Probably from a sense of guilt, the War Relocation Authority, the organization responsible for running Camp Minidoka and the rest of the camps, offered us heavier clothing, long johns included. The coat, which Tommy said was a leftover WWI Army issue, was several sizes too big. Its hem fell nearly to my feet and my hands were completely covered unless I folded the ends of the sleeves several times, but it provided great protection from the wind and cold. I'd long since gotten over feeling ridiculous in it.

When we stepped inside our barracks, I took a handkerchief from my pocket and wiped grit from the corners of my eyes then handed the handkerchief to Mako. "While you've been training, I'll bet you forgot these wonderful wind storms."

Mako shook his head. "No. I haven't forgotten anything." His eyes held mine for a moment, before I looked away. "I'll see you tomorrow," he said and we both retreated to our separate quarters.

The bare light bulb hanging from the middle of the ceiling, the only light inside of our apartment, was turned off, but I made out the silhouette of my father sitting at the table. He appeared deep in thought. "Papa, what are you doing up so late?" I drew closer and saw his cheeks were slick with tears. "Papa?"

He said nothing, simply took my hand and held it. Finally, he answered. "I was thinking of your mother and how much she loved me to read to her in the evenings."

I dropped to the floor and rested my cheek on his knees. "Oh Papa, I miss her, too."

Mako knocked on our door early the next morning and invited me to go to the movies with him that night. I spent the day trying to decide what to wear. My options were limited. The winds of the night before had given way to black, threatening clouds. I suspected the walkways between our barracks and the cinema, where the movie would be shown, would be a muddy mess by evening. I'd need to wear my *geta*, wooden platform shoes lots of us girls wore to keep our feet out of the mud. The temperature remained in the twenties, so the WRA-donated long johns would be called for under a pair of wool slacks. I decided one of the two pair I owned might be presentable after a little brushing. I went to the laundry building where I washed and ironed a blouse. A sweater would complete my outfit.

By evening, I felt like a nervous wreck. When the dinner whistle blew at five, I told Papa I wasn't hungry, but in truth, I couldn't have swallowed a bite of the food they served in the dining hall. I ate a few crackers and drank a cup of tea instead.

Tommy made fun of me. "What's the matter? Got an upset tummy just because your heartthrob asked you out?"

I didn't rise to the bait he continued to throw out, and Papa finally insisted he stop. The two of them left for the dining hall, but not without Tommy giving me a wink and a knowing grin first.

I crossed to my dressing table, covered with lipsticks and bottles of nail polish and cologne. Tommy had made it for my eighteenth birthday. One of the legs was a shade shorter than the other three, but I loved it. I looked in the small mirror on the wall above and shook my head in despair. Suki and I had given each other home permanents the week before and I think we left the solution on my hair too long. I ran the brush through it, trying to straighten the frizzy ends. I gave up. In the middle of fastening a yellow crepe-paper flower above my ear, hoping to distract from the mess I'd made of my hair, a knock sounded.

Mako stood at the door, another crepe-paper flower in his hand, this one red. He smiled and held it out to me. "I wish this could be a real one. I tried, but I guess the season is wrong for fresh-cut flowers."

"A fresh flower would only die. This I can keep." Reminding me of our first date, I added to myself.

Mako would leave soon and the months following were sure to find me listening to the nightly radio broadcasts and searching the *Pacific Citizen* to glean whatever news I could of the 442nd, but for now, at least, he was here, with me.

I was so aware of him sitting next to me in the cinema, I couldn't focus on the movie, even though it starred Cary Grant, one of my favorite actors, and people laughed a lot.

After the movie, we went to the canteen with a group of friends, many also in uniform and on leave. Mako wasn't the only one going away to fight. Nearly every boy I'd graduated from high school with had signed up. We drank Cokes, played the jukebox, and talked.

"What are we going to do about those *Buddhaheads?*" one of our old classmates asked Mako.

Many of us girls looked puzzled. "What are *Buddhaheads?*"

Mako translated for us. "They're Nisei from Hawaii. They call us kotanks. They say our hollow heads make that sound when they hit us."

"Hit you? When you're training, you mean?" I asked, even more mystified.

Another former classmate chimed in. "They're always picking fights with us. They're jealous because mainland Nisei were made NCO's before they even got to camp."

"He means non-commissioned officers," Mako said.

"Is that what you are?" He had two red stripes on the arm of his uniform jacket, stripes the others didn't have.

Mako nodded, looking embarrassed.

A friend of Mako's laughed. "Your boyfriend's a rank-grabber."

They told us about Mississippi and Camp Shelby, where they'd taken their basic training.

"All the officers are white," Mako said. "The Hawaiian *Nisei* call them *haole*. It's a Hawaiian word for white people."

"What about the people in the town near your base? How do you get along with them?" Even on the West Coast, we knew about the Jim Crow south.

"Not so bad. I guess we're kind of an oddity to them, yellow instead of black. The Negroes are who they treat like dogs. Our officers tell us we need to mind our own business when a colored soldier is disrespected by some store clerk or a bus driver or someone who thinks he should have the sidewalk to himself. It's hard, though."

"Why?" At the sound of his voice, I turned to look at Ralph Naito, another former classmate. He'd been quiet most of the evening. "Not so long ago we got the same treatment, or near enough, if we wandered too far away from Japantown."

Later, Mako and I hurried back to our barracks. The anticipated rain began while we were watching the movie and now came down in buckets. Mako held my hand, keeping me from slipping in the mud. We side-stepped the many puddles.

I lay awake again, this time thinking of what our lives would be like when the war ended and everyone returned home, though where home would be I didn't know. I also thought of what Ralph Naito had said about how we were treated whenever we left our places. Whether Portland, Seattle, or Tacoma, each had a Japantown. Would they be the same after the war, or would things be worse?

Mako returned to duty the day after Thanksgiving. He promised to write whenever he could, though he told me he didn't know if he'd have much opportunity once he got overseas.

I gave him the picture Virginia had taken of me. "I'll write often, too."

Mako worried about his mother. They'd still heard nothing from or about his sister. "I think her ship sank. It must have gone down. Otherwise, the Red Cross would have been able to find out something." Tears were in his eyes when he told me. He didn't try to hide them. I promised I'd continue to look in on his parents.

After he left, I always filled Mr. and Mrs. Ito's coal scuttle whenever I went to get coal for our apartment. Tommy did the same. I often sat with them in the evening, too, after I returned from work. I'd taken a job with the camp newspaper. Not writing articles or stories, but helping in the office.

John Sato worked for The *Minidoka Irrigator* as well, but as a reporter. We met each other nearly every day and frequently talked about our shared experiences the previous summer at the Franconi farm. I think he had an eye for Virginia. He didn't say as much, but he often turned our discussion to her and Bella.

"I wonder if her husband is still alive," he said one day.

Thinking of the nasty things the old man said about whores and bastards, I thought it unlikely Virginia had a husband. I didn't say as much to John. If Virginia wanted him to know, she'd tell him. I shrugged instead.

Tommy, now in his final year of high school, claimed he planned on signing up as soon as he graduated. We argued about it.

"I'll probably be drafted anyway."

He was right, but I still hated it. "You could try to get a deferment, say you're needed to help look after Papa."

Tommy snorted. "Do you honestly think Papa would stand for that? He's perfectly healthy. Besides, you're here."

"What if I want to go to school somewhere?"

He knew I had no such plan and shook his head at me.

"Anyway," I said. "I don't know why more Nisei don't simply refuse the draft. It shouldn't be legal. Those men at Heart Mountain are right."

Some men at the Heart Mountain camp had formed what they called the Fair Play Committee. They issued a statement saying they'd gladly sacrifice their lives to protect and uphold the principles and ideals of their country, as set forth in the Constitution and the Bill of Rights, but for the fact they'd been denied the basic freedom, liberty, and justice those documents promised for all citizens, including Japanese-Americans.

"The camps aren't our homes and the government shouldn't be able to draft people from them. You should refuse to go."

Tommy looked at me like I'd gone crazy. "Are you kidding? I'd never do that."

I didn't say anything more. I was outnumbered. Even Papa said he thought the draft-resisters should become conscientious objectors or serve as corpsmen.

Contrary to most Nisei, especially the Japanese-American Citizens League, which called all draft resisters unpatriotic and un-American, I admired the men from Heart Mountain for standing up for their principles. I wondered what John Sato would do if or when his number came up and he got drafted.

Papa, Tommy, and I attended a special church service on Christmas Eve. At New Year, the dining room cooks attempted to prepare *osechi ryore*, a feast of delicacies traditionally served in a three-tiered lacquered box on New

Year's. Everyone appreciated their efforts. Otherwise, the holidays came and went with little notice.

No letter came from Mako after he wrote to me they were shipping out. I searched the *Pacific Citizen* each week for news, but learned little of where the 442nd was or what they were doing. Although we didn't have a radio, one of our neighbors had ordered one from Sears Roebuck and often invited me to listen. Sometimes my father and Mr. Ito joined us.

"Would you like more tea, Keiko-san?" Mrs. Ashida asked me one evening following the nightly newscast.

"Thank you, Ashida-san, but I need to go home and check how Papa is faring. He's caught a nasty cold and didn't want to infect anyone here tonight." Since we lived so close together, colds and flu traveled quickly through the camp. "He'll want to know American troops are fighting successfully in Italy."

Later in the evening, Tommy came in stomping snow from his feet and brushing it from his hair and shoulders. "Where's Papa?"

"Gone to bed," I said. "His cold isn't any better. Did you listen to the news tonight?"

Tommy took off his jacket and went to stand in front of the stove. "Sure. We were at Billy's place. His folks have a radio."

"Where exactly is Anzio?"

Tommy thought a minute. "Well, if Italy is a hip-length boot—like those the three Musketeers wore—Anzio would be around the knee."

I tried to picture a map of Italy in my mind. "They've

been in Italy since the end of January. I wonder what it's like, what the countryside is like, the weather, how the people treat them, now Italy's surrendered."

Tommy shrugged. "I don't suppose the Americans see many Italians. They're too busy fighting the Germans."

I wondered if Mako fought in Anzio. "I'm going to bed," I said.

Tommy went outside and a short while later the door opened and closed and coal rattled out of the bucket and into the stove. Moments later, I heard him undressing and climbing into his bed. "Are you still awake?" he asked through the curtain separating us.

"Yes." Outside, the wind blew. Sometimes the wind blew so hard it sounded like a train rushing between the rows of barracks, plowing through whatever got in its path. It was calmer, for now at least. Tumbleweed or a small animal gently brushed against the wall behind my head.

"Don't worry about Mako," Tommy said. "He's tough. I'm sure he's okay."

# 8

# VIRGINIA

The setting sun streamed in the window behind Marc. All I could see was his silhouette. "Those two men from the sugar company came back," he said, unconsciously rubbing and rotating the shoulder he'd injured when the hay derrick fell on him. "They want us to plant the entire farm in sugar beets next summer, all but the hayfield."

"Why sugar beets?"

"Part of the war effort. I guess they can make an industrial-grade alcohol from them, used in making explosives."

Marc was ten times the farmer our father had been, but given its history, planting the whole place in one crop seemed like a huge risk. "You're not thinking of doing it, are you?" I asked.

"They made sugar beets sound pretty lucrative."

"You'd be putting all your eggs in one basket, though. Besides, you'd need special equipment, wouldn't you?" I frowned, but wasn't really concerned…not yet.

"I have most of it. I've talked to the bank about getting a loan to buy whatever else I need—if I can find it."

With factories busy producing tanks instead of farm equipment, and doubtlessly demand heavy for anything used, Marc had reason for concern. He stepped away from the window and I finally saw his face—hopeful, also determined.

"I might be able to get something to at least top the beets if I act right away and if we can afford it. Otherwise we'll need to do all the work by hand—thinning and blocking in the spring then harvesting in the fall."

Now I was beginning to worry. "I can't believe you're even considering this; the whole farm in one crop is crazy. What if blight strikes, some disease that only happens to sugar beets? You could lose everything, including the farm." Even as I said this, I knew he'd appreciate the irony of me worrying about a place I'd once claimed to hate.

"Farming is always a gamble, Virginia."

"A gamble, yes, but you needn't risk the entire farm—and what about labor—will Camp Minidoka supply all we need?"

Marc shrugged. "Why not—we had no trouble getting Keiko and John Sato and the boys. I'll probably ask for at least four more to help thin and block the beets when they first start coming up, and later, when we harvest. The rest of the time we can manage with the group from last summer—maybe one more."

"John might be drafted and the boys are seniors this year—they'll probably enlist when school is out." My arguments meant nothing, though. He'd already decided—probably before he said anything to me.

"Well, if not them, we'll get someone else. The sugar company men said Camp Rupert is going to be letting some POWs do field work."

"No Germans, Marc. I wouldn't sleep a wink with Germans here."

"Now how would Germans be different from Italians?"

Heat rose in my cheeks. He'd dismissed my fears about the sugar beets without even considering I might be right. This, too, he found cause for derision. "You know perfectly well why they're different; our brother is fighting them. He isn't fighting Italians—they've already surrendered."

I hoped Leo had never fought them. We probably had cousins in Italy. Something was wrong being at war with a country where we had cousins. I blinked, suddenly brought up short realizing how torn Japanese-Americans had to be, German-Americans too. Why hadn't I considered that before? It might even explain some of Dad's anger. On second thought, probably not. War with the country of his birth was likely only one in the litany of excuses he used to justify his foul temper.

"Okay, I get it," Marc said. "By the time they get here, though, I suspect the fight has gone out of them, Italian and German alike. I seriously doubt whoever we might be assigned is going to have the energy to cause trouble."

I scowled. At least on this I'd stand firm. "No Germans." Even though he clearly thought me unreasonable, he said no more about them.

Without discussing his decision with our father and with my reluctantly given and probably unnecessary agreement, Marc signed a contract with the sugar company. For what remained of the fall he plowed and ridged all the fields except for the hayfield where the big hay stack remained, surrounded by the fence the men had erected, and where the few head of cattle we had were feeding on hay stubble. Marc said he'd been told that preparing the land in the fall would give him more time to plant when the danger of freezing passed in the spring. Still favoring his left shoulder, he worked long hours. Even after I'd gone upstairs to bed at night, the lights on the tractor poked through the dark. He got up early, as well, often putting in two or three hours of work before coming back to the house for breakfast.

He finished plowing the fields just as winter arrived. Then, if not out in the barn taking care of the animals, he did paperwork. When he wasn't bent over his ledgers and journals, he read article after article on raising sugar beets. Sometimes he'd drive off to consult with other farmers. Marc wasn't the only one the sugar company had convinced to devote their entire acreage to raising sugar beets.

I concentrated on Bella's first Christmas, wanting it to be special. I loved how the tree lights were reflected in her wide, unblinking eyes. On Christmas morning, she enjoyed the crinkle of the paper when I unwrapped her presents: a brush and comb set from her Aunt Irene, a trio of wheeled ducks on a string from her Uncle Marc and a pair of rather amateurishly knitted pink booties and matching hat from her mama.

"Here," said Dad and dropped a package in my lap.

"What's this?"

He nodded at Bella. "It's for her." I looked from him to the oddly-shaped object wrapped in newspaper and tied with string. "Open it," he said.

I untied the string and took the paper off to find a carved and painted bird mounted on a piece of twisted greasewood. "Did you do this?"

He nodded.

"This is beautiful, Dad. Thank you." I was truly impressed and touched at his unexpected gesture.

"It isn't much, just something to do. A white-breasted nuthatch—they used to perch on our window sills in Philly."

I admired the way the little bird's head cocked, as if considering an important question. I drew a breath and smiled at my father. "Bella will treasure this one day."

After I'd cleared away the wrapping papers, Marc retreated to his farming journals and Dad to his room. I turned on the radio and listened to Christmas music while I finished stuffing the chicken I'd killed. I slid it into the oven then began peeling potatoes. Later, when the three of us sat down to eat, my mind flashed back to a time when seven of us were at the table, Dad at one end, my mother at the other, all five of us kids arranged along the sides.

Growing up, meals were generally silent, one-course affairs at our house. Christmastime was different. On Christmas Eve, my mother prepared what she called smorgasbord, with Swedish meatballs and sliced ham, scalloped potatoes, and a variety of vegetables, pickled and plain. She'd make some Italian dishes, too, though Dad always said they weren't as good as his mother's. Before Christmas, we kids would help Mom make taffy and popcorn balls and we'd decorate the Christmas tree with strings of cranberries and popcorn.

Christmas Eve may have been Swedish and Italian, but Christmas day was all-American with turkey and trimmings: cranberry sauce, sweet potatoes with marshmallow topping, mashed potatoes, a molded salad and on and on. Every year, Paul and Irene argued about who would get the wishbone while the rest of us egged them on. Mom sometimes told stories about her family. Many of her relatives still lived in Sweden.

After Mom died, all that changed—no more popcorn balls, no stringing popcorn and cranberries, no tree. Christmas Eve and Christmas day became the same as any other day, with Leo taking off in the truck to visit friends the minute we finished dinner. Marc and I soon followed his example. I felt guilty leaving Irene and Paul to deal with Dad, who grew even more belligerent and bitter after Mom's death, but I still went. I sighed, wishing it possible to go back and change things.

Things went back to normal after Christmas. From the nightly newscasts on the radio I learned I'd been wrong thinking Leo wasn't fighting in Italy. He might well have been among the troops landing near Anzio or even earlier, in Sicily. Only after the war did we learned our brother had been transferred to the 63rd Infantry Division and eventually took part in the liberation of Jews from concentration sub-camps in southern Germany. The horrors he discovered in those places never left him.

We didn't know Paul's location either. Somewhere in the Pacific, the Gilbert Islands maybe, Tarawa or New Guinea. Marc and I tried to locate some of these foreign-sounding places on a large map of the world he'd pinned to a wall in the living wall. Paul almost never wrote, but the few heavily censored letters we got from Leo, though trying to sound upbeat, brought us little reassurance.

Irene on the other hand appeared to be thriving in Portland and more than once invited Bella and me to come for a visit. By April, I was sorely tempted. To Marc's delight, saying the soil would be better prepared for the sugar beets when he planted them, the rains were unrelenting. Rather than visit my sister, I managed to find some paint and spent the next couple of weeks painting the walls of my bedroom sunshine yellow, the window sills and trim hot pink.

The colors reminded me of Mexico. Despite Tucker, I'd loved the place and its people. They may have been poor, for the most part, but they showed an honesty and resilience I admired. It spoke to me in the colors they favored. After I finished, I called Marc in to show him the results.

"Where in the hell did you get this color scheme?" He shook his head and laughed. "Can't you picture Mom's face if she was here?"

I bounced Bella in my arms. "She'd be shocked at more than the color of this room."

Marc quickly sobered. "Not as shocked as you might think."

His quietly spoken words gave me a strange comfort. I hoped he was as insightful as he sounded, but we'd both been in our mid-teens when our mother died, not an age known for observation or introspection.

One afternoon I drove out to Camp Minidoka to check on Keiko and her family. Only eighteen, which made me feel ancient, it surprised me to discover I thought of Keiko as a close friend. I'd grown away from the girls I'd known in high school, most of whom were married and involved with their own families, or, like Irene, had moved away.  Keiko's maturity intrigued me. At her age, I'd been all about parties, clothes, and boys.  Keiko was different. She had plans for her future. I admired that.

After visiting with Mr. Ugawa and enjoying a cup of his tea, Keiko and I went to the recreation center and she played some songs on an old piano. The music she produced from its yellowed keys amazed me. Bella appeared entranced, holding still on my lap instead of lunging from side-to-side, trying to grab at things.

I hoped to visit with John Sato, too. Keiko told me he worked for the camp newspaper, *The Minidoka Irrigator*, so we made our way over to its office, carefully avoiding the puddles along the walkway. Unfortunately, John had gone out on an interview.

"What is this 'No-No' business the editor mentioned?"

Keiko and I were headed back to where I'd parked the truck. The weather had suddenly turned cold again and a light snow drifted down, disappearing as it landed on the still wet ground. Bella opened and closed her outstretched hand, trying to catch a flake.

Keiko explained. "No-Noes are young men refusing to be drafted unless the government releases them from the internment camps first. John has been doing a series of interviews for the *Irrigator* and the *Pacific Citizen*, a newspaper published by the Japanese-American Citizens' League. John is sympathetic to the No-Noes, which is causing him problems,  because the *Pacific Citizen* and the

JACL are not. They claim all No-Noes should be rounded up and sent to Tule Lake."

"Are there many of them?" I was a patriot, right down to the ground. I wanted America to win the war. We had to. But considering their situation, I thought I also understood the stance of these young men refusing to be drafted.

Keiko shook her head. Her words surprised me. "Most young Nisei men are pleased to be going into the Army or Navy, eager to show their patriotism."

"What will happen to those who refuse, these No-No boys?"

Keiko frowned. "I suspect they'll go to jail," she said. "Many have already been arrested and are awaiting trial."

I thought about Keiko's and my conversation in the days following and one evening, after listening to the nightly news, I talked to Marc about the No-Noes. In his usual thoughtful way, he considered what I'd learned. "I guess I get their point, but I doubt it will make a difference to the government."

"They'll be convicted you mean?"

"I expect. Imprisoned, too."

"Well, they already are in prison. They're surrounded by barbed wire and guard towers with rifles pointed at them. If that isn't being in a prison, I don't know what you'd call it." The futility of the situation struck me as crazy. "They say they'll enlist if they're freed from the internment camps first and the government says they'll go to prison if they don't enlist first. You'd think they could work out a compromise." I sighed, thoroughly disgusted with the pigheadedness of most men.

"So, will Keiko be back?"

I got up and poured us both another coffee, glad it was no longer rationed. "She says so, but she's worried about leaving her father on his own—I guess her brother is determined he'll enlist as soon as he graduates. I'm not sure about John Sato. He's working for the camp newspaper now, plus he expects to get his draft notice soon. Keiko thinks he might be a No-No—certainly he's sympathetic to them—so who knows what will happen to him." I'd been more than a little disturbed when Keiko told me this. I liked John. A lot. I didn't want him to be in trouble with his own people or with the government.

Marc went outside, saying he'd forgotten to do something in the barn. Left alone, I wondered why some Japanese-Americans eagerly went off to war, like Keiko's boyfriend and her brother, while others remained reluctant. I was sure both responses had little to do with courage and much more to do with a culture I'd only glimpsed.

In early May, I went to visit Keiko again, and this time had the chance to visit with John Sato as well. While Keiko entertained Bella, John and I talked over tea in the canteen. I learned he'd graduated from the University of Washington with a degree in engineering.

"I couldn't get an engineering job, though, so I went to work in the lumber mill near Puyallup where my father and brother worked and where I'd worked summers."

I didn't know he had family. Keiko told me he lived in a barracks for single men. "Where are your parents and your brother now?"

He studied his tea cup for a minute before he spoke. "My brother was killed in an accident at the mill."

"Oh, John, I'm so sorry."

"My father blamed himself."

"What a shame." My words were inadequate, but I could find nothing else to say.

John nodded and took another sip of tea.

"Did your father get sent to Fort Missoula?" Keiko once told me many of the older men, especially community leaders, were sent to Montana right after Pearl Harbor, to a camp run by the Department of Justice. Even Keiko's father, wise and considerate Mr. Ugawa, had been among those arrested. Luckily, they released him and he returned to his family. "What about your mother?"

John shook his head. "They were both desolate. A month after my brother's funeral, they packed up and went back to Japan."

Stunned, I stared at him. "Why?"

"I think they always planned to go back at some point. Many came to America for no reason other than to earn money to send home. In the early 1900's, the part of Japan my parents were from underwent a terrible draught. People were starving. I suspect my parents found America harder than they'd imagined, still, they sent money home. They were frugal. They saved for themselves, plus they put me through college and would have done the same for my brother, if he'd lived. Frankly, I don't know how they did it." He stopped talking a moment while he poured us more tea. "They wanted me to go with them. I wouldn't. America is my home. I was born here."

"Have you heard from them since they went back?"

"Not since a couple of months before the war started. They're from a small village in the mountains near Hiroshima. I worry the government might think they're spies since they spent so many years in America. I suspect they're rich by comparison to the other villagers. Who knows what someone's jealousy might lead to?"

I told him then about a family in Keiko's barracks, the Itos. "Their daughter traveled to Japan before the war and was on her way home when Pearl Harbor happened. Her parents don't know if her ship sank or returned to Japan. They only know it didn't get to San Francisco. They haven't had word from or about her since."

John showed no surprise. "This war has torn a lot of families apart." I was fast learning just how much, along with how little, if anything, we could do about it.

I hesitated to ask about his plans, but did anyway. "Will you go into the Army if you're drafted?"

He didn't appear offended, merely thoughtful. "I don't know. I'm torn. We Nisei are like half-breeds, neither one nor the other. My Japanese half will reject me if I refuse to serve and my American half has already rejected me or I wouldn't be here." He nodded around the room, but I understood he meant the entire camp. "I'm no longer sure how or where I fit."

Keiko returned with Bella before I could reply. "I think she's hungry," Keiko said as Bella stretched out her arms for me. I took my daughter and tried to settle her on my lap, but she squirmed to face me and pulled at my blouse.

John stood. "I need to return to work," he said. "I enjoyed talking with you, Virginia."

"You, too, John." He left and I hurried to carry Bella out of the canteen before she began to throw a fit, something she was quite capable of doing.

"You can feed her at our place. Papa has gone to visit a friend." A few minutes later, Keiko left me and I was glad to be alone, to think about all John had told me.

Marc declared the time had come to plant. "Since I plowed and ridged the fields in the fall, I won't need to disturb the dirt—just enough to plant the seeds—and it will be more compact, allowing the water to flow more freely in the ditches." I'd finished the dinner dishes and was wiping up the counter. "I'll fertilize better, too. I tried to raise sugar beets a few years ago, but failed because I didn't put down enough nitrogen at the right time. That's why they didn't develop like they should have done, why their sugar content was so low."

Even though I still worried about devoting the entire farm to one crop, the way he spoke amused me, like a teacher at the front of the class. "So where did you get all this knowledge about sugar beets?"

"From the sugar company guys and some farmers who were more successful with them than me."

"Oh." Finished with cleaning up, I sat at the table across from him and reached for the front page of the Twin Falls newspaper, tired of thinking about sugar beets. All I could do was hope they would be a winner this time.

True to her word, Keiko came back to us, this time with a girl named Suki. I gave Suki Paul's old room, but told her she would be needed in the fields not in the house, like Keiko.

"That's okay. I like being outside."

"Well, come August you might not like it so much. By then, though, we'll all be outside suffering with you. Well, July, too. I'm told the beets always need thinning or weeding or something done to them."

We got four teenaged boys and a couple of older men to help in the fields as well as Suki; Keiko and I would obviously be kept busy most of the time simply preparing food. I asked about John Sato while we fixed breakfast the morning after they all arrived. "Is he still busy with his job at the camp newspaper?"

Keiko opened a cupboard and brought out a large bowl. "He got his draft notice. I'm not sure what he's decided to do. With most people against the resisters, the decision will be hard for him."

I nodded. I'd thought often of John and the decision he would need to make. "So how do you feel about them, the No-Noes and the draft resisters?" I stirred the oatmeal while Keiko opened some jars of peaches she'd helped me can the summer before.

"If I were a man, I'd be one." She poured the peaches into the bowl.

"Oh? You don't strike me as someone who would go against authority."

Keiko shook her head and pursed her lips, but she didn't say anything more.

I gave the big pot of oatmeal a final stir and moved it off the heat. "Let's get this stuff to the picnic table. I see them coming out of the prove-up now. Marc's already eaten and gone out to the fields."

Suki tried, but she found keeping up with the men in the fields nearly impossible, so Marc told me to teach her to milk the cow and put her in charge of the barn. She was soon happy slopping the pigs, dealing with the new calf, and taking care of the chickens. Then I put her to work in the garden. Earlier, Marc had plowed an extra quarter-acre.

With all the people to feed now, the vegetables the expanded garden produced would be essential. Besides the usual corn, carrots, radishes, and potatoes, we planted squash, cabbage, zucchini, peas, cucumbers and even eggplant. I'd found my mother's recipe for eggplant parmesan and looked forward to trying it. The year before, Keiko and I put in two rows of strawberries and now the off-shoots needed to be replanted. Also like the previous summer, we devoted a portion of the garden to watermelon and cantaloupe. Between weeding and watering the garden and taking care of the animals, Suki had plenty to do, freeing Keiko and me to work inside.

We were canning baby dill pickles one morning—the kitchen smelled of vinegar, and the fan, on high speed, did little but shift the hot and steamy air around. Sweat beaded on our foreheads and my back felt slimed. A car horn blared as I tightened a lid. I peered out the open window, puzzled when Mr. Hargrove, our mailman, drove toward the house. Normally he simply put what little mail we got, mostly farming brochures and seed catalogues, into the box at the end of the lane.

"He must have something he wants me to sign for." I wiped my hands on my apron before untying and hanging it over an open cupboard door. "I'll be right back." I figured

Marc had ordered something and failed to mention it to me. "Afternoon, Mr. Hargrove."

He answered in his usual gravelly voice. "Got a letter you need to sign for."

I frowned and took the letter, addressed to both Marc and me, and saw Letterman Army Hospital in the upper left -hand corner. "Who in the world is writing us from an Army hospital in California?" Leo was in the Army, but in Europe and if anything happened to him, we would have heard. The same went for Paul, we would have heard. He was in the Navy, anyway.

Mr. Hargrove didn't answer, but pointed with a shaky finger to the line where I needed to sign. Everyone knew he should have been retired from the postal service years before. Partially deaf, his driving worse than Dad's, he terrorized everyone who had the misfortune of sharing the road with him. Marc claimed they kept him on because of the war. After I signed his receipt, he backed up then started down the lane. My eyes followed his progress only a moment before returning to the letter. I turned it over several times— as though the envelope alone would reveal some clue— before I tore the seal and took out the letter.

Marc came running as soon as I rang the farm bell. I watched as he read. "We should have been notified immediately," I said. He shook his head, continuing to study Major Phillip Trotter's letter. I tried again. "It doesn't make sense. Paul would surely have listed you or Dad as next-of-kin, so why didn't the Navy tell us he'd been hurt?"

Marc folded the letter and returned it to its envelope. "Obviously, he didn't list us. But at least he's asked this doctor, Major Trotter, to notify us he's well enough to come home."

I still couldn't believe our youngest brother had purposely denied his family's existence. "We should have been notified the minute he was wounded."

Marc continued to frown. "I doubt they could have notified us right away, even if they'd known we existed. I imagine it's pretty crazy when an airplane crashes into a ship"

Instantly chagrined, I thought of the families of the men who'd died. Paul was lucky not to be one of them. We were lucky.

In his letter, Major Trotter told us a little of what to expect. *"His right arm and hand are pretty much useless right now. We've done several surgeries. Orthopedics is a specialty here at Letterman, which is why your brother was sent to us from Balboa Naval Hospital. We've done all we can. Now the hand and arm need time and gentle exercise to heal, as much as they're going to. The ophthalmologist treating him believes with time, your brother's eyesight might partially return."*

The last line stunned me. Our brother was now blind and the doctor mentioned the fact like an afterthought. Paul, who, even as a boy, had been a voracious reader, would now be unable to see the books he loved. My throat closed at the thought of how miserable he must be. Tears stung my eyes. "I'll move Suki in with Keiko," I said, struggling to get the words out. "And make sure his room and all his things are as he left them."

The letter, which Marc folded and returned to its envelope, said Paul would be arriving at the air base near Mountain Home the following week. "Do you think you can get him? I shouldn't leave the men on their own right now." Although he didn't say as much, I suspected my brother worried this second attempt at growing sugar beets might lead to another failure. In addition, interest would soon be due on the bank's loan.

"Sure. Keiko can manage lunch with Suki's help. The letter says his plane is due around noon. I'll take Bella and plan to leave right after breakfast. I'll have plenty of time. With luck, we'll be home by late afternoon."

I stood on the tarmac and squinted at the sunlight glinting off its wings as Paul's plane touched down. Bella bounced in my arms, throwing herself from side-to-side, her favorite game. The plane taxied toward us. Unprepared for the noise and the blast of air from the plane's propellers and disregarding Bella's protests, I held her face to my chest, covering her ears as best I could until the engines were cut.

A nurse stood next to me with a wheelchair. "He'll need to be seen by one of the doctor's here before he's released."

"Will it take long?" Nervous, I wondered how much Paul had changed, not only by the war and his injuries, but simply by time. I hadn't seen my brother in years. He'd barely turned thirteen when I left home. On the drive to Mountain Home I'd tried to remember what he was like back then, but I'd been too caught up in myself and my plans to pay attention to a young boy. Now, all I could picture of him were his green eyes always watching me, or others, when they weren't glued to the pages of a book.

"Not too long," the nurse said. "The doctor will need to make sure his condition wasn't worsened by the flight."

"Worsened by the flight? Is that possible?"

She hastened to reassure me. "Given his injuries, it's unlikely."

Two men rolled steps to the door of the plane. Several passengers and crewmen exited before a uniformed young man helped my brother down the steps. They walked toward us, the young man guiding Paul's hesitant steps. Paul's right arm was in a sling. He looked thin enough to snap in half.

"Paul?" He turned his white-blond head toward the sound of my voice and I saw myself reflected in his dark glasses. My throat thickened. Muscles jumped beneath my skin. "It's me, Virginia." Tears pooled in my eyes. I tried to blink them away, but they spilled over, onto my cheeks. "Paul," I said again and reached out with my free arm to embrace him as Bella drew back, clinging to me. At my touch, Paul stiffened and I dropped my arm.

The nurse frowned and shook her head at me. "We'll get you over to the infirmary where the doctor can check you out," she told Paul, her voice bright with forced cheer. "Then you and your sister can head home. And your little niece—Bella, isn't it?" This directed to me. I nodded, unable to speak.

We were both silent as we drove away from the base an hour later. I stopped at a gas station in Grand View to fill the truck's tank. Paul still hadn't spoken. His thin lips appeared sealed together. "Are you hungry?" I asked. He shook his head. "Marc wanted to come, but couldn't get free. Except for a few acres of hay, he's planted the entire farm in sugar beets this year. Lots of farmers are doing it instead of the usual hay, barley or potatoes." He still made no reply.

I began to resent the lack of response and fell silent myself as we drove out of Grand View and then for several miles after. I'd fed Bella and changed her diaper while the doctor checked Paul. Now in the harness strapped to the seatback, she lay asleep, curled up beside me, her head in my lap. I stroked her silky-fine hair with one hand.

I tried again. On the bridge over the Snake River, near Bliss, I spotted a couple of Bald Eagles riding the wind currents high above the turbulent, muddy-green water. "The river is full. I'm almost surprised, considering how much water is being siphoned off and flowing through the irrigation canals."

When Paul still showed no sign that he'd heard me, I gave up.

Only the noise of the truck's tires filled the cab as we drove mile after mile on the narrow highway, bordered by sand and sage. When we eventually came to Shoshone, I turned south, toward the farm. Bella slept on.

*9*

# *KEIKO*

Virginia got out of the truck first, her back stiff. Marc helped their brother out. Razor-thin, his face set in a grim mask behind dark glasses, I wondered if he was angry or simply in pain. Maybe both. The old man stood to one side, shuffling his feet. Bella asleep and cradled in her arms, Virginia followed the other three into the house. I quickly moved away from the window.

Voices and shuffling feet sounded above my head as they got the brother settled in his room. A minute or two later, Virginia came downstairs and into the kitchen. I asked how the drive went.

"Okay. Long."

A few minutes later, Marc stuck his head in and said he was going back out to the fields.

Virginia stared at him, frowning. "Is he okay on his own?"

"He said he wanted to sleep. I'll be back in a couple of hours. Ring the bell if you need me for anything."

After he left, Virginia remained quiet for several minutes. A couple of times I thought her about to say something, but each time she changed her mind. I put the salt and pepper shakers in the cupboard. She sighed. "I think

*135*

I'll take a nap as well. I'll be down in time to help with dinner."

As she walked away, her shoulders shook.

I'd already peeled the carrots and cut up several cantaloupes Suki earlier brought in from the garden—it was all I could do toward preparing the evening meal. I went into the living room to dust. I'd picked up the carving of a bird mounted on a twisted stick, when the old man came into the room.

"Put that down."

The harshness in his voice startled me and I nearly dropped the little blue and white bird. "I was about to dust him. A nuthatch?"

The old man frowned, but nodded. "Be careful."

"I've seen you carving, out on the porch." For some insane reason, I wanted to keep the conversation going. "I didn't know you painted what you carved. I like the way you posed him—like he's considering an important question."

The old man gave another grudging nod before he settled into his overstuffed maroon chair by the window, the chair so old and well-used the seat cushion was permanently indented, molded to his skinny form. He picked up an old copy of Life magazine and turned a few pages, pretending to take an interest in the articles and pictures. I returned to dusting, moving a lamp and a small bowl out of the way, conscious of his eyes flicking between the magazine and me. The scowl never left his face. I quickly finished dusting and left the room.

That night, long after the family retired to their separate rooms, Suki and I sat on the front porch and visited. The light from Virginia's window fell onto the rose bushes in the front yard, in full bloom and healthy, now weeds no longer choked them. Suki talked about friends from camp, so many of them back east now preparing to enter various schools. My mind on the blind man upstairs, I only half-listened to her. He was so distant from the family, I struggled to think of him as Marc and Virginia's brother. Virginia had been visibly upset when she brought him home that afternoon. He barely ate dinner and didn't speak, not even when Marc asked him a direct question. Instead, he either shrugged or shook his head, yes or no.

Sometimes the blind man sat near the garden, where Suki had stretched a sheet between four poles above a wicker chair she carried from the porch. Several times the wind knocked the poles down, but Suki always managed to get them upright again. Often the old man stared at the pair from where he sat on the porch and several times I caught Virginia watching the two from a window, a perplexed expression on her face.

Even Marc, who seemed unfazed by anything, avoided his brother, burying himself in his paperwork or journals when he wasn't in the fields working. Only Suki seemed to know how to talk to the man. I wondered why he held himself apart from his family. I didn't think the war caused the distance, but something else, something that happened before he went away. I wondered what it could be.

Suki and I were once again on the porch after everyone else went to bed. The night hot and sultry, Suki fanned herself with a newspaper.

"What do you two talk about?" I asked.

She continued to fan herself. "Nothing much. I tell him about the clouds, the color of the sky, how my forehead feels pressed against the warm side of the cow, the sound of milk squirting into my bucket. Things like that. Sometimes he tells me about being at sea. He says he liked going out on the deck alone at night, seeing the stars and moon shining on the water, hearing the ship cut through the waves." She stopped waving the newspaper and turned to me. "Can you imagine how awesome that would be, Keiko? Nothing but ocean as far as the horizon, as far as you could see in every direction?"

Never having seen the ocean, nor a body of water wider than the Columbia River in fact, I couldn't imagine. "Is he aware you're Japanese-American?"

"Oh, yes. I've told him all about how my family was brought to Camp Minidoka from Seattle. I've told him about the workers in the fields being Japanese-Americans, too. He laughed, like it was all a big joke."

Well, to him our internment might be a big cosmic joke. He and God might both see the humor, but I didn't. As soon as the thought crossed my mind, I tried to un-think it, knowing I blasphemed. But the image of God slapping his knee and laughing at our stupid squabbles down here on earth wouldn't go away.

One morning Virginia told me we needed to think about preparing food that would keep for several days at a time.

"Why?"

"Marc needs everyone's help in the fields next week. The weeds are getting ahead of him—with irrigation, they flourish right along with the sugar beets. He'll probably need us off and on all summer."

I thought a minute. "Instead of making up sandwiches every day, we could carry out the ingredients and have everyone make his own for lunch."

Virginia nodded. "That's a good idea. How far ahead can we make rice balls?"

"Depending what's in them, they'll keep for a day or two, but any longer and the rice dries out."

"Could we make them the night before? If so, we'd only need to come back a few minutes before the others to put everything on the table."

In the end, Virginia stayed at the house with Bella and her brother while Suki and I joined the men in the field.

The sun beat down. The muscles in my back and shoulders screamed from bending over the hoe, digging up the weeds and redirecting the water. When the water flowed in the shallow ditches between the bushy rows of sugar beets, my feet sank into the gooey mud, reminding me of the walkways at the camp after it rained. I straightened and stretched my muscles, looking for some relief. For this, we earned sixteen dollars a month—I'd never worked so hard in my life, not even the summer before, digging and bagging potatoes.

I leaned on my hoe and stared into the distance where puffy white clouds obscured the view of the mountains. A welcome but stiff breeze sprang up, drying the sweat trickling down my back, also nearly blowing the broad-brimmed straw hat I wore off my head. I tightened the string under my chin and returned to work.

The boys, though they were city boys, seemed inured to the hard labor. They teased one another and Suki and me, and we soon learned to tease them right back. Even Marc sometimes loosened up enough to poke fun at one or another of us, but for the most part he remained aloof. Virginia told me he worried about the gamble he'd taken, planting the entire farm with one crop. Until then, I didn't realize farmers took risks.

Aside from the teasing camaraderie in the fields, the hoeing allowed plenty of time to think. As I tried to ignore my aching muscles, I pondered what had occurred that spring. I hadn't told Virginia everything when she asked about John Sato and the No-Noes.

Over the winter and spring, John and I had become friends—or perhaps 'confidants' better described our relationship. In large part I shared his anger at our situation. I was angry and resentful. But I feared I might be growing resigned as well, because at times, I simply wanted to go home, wherever that might be. Still, I lent a willing ear and John often discussed with me the growing No-No movement.

The movement may have started at Heart Mountain with the group that called itself the Fair Play Committee, but it was spreading to all the camps, a few at a time. "We have half-a-dozen young men here at Minidoka—probably a few more who haven't spoken out yet," John told me.

"They'll be arrested." We were sitting across from each other at his desk at the Irrigator.

John nodded. "Tried and put in prison, too. They know that, the same as Minoru Yasui, Fred Korematsu and Gordon Hirabayashi knew what they were risking."

Each of the three men he spoke of had sued the government. Yasui's and Hirabayahi's even got as far as the Supreme Court, unfortunately to no avail. Korematsu's suit was still pending. The case of a woman named Mitsuye Endo waited as well. Her case sounded the most promising to me.

"Some things are worth standing up for," John said. "The Constitution is one of them."

"You're right." I thought of my many arguments with Mako. I'd said much the same about the Constitution—for all the good it did me.

That night, the rain had come down hard and the wind rattled windows. Three No-No boys, making their way back to their barracks from the canteen, were overtaken by a gang of other young men. The No-Noes were severely beaten. Torn away by the wind and rain, their cries for help went unheeded. Two No-Noes ended up in the hospital. The third died in the mud, between two barracks.

The young men who did the beating were arrested and charged with manslaughter. Their parents were devastated.

I'd gone to school with all three No-Noes, including the one who died, Richard Sawada. Papa and I were among the few who attended his funeral. Mr. Sawada wouldn't acknowledge condolences. "Do not bother with your sorrow," he told Papa, his eyes hard and glaring. "Instead of answering the call to serve his country, my son brought shame to his family."

Poor Mrs. Sagawa stood at her husband's side, her head bowed, weeping.

Sad for each of them. I wondered if they would ever be whole again.

Not long after the beatings and Richard's funeral, a camp administrator gathered us around the flagpole in front of the administration building. We huddled together in the wind and waited as the administrator paced back and forth before the flagpole. He finally stopped pacing and faced us. "You people killed my son. He was on Guadalcanal less than a week, and you killed him."

Bile rose in my throat. I choked back the words I wanted to fling at him. How dare he even think that? His son wasn't the only one lost in this war. Every barracks block held at least one grieving family, mothers and fathers who'd never see their sons again, wives who'd never again share a bed with their husband, children who wouldn't know their fathers.

I appeared alone in my outrage. As we walked away from the administrator's accusation, a friend of Tommy's said he wasn't going to wait for his draft notice. "I'm going to enlist right away. I will prove I'm American." Those with him nodded. But others, mainly young boys, fourteen- and fifteen-years old, turned hostile. They'd always gone around in gangs, but now they started playing hooky from school, caused trouble and worried their parents. The self-imposed discipline that once ruled the camp was coming apart, and everyone remained on edge.

As promised, Tommy enlisted the day after graduation. Torn between anger and sadness, I cried when he leaned out the bus window and waved goodbye. Papa tried to stay brave, but he, too, could not hold back the tears.

I whacked at more weeds with my hoe as my thoughts spun on to thinking about where he and Mako might be at that moment. I wasn't sure Mako got all my letters, and I didn't want to worry him when he could do nothing, but his mother's health had deteriorated after receiving a letter from a woman who used to be their neighbor. Anti-Asian laws on the West Coast made owning property impossible for Asian immigrants, so for nearly twenty years the Itos had leased their farm. The owner, who'd promised to sell the farm to Mako one day, had sold it to someone else. With that news and still not knowing what had happened to her daughter, Mrs. Ito simply gave up. I doubted she would be alive to greet Mako when he returned from the war.

I glanced up and discovered I'd come to the end of another row. "Let's go eat," Suki said from the row next to mine. The others, too, were walking toward the house.

We washed our hands with a bar of soap and water from a hose at the side of the house. I cupped some water in my hands and dabbed my face and neck as well.

Suki got the blind man from the porch. I still had a hard time thinking of him as Paul—that name seemed too benign for this angry boil of a man. Suki didn't agree. "You don't know him—he's kind and thoughtful." She walked with him to the picnic table, barely touching his left arm to indicate where he needed to go. She fixed his plate and set it on the table in front of him, telling him where things were located as if the plate was the face of a clock.

I helped Virginia bring the rest of the food from the kitchen then got Bella out of her playpen and brought her outside as well. I'd spread a blanket on the grass, but Bella was crawling now and, blanket abandoned, would no doubt keep both Virginia and me busy as she explored whatever caught her attention, an ant, a flower, a blade of grass.

The three teen-aged boys took their plates over to the tree next to the rusted farm equipment. The old man came to the porch door and yelled at them to keep away from his truck.

Virginia rolled her eyes. "I don't know what we're going to do with him," she said to Marc.

"Lock him up."

My eyes flew to the blind man. At least in my presence, this was the first time he'd voluntarily spoken.

Virginia and Marc were surprised as well. "Why should we lock him up?" said Virginia.

The blind man's mouth looked like he wanted to spit. "Never mind." He retreated into silence once again. Suki, next to him, said nothing, merely continued to eat her lunch.

Virginia frowned. Marc shrugged and took a bite of his sandwich.

I seemed to be alone in understanding what the blind man meant. Their father was a lunatic, I was sure. Perhaps he *should* be locked up. With all the hatred that roiled inside him, I could only imagine what growing up with him must have been like. But the blind man's words sounded nearly as hateful as his father's words did. Once again, I felt certain whatever lay between them was nothing to do with the war.

Something soul-shattering must have happened to cause so much anger and hatred.

The rows of sugar beets stretched to the horizon. With nine of us working, Suki and me, the two older men and the teen-aged boys, plus Marc, who continued to work with a fury we were hard-pressed to match, we finished hoeing the fields by the end of the following week. The others went back to the beginning, to do the whole thing over again. Suki and I returned to our normal chores. She said the cow and calf were pleased to see her back.

The heat continued without respite. One mid-August day Virginia and I went outside to help Suki in the garden. While I picked plump, ripe strawberries, sweet as honey, Virginia weeded. Suki hoed. The blind man sat beneath his shady sheet with Bella asleep on his chest. Watching them together, as I'd done the last couple of weeks, I found it easier to think of him as Paul. It was obvious in the way he spoke to her and stroked her hair with his good hand that he loved his little niece. Bella seemed to understand his limitations, never lunging from his grasp as she did with the rest of us.

A car came down the gravel lane, breaking into the silence. A man got out. Virginia, several rows over from me, gasped. The man headed in our direction.

Under her straw hat, Virginia's face flushed and lines appeared to carve down like parenthesis from the sides of her nose to her tightened lips. Her eyes darted to Bella. "What are you doing here, Tucker?" I'd never seen her so shaken.

"Is that a way to greet an old friend?" I wasn't good at judging men's ages, but thought him to be forty-five or maybe even fifty. I didn't like him, but not because he was slim, tanned and rich-looking. Suki stepped from behind a cornstalk. We both stared at him.

Virginia's chin lifted. "I asked what you're doing here, Tucker. How did you find me?"

He stood on the lawn at the edge of the garden. "Your old roommate, Callie, gave me your address. I was in the area and thought I'd stop in." His eyes traveled over her. "I like the farmer's daughter getup, but I'm surprised you gave up Phoenix for this. The place doesn't do you justice."

If his remark was intended to be a compliment, it didn't work. Virginia scowled. "I thought I made it clear in Mexico I wanted nothing more to do with you. We're busy here, please leave." She started to kneel and begin weeding again when Bella woke up with a startled cry. Virginia's hands shook. She straightened and took a step forward then stopped and stuck her hands in her pocket—a failed attempt to appear nonchalant.

I went to Bella, now fully awake, trying to sit upright on her uncle's lap.

"Who is this man?" Paul said under his breath.

"I'm not sure," I whispered back. I took Bella and bounced her on my hip then headed toward the house. "She needs changing," I said over my shoulder.

As I started to pass him, Tucker reached out and gripped my upper arm. "Who do you have here?" Before I could react, he took Bella from me. "She's mighty cute. How old is she?" When no one answered, Tucker's gaze swung to Virginia, his eyebrows raised. "Mine?"

Virginia shook her head. "No, Tucker. She's not yours." As though suddenly released, she walked over and reached for Bella. "She's mine."

"Hold on." Tucker wouldn't let Bella go. Bella whimpered and reached out for Virginia.

Suki went to Paul's side and whispered something to him. Paul rose and they both crossed the patch of lawn separating us. Paul held out his left hand. "We haven't met. I'm Virginia's brother."

Tucker stared at Paul's outstretched hand before taking it. Suki disappeared around the corner of the house. A moment later the farm bell began ringing like mad.

Tucker frowned. "What the hell is that about?"

Bella reached out for Virginia and this time Tucker let her go. Holding her daughter, Virginia moved away. "You need to leave, Tucker."

He brushed an imagined speck from the front of his shirt. "I can't believe you'd rather hang out with a crippled blind man and a couple of little Jap girls. Why work yourself ragged when you can enjoy life? I'm on my way to Montana, to see about some beef for the Army, but then I'll be heading back to Phoenix. Come with me. We'll have fun again. You can even bring the kid."

The farm bell was still clamoring when Marc's truck skidded to a stop, dust swirling up around it. Marc jumped down. "What's going on?"

Tucker's eyes narrowed. "The troops have arrived," he muttered.

Marc strode up to him. I didn't even notice his limp anymore. He scowled. "Who are you?" I'd never heard his voice so harsh.

"Virginia and I are old friends." Tucker tried to put his arm around Virginia's shoulder, but she shook him off.

Marc nodded. "I've wanted to meet you for a long time." He pulled back his fist and drove it into Tucker's stomach. I gasped, hardly able to believe what he'd done.

Tucker grunted and grabbed at his midsection before collapsing to his knees.

"Leave," Marc growled. "Unless you want more."

Tucker shook his head. "Bastard," was all he managed to get out. He was struggling to his feet when a loud blast rang out followed by a bunch of pings.

I whirled around, my heart in my throat.

The old man stood at the corner of the house, under a poplar tree. His thin legs were spread, his feet planted. He held a shotgun. "Get out. You come back, I won't be firing no warning shots."

Tucker managed to stand upright, wobbling only a little. "You're crazy. You're all crazy." He turned and headed toward his car, one hand still lodged against his stomach. When he got to the car, he swung around and glowered at Virginia. "Don't worry about the kid. I already have a couple of brats. I don't need another." With that, he got in the car, slammed the door, and started the engine. A moment later, spitting gravel, the car tore down the lane.

We all stared after him except for the old man, who'd gone back in the house, the screen door slamming shut behind him. A v-shaped pattern of dark spots were on the side of the house near where he'd been standing.

Marc opened and closed his fist. When Tucker's car turned onto the highway, he grinned at Virginia. "I told you I'd make him pay."

Virginia closed her eyes then buried her face against Bella's neck. Bella, who'd let out a frightened wail when the old man fired the shotgun, quit crying, and pulled on her mother's hat string. After a few moments, Virginia looked up. "Thank you. Thank you all."

Marc nodded. "Guess I'll go back out to the field."

Suki helped Paul to his chair then picked up the hoe and went back to work.

"Are you okay?" I asked. Virginia nodded. I walked back to my basket, knelt, and began picking strawberries.

Virginia put Bella in her playpen and returned to weeding.   In the companionable quiet came the far-off sound of the tractor starting up.

The phone in the hallway rang. Virginia went to answer.

"Hello. Yes, she's here, Mr. Ugawa. Just a moment. Keiko, your father needs to speak with you."

My hands trembling, I stood on tiptoe to speak into the mouthpiece of the phone. "Papa, what is wrong? Has something happened to Tommy?"

"No, your brother is fine." His voice sounded tinny. "Mrs. Ito died this morning. I thought you would want to know."

I explained to Virginia and asked if I might go back to Camp for a few days.

"Of course. Suki can help me in the kitchen until you can come back. Go pack what you need while I finish the dishes."

When we got to Camp Minidoka and parked the truck, an Army bus stood near the reception building and several people milled  nearby, men  with suitcases, mothers or wives clutching their sleeves, some crying, some silent, all waiting.

Virginia came to an abrupt halt. "There's John."

He stood alone, his suitcase at his feet.

"You've decided to go," I said when we reached his side.

John nodded. "The American part of me wanted to stand up and fight despite facing three years in prison, but apparently lacked the courage of its convictions. My Japanese side won the battle and is now happily ready to face the enemy in Europe." He forced a smile.

"I'm glad we got to see you before you left." Although I was unaccustomed to showing affection toward someone unrelated to me, especially a man, I hugged John then took Bella from Virginia's arms so she could do the same.

Virginia's lips trembled slightly as she stepped forward and put her arms around him. John hesitated for only a second before returning her embrace. They stood together almost a full minute before John dropped his arms and stepped back. Without another word, he picked up his suitcase and moved toward the bus. "Take care," Virginia whispered. Five minutes later, we stood waving with the others as the bus pulled away from the parking lot and out the gate.

# 10
# VIRGINIA

Damn, damn, damn. Damn. I pounded the truck's steering wheel with the heel of my hand before I collapsed against it. I couldn't stop my tears. Tucker showing up without warning left me rattled and drained. Now to say good-bye to John Sato, to see him get on that bus, knowing where he was going….it was too much. I leaned back against the seat and Bella patted my tear-wet cheeks. "Ma-ma," she said. "Ma-ma."

I couldn't stop sobbing. Bella continued to pat my cheeks and hair until I turned to her and sniffed mightily. She laughed. I wiped my cheeks and tried to smile, but the smile wobbled on my face. I pulled her into my arms. "You and me now, baby girl, just you and me." Releasing her, I started the truck once again and eased back onto the road toward home. I'd gone less than half a mile before I realized what I'd said was untrue. Bella and I weren't alone. We had Marc, Paul, Suki, Keiko and even my crazy old father. Straightening my shoulders, I gave my daughter a real smile. "We're going to be okay."

The leaves on the poplar and cottonwood trees started to turn yellow, and the crew finished defoliating the sugar beets. Time to harvest them. Keiko called to let us know she was ready to come back, which pleased Marc. He would still be short-handed though, so arranged to get the help of three Italian POWs, from Camp Rupert, the prisoner of war camp about forty miles away.

As soon as the Italians arrived, Dad acquired a sudden interest in helping—he volunteered to interpret. His Italian seemed a little rusty at first, but soon he communicated easily with the three men—no doubt finding it helpful that one of the Italians spoke fluent English.

The fourth day they were with us, I sat at the picnic table next to the English-speaking Italian. We'd finished lunch and were drinking a final glass of lemonade before everyone went back out to the fields. Dad and the other two Italians were under the cottonwood tree, examining Dad's truck. I watched them for a minute before returning my attention to Niccolo. He was movie-star handsome. Suki and Keiko both agreed. Suki liked his dimples. They flashed whenever he laughed, which he did with regularity. Keiko found his curly hair the main attraction.

"So how did you learn to speak English so well?" I asked.

"My mother was Canadian."

"Oh? Is she in Italy now, or Canada?"

Niccolo crossed himself and the laughter faded from his dark brown eyes. "She was not called upon to witness the two countries she loved at war with one another."

"Oh, I'm sorry." I instinctively reached over and covered his hand with my own. "Marc and I lost our mother, too, when we were teenagers." He turned his hand over and squeezed mine. After a moment, I pulled my hand away. "Where in Canada was your mother from?"

"Montreal—in Quebec, just above the state of New York." I'm sure he guessed that like most Americans, I didn't know as much as I should about Canada's geography.

"Does she have relatives still living there?"

The laughter returned to his eyes. "Many—I have Canadian aunts, uncles and cousins by the score."

There it was again. Another reminder of our interconnected world and the many families being wrenched apart by the war. "When this is all over, maybe you can visit them."

"I would like to see them all again."

"You've been there?"

"Oh yes, many times."

"Where in Italy is your home?" I didn't know any more about Italy's geography than Canada's.

"Tuscany. You've heard of the Leaning Tower of Pisa?" I nodded. "The family farm and vineyards are north of there," he said. "We also own an apartment in Rome."

I found it surprising that he came from a farm, too, though obviously a more successful one than this. "You must miss everything. What about brothers or sisters?"

He smiled again, the dimples flashed. "Oh yes—a brother a few years younger than me, but he is a priest so not in the army, thank God. Also, two younger sisters." Once again, the laughter drained from his eyes, fled from his lips. "I have no idea how they are faring, nor my father." He sighed and lifted his eyes heavenward. "I can only hope He is watching over them."

"Okay, let's go." At Marc's shout, everyone, including Niccolo, rose and headed for the truck to take them out to the fields once again. Keiko and I would be joining them as soon as we put the lunch things away and I got Bella down for her afternoon nap. Suki would remain behind to mind Bella and look after Paul.

I still didn't understand what made Paul so resistant to all of us when he'd first come home. At least he'd let down his guard with Bella. He often held or played with her. Suki, too, had a way with him the rest of us couldn't match. She spent many hours sitting next to him in the evenings, in the living room while listening to the evening news on the radio or on the front porch, always gently massaging his hand, stretching out the muscles in each finger, bending his elbow and forcing him to pull against her strength. With Suki, Paul never complained of being too tired or ready to quit.

Overwhelming gratitude brought the sting of tears to my eyes, gratitude for each of them, Suki, Keiko, the workers in the field, Japanese-American and Italian POWs alike. Where would we be, how would we run this farm without their help?

Keiko stood behind me and held onto to my shoulders as I drove the tractor and wagon out to the field. As soon as we got there, she jumped down and grabbed a shovel. I jumped down, too. With one of us on each side of the trailer, we pitched shovel-full after shovel-full of sugar beets into it.

Late in the afternoon, the wagon and the big farm truck Marc had borrowed were full. Even Dad's old truck was filled and sputtered along. Lined up like a parade, we drove out of the field and down the lane, heading for our sugar beet dump. It was one of many along the railroad line running parallel to Highway 25.

Like the day before and the day before that, we would reach the dump around five, and it would probably be close to eight before we got back to the house, assuming the line to off-load wasn't too long. The others would have eaten, but plates would be kept warm for Marc, Dad, and me. The next day, we'd get up and do the same thing over again.

Despite being exhausted, as we all were, Marc beamed, ecstatic with the tonnage of the beets we'd produced. "Let's just hope the sugar content is high enough to make it all worthwhile," he said.

We'd been hauling the beets out of the field for ten days when Niccolo asked if he could speak to me in private. "I must tell you something important," he said.

With the rest of the crew outside eating breakfast, I invited him into the kitchen. "What do you need to talk to me about?"

"Your father."

My stomach clenched. "What about him?" I held my breath.

"He is trying to talk us Italians into escaping."

"What? What do you mean, escaping? When? How?"

"He says he will drive us to where you take the sugar beets. He says we can hide until the train arrives. When people are busy elsewhere, loading, he tells us we are to slip aboard."

Relief swept over me and I started to laugh. "That's crazy. The train only goes to the processing plant in Twin Falls. Where would you go from there?"

"Not I! I have no intentions to take part in this. Stefano and Michel may. I thought you should know."

I stopped laughing and thought of all the trouble this would cause. Marc was the one responsible for these men. If they tried to escape, he'd be in hot water with the Army, maybe even arrested. It wouldn't be Dad, the one who deserved to be. "Thank you for coming to me with this," I said, fully sober now. "I'll let my brother know what you've told me. I'm sorry to say, but my father is a little crazy."

His dark eyes filled with sympathy. "I know."

"I suppose we'll laugh at it one day," I told Marc after dinner, when we found ourselves alone and the others occupied elsewhere—Dad in his bedroom, Suki and Paul on the porch and Keiko in the living room listening to the radio. "What are we to do in the meantime?"

"I'm not sure," Marc said. "I wish we had John Sato here. He'd keep an eye on them for us."

"Well, I think Niccolo is trying to, at least he warned us." I blinked away the sting in my eyes at the mention of John Sato. "I suppose we could hide Dad's keys."

"Or I could make sure his truck doesn't run, but we'd need to keep the other keys away from him—no more leaving them in the ignition or on the seat. And I suppose I'll need to take the spark plugs out of the tractor at night."

"Why don't we talk to him, explain to him how much trouble you'll be in if they run off." My naivety struck me the minute the words left my mouth. Once Dad got an idea in his head, nothing deterred him. If contrary to his own, viewing anything from another person's perspective lay far beyond him.

"Let's think about it a bit." Marc's voice was resigned. "In the meantime, I'll go fix his truck." A while later, after I'd gone to bed, he knocked on my door before sticking his head around it. "I disconnected a wire under the dash and loosened a sparkplug," he said. "I also put his tools where he won't be able to find them, at least for a while."

"Good—that should keep him out of trouble for a day or two anyway."

The next morning, Dad stomped into the kitchen from outside. "My goddam truck won't start." I stood in front of the stove stirring the now customary pot of oatmeal. Keiko buttered toast. He ignored Keiko and spoke to me. "I'll drive the tractor today—you can help load."

"Why not work on the truck?" I said, trying to sound innocent. "Maybe you can get it running again. Then you can drive it out and join us."

Keiko continued to butter toast. She'd already sliced and arranged the cantaloupe on a large tray.

Dad thought for a minute. "You're right. The goddam thing ran like a charm yesterday—can't be too much wrong."

Marc was right. He'd found the best way to keep our father in line. I just hoped Dad wouldn't figure things out. If he did, there'd be hell to pay. At noon, when we came back to the house for lunch, I spotted Dad leaning under the truck's hood. He'd found his tools and now beat on something with a wrench, cursing a blue streak. I glanced at

Marc and found it hard not to giggle. My brother frowned and shook his head.

Unfortunately, we congratulated ourselves too soon. A short time after midnight, Marc shook me from a sound sleep. "Dad's gone, his truck, too."

I woke instantly, fully alert. "What about the Italians."

"Gone, except for Niccolo—he came and told me."

"I'll be right down." Marc left and without turning on the light, I dressed and tiptoed out of the bedroom, gently closing the door behind me so I wouldn't wake Bella. Keiko was up and in the kitchen by the time I got there, bathrobe belted around her waist, slippers on her feet. I clasped her hand and smiled my thanks.

"What are we going to do?" I asked Marc.

"He's probably taken them to the sugar beet dump like he planned. I need to call Camp Rupert and let them know what's happened. After I make the call, we'll go look for Dad. I won't tell them about his involvement if I can avoid it."

"How did he get his truck started?"

Marc shook his head. "He must have discovered the loose wire behind the dashboard." He went to make the phone call.

Keiko handed me a thermos of coffee, smiling her sympathy. "You might want this."

We found Dad sitting in his truck, next to the highway.

He scowled and thrust out his chin when we approached him, "What the hell are you two doing here?" He gripped the steering wheel, as though we were going to pull him out of the truck.

Marc might well have wanted to do exactly that, but managed to restrain himself—barely, judging by the expression on his face.

"Better question is what the hell are you doing here, Dad?"

"Out of fuel. Damned rationing."

"So where are the Italians?"

"What are you talking about?" Dad tried to look innocent. "You mean our Italians? How the hell should I know where they are?"

"You don't lie well, Dad. Where are they?"

Although Dad remained unforthcoming, we found the two men hiding in a gully near the beet dump. We hustled them into the back of Marc's truck, siphoned fuel from that truck into Dad's, and got out of there as fast as possible. When we arrived home, Marc called Camp Rupert and told them his earlier call was a mistake, a false alarm. He said we'd found the missing Italians asleep in the hayloft with an empty liquor bottle between them. He got chewed out for wasting their time and for not keeping a better eye on their POWs, but fortunately nothing worse. Or so we thought.

The next day an Army captain showed up with two military policemen. They interrogated everyone, including all three Italians. Eventually, the truth came out and the Italians were taken away in handcuffs, even Niccolo.

Marc's ears reddened and a muscle in his cheek twitched as he tried to control his exasperation. "He didn't run off. He even warned us. I need him."

"Makes no difference," the captain said. "You folks obviously aren't up to providing the kind of security needed with these people.  Just be glad we aren't going to arrest your father for interference and failure to cooperate."

"They shouldn't be locked up anyhow." Dad, belligerent as always, continued to deny blame. "They aren't our enemy—not since Italy surrendered. It was all Mussolini's fault anyway. Those boys would never have fought against the U.S. if it wasn't for that bastard Mussolini."

The captain remained unimpressed. "Regardless of what you think, Mr. Franconi, they are prisoners of war and they'll stay POWs until President Roosevelt says different."

After they left, Marc slammed his hand against the doorjamb. "So, here we are short-handed again. Guess that means you'll need to get your skinny butt out there, grab a shovel and help load sugar beets tomorrow, Dad."

We'd just finished the final load of the day when Marc announced we were down to our last five acres. "We should be done by the end of the week." A cheer would have gone up except everyone was about ready to drop. Keiko, with the men, walked wearily toward the house where she'd help Suki put dinner on the table. No less tired, Dad, Marc and I set off to deliver the day's last load of sugar beets.

At the beet dump, we pulled into the long line of trucks and horse- and tractor-drawn wagons to wait our turn to off-load. We hopped down, Marc and Dad from their trucks, me from the tractor, and joined one of several clusters of farmers.  They weren't discussing the weather or the sugar-content of their beets, the common topics of conversation in these daily gatherings. Politics, in the form of the upcoming elections, was on everyone's tongue.

No matter his success in ending the Great Depression with the New Deal, the country's record two-percent unemployment and our many recent battlefield wins, President Roosevelt's election to an unprecedented fourth term was not a foregone conclusion, not in our part of the country.

"Harry Truman—never heard of him," a farmer from a few miles out of Eden said, spitting out a stream of tobacco juice for emphasis.

Another farmer agreed. "Yeah, something fishy goin' on there—why not keep Garner? Why switch now?"

"Garner is a crazy SOB is why. Dewey's gonna win anyway."

The talk against Roosevelt went on and on, with complaints about the government getting too big on one hand and not doing enough for farmers on the other. That damned Roosevelt, as they all referred to him, was too friendly with this group or not friendly enough with that group. And everyone united in opposition to the New Deal, the common thread being "The government needs to stay out of our business."

I didn't join in the discussions, either for or against. My feelings about President Roosevelt were mixed. I didn't think anyone could have done a better job getting us out of the depression, and I thought he'd done well against formidable odds in the war. I also admired how he'd fought and beat polio. I couldn't see the barbed wire and guard towers around Camp Minidoka, though, or picture them in my mind without feeling outrage. I wasn't sure but what that one solitary act, signing the order creating the camps, didn't nullify every good thing he'd done.

I'd have asked the men their thoughts on the subject, but I already knew their answer would be that at least he'd gotten that right.

I looked at the hundred-foot long stack of sugar beets we were waiting to add our own loads to, just one of many stacks scattered along the railroad tracks waiting to be hauled away. In addition to the stacks, trucks rattled past us on the highway, heading straight for the processing plant in Twin Falls. Each stack, each load spoke to how much local farmers, our family included, owed to Roosevelt's order. Without the order and without the Japanese-American labor the order brought, all those tons and tons of sugar beets would be rotting in fields.

We got home well past dark. Bella was already down and asleep for the night. I'd barely seen her in the past two weeks. Upstairs in our shared bedroom, standing next to her crib and stroking her hair and cheek, my eyes filled with unshed tears. I wanted so much for this child. I didn't want her life to be easy, full of indulgence. But unlike me, I hoped she'd make good decisions.

Dad had eaten and gone to his room and Marc was half -way through his dinner by the time I joined him. He wanted to talk more politics, but I couldn't muster the energy to do anything except eat the chicken and dumplings kept warm for us. After I finished, I took a quick bath and fell into bed.

As things turned out, what I thought about FDR mattered little. On November 7th, he handily beat Thomas Dewey, winning his fourth term.

Soon after, Marc and I were taken by surprise when an announcer on the nightly news reported that per the Roosevelt Administration, there was no longer a need for the internment camps. The camps, including Camp Minidoka, would close the following spring. Marc looked stunned. He began pacing the living room. Several times he thrust his hand into his hair or slammed his fist onto the back of the couch or chair. Several minutes passed before he spoke. "So where in hell are we supposed to get the help we need next summer?"

# 11
# *KEIKO*

Was what the man said true? Could the camps really be closing? Gathered around the Ashida's stove, listening to the nightly newscast, we stared in wonder at one another, hardly able to believe what we'd just heard.

"Where are we to go?" Mrs. Ashida voice quivered as she asked the question foremost in our minds. Mr. Ashida's eyes darted to Papa and Mr. Ito, his brows raised.

No one had an answer. Our Japan-Chinatown apartment was doubtless rented to someone else. The Ito farm had been sold. Mr. and Mrs. Ashida once owned a grocery store in Tacoma, but they were forced to close before being sent to the Puyallup Assembly Center, euphemistically referred to as Camp Harmony, before coming to Camp Minidoka. Their store had been rented to a Chinese-American couple.

Our stories were repeated across the entire camp—homes, farms and businesses gone, families scattered. I thought of my friends, away at school, no doubt establishing themselves in other parts of the country. Perhaps I should have done the same. I might be in Chicago now, or Atlanta or even Providence, Rhode Island. Instead, I'd insisted on remaining at Camp Minidoka with my father, planning to return to Portland and my music. Those plans seemed impossibly naïve now.

I didn't sleep that night and beyond the curtain separating us, Papa tossed and turned as well.

The next day, Virginia came to visit us. "I told them at home I needed to go to the store in Jerome, but I wanted to talk to you."

"You've heard the news."

Virginia had a strange expression on her face when she put Bella down. "We did. Do you suppose President Roosevelt really did wait until after the election to make the announcement, because he didn't want to upset West Coast voters?"

I shook my head and shrugged, unable to give her an answer. "I guess we can't complain about the timing of the announcement so long as the camps are closing."

"What will you do? Where will you and your father go—back to Portland? Oh, Keiko, I will miss you."

I'd miss Virginia, too. We'd shared so much over the past two summers, Bella's birth, dealing with her father, Paul, the sugar beets—she'd become like my sister and I thought, or at least hoped, she felt the same about me. I poured us each a cup of tea. Bella, who walked on her own now, played in the curtains separating our sleeping quarters, batting at them, wrapping herself in them, all the while gurgling her contagious little belly-laugh. Virginia called her away.

"She's fine," I said. "She won't hurt them."

Virginia took a sip of tea before repeating her question about where Papa and I would go. "Do you know yet?"

My stomach clenched once more, my lips twisted. "I'm not sure. Most young people are already gone from here. The boys to fight the war and the girls, including most of my friends—well, all but Suki—have gone off to universities in the East or Midwest. Only old people and children are here now." I threw myself back against my chair. "I suppose we'll go back to Portland, at least eventually."

Virginia's amazing navy-blue eyes studied me, her head cocked to one side. "You don't seem excited."

"I'm not sure what to think. All the while we've been here, that's exactly what I wanted—to go back to Portland and win a music scholarship. Now I'm not sure I even want to study music."

"You play so beautifully, though—if not music, what would you study?"

"I've been thinking about law."

"Become a lawyer you mean?" Virginia sat back in her chair, her eyes wide, her brows raised in surprise. "I guess I never thought about a woman as a lawyer. Can you be one?"

"I'm not sure," I said with a little laugh. "Well, there are some women lawyers, but I don't know if any are Japanese-Americans. I might be the first."

Virginia laughed with me and then sobered. "Well, I think you'd be a great lawyer."

I walked back to the truck with her. Neither of us said much. Virginia looked pensive, while I couldn't stop thinking about the future. I tried to put my own jumbled thoughts aside. "You look worried. What's troubling you?"

"I don't want to burden you with Marc's and my problems."

Bella had wanted to walk on her own when we left the barracks, now she stopped and plopped to the cold ground, refusing to get up. I scooped her into my arms, but she reached for her mother and Virginia took her.

"Tell me," I said.

"Well, I don't want you to worry, but with the camp closing, Marc's afraid he won't get the help he needs next summer. I'm sure something will turn up, though."

"Oh." I could think of nothing else to say and we were both quiet again. In some ways, the farm had come to feel like home to me, though I had no desire to live there the rest of my life. Still, I hated thinking someone would replace me.

We passed the restroom-shower building. Virginia's eyes darted to it and away. She didn't comment.

Several young girls with schoolbooks in their arms walked toward us. A milder than normal wind tugged at their jackets and coats, blowing bobbed black hair this way and that. I nodded to two who lived in the next barracks to ours.

Virginia shifted Bella to her other hip. "Have you heard from Mako since his mother died?"

"No. Papa helped Mr. Ito send him a message, but I'm not sure he received it. I worry about him. I worry about all of them." I quickly blinked away the tears that pricked my eyes.

Virginia stared ahead. "I keep thinking of my brother, Leo, too. We hardly ever get a letter from him anymore." She drew a breath. "And poor John Sato, with his parents returned to Japan and never hearing from or about them— like the Itos never having word of Nobuko's fate."

We'd reached the truck by then. Virginia buckled Bella into her harness. "I'll try to get over whenever I can. Perhaps you and your father can come and spend Thanksgiving with us?"

"We'd love to." It would be just the thing to take our minds off where we were going to live.

"I'll ask Suki, too."

I laughed. "Paul will like that."

Virginia tried to start the truck, but the engine was cold and she needed to press the ignition a couple of times before it caught.  She shivered and eyed my long WWI coat, nearly dragging along the ground. "I think I actually envy you that."

"Shall I check with the WRA—they might have another one in stock?" We both laughed as she backed out. A minute later, she was gone.

Without Virginia and Bella to distract me from my worries, my head down, I started trudging back toward our barracks. A sudden loud bang had my head whipping up, my eyes searching. A rifle shot. I knew it instinctively. Several people screamed. Without stopping to think, I ran toward where I thought the shot was fired, one of the towers. MPs and guards were running, too, blowing their whistles.

A man lay on the ground. It took only a minute to recognize Mr. Sano, Papa's bird-watching friend. He was bleeding from his hip. Papa, covered with blood, knelt beside him.

"Papa," I gasped and rushed to his side. "Are you hurt, too?"

He shook his head. He tried to stop Mr. Sano's bleeding by pressing on the wound with a handkerchief, already soaked through. I tore my scarf from around my neck and handed it to him.

The guard scrambled down from the tower. I recognized the young man with the pale blue eyes and angelic face, the one who didn't look old enough to be in the Army. "He wouldn't stop. He was trying to escape."

Papa looked up, his brows drawn together in a frown. "He's deaf and he was intent on watching a Goshawk being harassed by blackbirds."

"He was trying to escape," the guard repeated.

Papa expelled a loud breath and turned back to Mr. Sano, renewing his efforts to staunch the bleeding.

Footsteps beat along the graveled path. Dr. Toma ran toward us followed by two nurses carrying a stretcher. They got Mr. Sano onto the stretcher and started to carry him away. Dr. Toma pressed a large white cloth against Mr. Sano's wound. My bloodied scarf lay abandoned in the dirt.

"Wait!" Running toward us was another MP, this one an officer. He arrived out of breath. "What's happened here?"

"He was trying to escape," the guard said for the third time.

"He was not trying to escape," Papa said, exasperation sounding in his voice. "I told you, he's deaf. He didn't hear you."

Dr. Toma was impatient. "I need to get him to the hospital. He's going to die if we don't get the bleeding stopped."

"Go ahead. You go with him," the officer told two of his men.

I stared at him. "Do you seriously think Mr. Sano needs to be guarded? Do you think he's going to get up from that stretcher and run away? The  man is barely breathing." The officer gave me a quelling look, but made no reply.

Dr. Toma and the nurses, the stretcher with Mr. Sano between them, rushed off, followed by the two guards and Papa. I hurried after them.

"This is so crazy. They just announced the camps are going to close," I said to Papa, catching up to him. "How could such a senseless thing happen?"

Papa said nothing, his mouth clamped tight as we hurried along.

At the hospital, Dr. Toma and the nurses disappeared through a door with Mr. Sano, still unmoving on the stretcher. The guards looked unsure if they were to follow or wait. After hesitating, each looking inquiringly at the other, they went through the door as well. Moments later, they were ushered back out. They stationed themselves on either side of the door. Papa and I took chairs.

Before long Mrs. Sano arrived, supported by two of her friends. Her eyes were wild and filled with frantic tears. Papa clasped her shaking hands in his. She was nearly breathless. "Where is he?" she finally managed to ask.

"They are taking care of him, Sano-san. We can't go in."

"What happened? Who would shoot my husband?"

"The guard says he was attempting to escape. You know that is ridiculous. We were nearing the fence, but only to watch some blackbirds badgering a Goshawk. Unable to hear the guard's order to stop, he continued."

Mrs. Sano wailed. "That is no reason to shoot him."

"The guard is young—that is the only excuse I can make for him." Papa's voice was filled with sadness. He turned to me. "Keiko-san, please get Mrs. Sano and her friends some tea."

I bowed my head then went to locate tea.

After what seemed like an eternity, Dr. Toma came and explained to Mrs. Sano it would be at least forty-eight hours and maybe longer before they could say if her husband would survive. "We got the bleeding stopped, but the bullet has done damage to the bone in his hip. How much, I can't say for sure." He sighed heavily and sat in the chair next to Mrs. Sano. "I doubt he will walk again," he said. Mrs. Sano gasped. "And he faces the danger of infection. Right now, his body is in shock."

Mrs. Sano continued to cry, though quieter now, wiping her eyes on a handkerchief. "When can I see him?" she asked between sobs.

"I'll have someone take you to him now," Dr. Toma said. He wearily rose and turned to Papa and me and Mrs. Sano's friends. "I'm sorry, but no one else will be allowed now. Maybe tomorrow or the next day."

We left, but the guards remained on either side of the door. I wondered if they'd stay in place all night.

When Papa and I were back in our apartment, I brewed a pot of tea for us. "Please sit, Papa. I need to talk to you." The hours we waited at the hospital with Mrs. Sano had convinced me. I knew what I wanted to do with my life.

"I still don't understand why you suddenly want to study law instead of music?" he said after I'd told him.

"The decision isn't a sudden one, Papa. I started thinking of it last winter, when John Sato first told me about Mitsuye Endo and Fred Korematsu." At the time, their cases were still waiting to come before the Supreme Court. "Fred Korematsu was a welder and classified IV-F because of some problem with his health. He had an Italian-American girlfriend and apparently didn't want to leave either his job or her. He was arrested for not obeying the evacuation order."

Papa held the tea cup in both hands. He took a careful slurp, but didn't take his eyes from me. I was encouraged to continue.

"Like Korematsu, Mitsuye Endo is also from California. After Tanforan, she was sent to Tule Lake and then Topaz." Topaz, a Utah internment camp, was as desolate and dusty as Camp Minidoka, but not for that reason did I identify with Mitsuye Endo.

"Like me, she doesn't speak much Japanese, doesn't write it, has never been to Japan, and she has a brother serving in the Army. She's also never been in trouble and complied with the evacuation order—in other words, she was a 'good' Nisei. Instead of continuing to comply as we did, though, she stood up for herself. She petitioned the government for her freedom." When John told me about her, Mitsuye Endo became my heroine.

Papa listened to me with great interest. "Other cases have been tried before the Supreme Court—like that man from Hood River," he said.

"In those cases, the Court only considered the curfew violations, Papa. They didn't rule on whether putting 100,000 innocent people in concentration camps was a violation of their rights. That's what Mitsuye Endo's case is about—the unconstitutionality of what our country did to us."

Papa nodded, but a deep frown showed his confusion. "I still don't understand, Keiko-san, why this makes you want to study law instead of music."

I took a deep breath. "Because, we can't let this happen again, Papa—what happened to Mr. Sano this afternoon makes that all the clearer. And the only way to make sure it doesn't is through the courts. Japanese-Americans need to be part of that. I want to be part of that."

I stared at my father, mentally pleading for him to understand. Music, nursing, and teaching were considered acceptable for Nisei women. Would he agree with my studying such a non-feminine and non-traditional subject as law? I held my breath, waiting for his answer. I let it out on a long sigh when that answer came.

"Very well, then. We will need to find a way to make that happen."

"Thank you, Papa. I promise you I will make you proud of me one day."

"Keiko-san, I am already proud of you. I only wish your mother had lived to see what a fine and courageous young woman you have become."

My lips trembled and my eyes filled with tears. I would treasure those words forever. "Thank you, Papa."

I was euphoric for at least a day, picturing my rosy future, but the reality of our situation didn't take long to come crashing down. In just a few months' time, Camp Minidoka would close, leaving us with nowhere to go.  And even though my father agreed to my plan to become a lawyer, where would I attend school? How would I pay for it?

My stomach churned and my nerves were rubbed raw by the constant, dust-filled wind, making me wish Mama was still with us. She would understand my mixed-up feelings.

I tried to keep my concerns from Papa.  Mr. Sano was still in critical condition and Papa spent hours at the hospital supporting Mrs. Sano. We hadn't had a letter from Tommy since he left Mississippi for Europe to join the 442nd.  No word came from Mako, either. Perhaps it was petty to be thinking of my own problems when so many others were facing even worse, but I couldn't help myself. Night after night, the wind blew. Night after night, I lay awake for what seemed like hours, thinking, thinking, thinking, before falling into a restless sleep.

# 12

# VIRGINIA

I drove home from the camp, my thoughts on my younger brother. Without Suki's constant and encouraging influence, Paul seemed to be sinking back into his former glum silence, and the icy gulf between him and Dad grew wider with each passing day.

Keiko once told me about Suki's aunt and uncle using her as their built-in babysitter. Maybe she'd like to come and stay with us permanently, or at least until she decided to go elsewhere. She could be a kind of nurse-companion for Paul. And I'd feel much better with her in the house if I decided to go to Portland, as Irene kept asking me to do. My mouth turned down in self-disgust…now who planned to take advantage of sweet, obliging Suki?

Still, I thought the idea a good one. I talked to Marc and got his agreement then wrote to Suki. She replied right away, saying she'd be happy to come. She assured me she would have no problem getting permission from the authorities since the camp would be closing soon anyway. She didn't mention needing permission from her aunt and uncle.

The one person I said nothing to about Suki coming to live with us was Paul. I wanted her arrival to be a surprise. It was, but not in the way I envisioned.

I spent the days before Thanksgiving giving the house a thorough cleaning and preparing both pumpkin and apple pies and drying out bread for the stuffing. I managed to buy a rather scrawny turkey for the centerpiece of the meal—I hoped there'd be enough meat on it to go around. I wanted cranberries, but neither the store in Eden nor the one in Jerome had any.

Dad was my only remaining concern. The scene he could create by going into a rant about Camp Minidoka internees living off hard-working, tax-payer's dollars, made my head ache and my stomach clench. At least he'd begun to forego his invectives about whores and bastards—Bella had softened him as the rest of us never could.

On Thanksgiving morning, Marc went to pick up our guests. I slipped on a jacket when I heard the truck coming down the lane, and went out to greet them.

Mr. Ugawa climbed down first, carefully managing the step before turning to assist Keiko and Suki. "Welcome, Happy Thanksgiving," I said.

Mr. Ugawa bowed and handed me a brown bottle. "It is sake—rice wine. I hope you will like it."

"Thank you."

Marc reached into the back of the truck for Suki's bag. I glanced up at Paul's bedroom window, imagining him lying on the bed, listening to our voices.

"We made the sake with rice we got from the dining hall," Keiko said, smiling. "Several of the neighbors contributed. We keep it hidden under the floorboards because alcohol in camp is taboo."

Mr. Ugawa smiled without comment while casting a curious eye over the yard and house.

Dark clouds threatened rain or maybe even snow. Shivering, we hurried inside. Mr. Ugawa wanted to remove his shoes, but I assured him it was unnecessary. Once coats, scarves and hats were discarded, I ushered our guests into the living room. Again, Mr. Ugawa's bright eyes took everything in.

"Where is Paul?" Suki asked.

"In his room. I'll run up and get him." As I'd known he would be, Paul lay on his bed, his sightless eyes closed. "Paul? We have company."

"I heard."

"Suki's here, too."

"I know. I heard her voice."

"Everyone wants to see you."

"No thanks."

I frowned. "What is 'no thanks' supposed to mean?'

"Just that, no thanks. I'm not an exhibit at the zoo."

"No one said you were. We just want your company." I crossed my arms against the strain of not snapping at him.

"All the same, I'll stay up here."

"For heaven's sake, Paul, will you stop being so ridiculously silly?" I looked at the ceiling and let out an audible sigh. "Suki is here. In fact, I've asked her to stay with us."

"I don't want her here. Tell her that."

I stepped away from the bed. "I most certainly will not tell her that."

Our voices had risen. Marc called up to us. "Are you two okay?"

I called back to him that we were fine before returning my attention to Paul, my voice lowered. "You need to come down. You can't stay up here and ignore our guests. We owe them too much."

"Oh? Like me losing my sight? Like me not being able to pick up a pen or pencil in this mangled hand? We owe them for that?"

I scowled at him. "What are you talking about?"

"Think about it. A damn Jap plane hit my ship, killed my friends."

My breath caught in my throat and I flushed with anger. "Paul Franconi, you know they had absolutely nothing to do with what happened to you. No one at Camp Minidoka did."

His voice remained unchanged. "I'm not coming down."

My teeth nearly snapped together. I needed to take a breath before I dared to speak. "Very well, stay up here and sulk. With your attitude, you won't be missed." I left, forcing myself not to slam the door on my way out. Perhaps I should have been more patient, considering all he'd been through, but I found his attitude impossible to understand. I was disappointed, too, with his rejection of Suki and what I'd expected to be a special surprise.

Marc waited at the bottom of the stairs. "What's up?"

"Our brother is sulking. He refuses to come downstairs—claims he isn't a zoo exhibit." I shook my head, trying to contain my growing frustration. "I don't understand what's got into him. He's saying crazy things."

Marc was calmer and more patient than I thought Paul deserved. "Let's leave him on his own for a bit. I'll go see him after I finish in the barn."

Though still angry with Paul, I managed a smile. "Maybe Suki will want to go out to the barn with you and visit Queenie. I think the two of them became life-long friends last summer."

I returned to the living room after checking the progress of the turkey, and found Dad with Mr. Ugawa. My stomach rolled over. Just what we needed—upstairs, Marc sulking in his room like a child, and downstairs, Dad starting in on one of his awful tirades. But my apprehension quickly turned to astonishment. Mr. Ugawa held the little nuthatch Dad carved for Bella, and the two were deep into a discussion about birds.

"If you want, I'll show you some of the others I've done," Dad said. "They're in my bedroom."

I stared, open-mouthed, as Mr. Ugawa put down Bella's bird and followed Dad to his bedroom, a place off-limits to everyone else.

"Is Paul not coming down?" asked Suki in her quiet voice.

I dragged my attention away from Dad's bedroom door. "Not just yet," I said and flushed, embarrassed by what she may have overheard.

She rested her hand on my arm. "It's okay. I understand."

More heat rose to my cheeks and I blinked back tears. "Well, I'm glad someone does."

"Don't worry, Virginia. He'll be all right." She spoke with a confidence I was far from feeling.

"I hope so." I took a deep breath and tried for a smile. "But for now, I'm ready to sit down and hear what you two have been doing. Then maybe you'll help me in the kitchen, Keiko, while Suki visits the barn with Marc. He'll be going out to milk shortly."

"Excellent," said Suki and Keiko together.

They filled me in on camp gossip and concerns. Suki spoke of problems with gangs of boys. "They're bored and restless and looking for trouble—a good thing the camp will soon close."

"You've heard about the shooting incident with the guard?" Keiko said.

"I did," I said. "Hopefully not someone you knew."

"He and Papa are friends. They were together, watching birds."

I reached over and gripped her hand. "Oh, Keiko, I'm sorry. Your father wasn't hurt, though? He looks well."

"No, but Mr. Sano is not in good shape. They allowed Papa to spend ten minutes with him yesterday, the first time since the shooting. Doctor Toma still can't say when they will release him from the hospital. It's unlikely he'll walk again." Dad and Mr. Ugawa returned to the living room in time to hear the last of Keiko's words. "I told Virginia about Mr. Sano," she told her father. She turned back to me. "And they are doing nothing about the guard, saying only he acted in the line of duty. It makes me angrier and more determined than ever to study law."

"So, you've decided."

"I have." She glanced at her father. He nodded confirmation.

Dinner was a success even without Paul, Marc having no more success with our brother than me. The conversation ranged from birds to Magic Valley history to reminiscing about Japan-towns in both Portland and Seattle. After dessert, we sampled the sake, served hot in thimble-sized cups Keiko brought. We all laughed and joked after two or three servings of the potent brew—even Marc, who put aside his worries for the following summer, at least for a while.

Later, Bella asleep in her crib, I lay in bed and wondered what we were going to do about Paul. His harsh words, words surely overheard by our guests—although they were too polite to say as much—still rang in my ears. Suki had appeared cool and unconcerned. Still, I doubted she'd stay, especially if Paul remained as recalcitrant and boorish as he'd been that afternoon.

Her tactics amazed and delighted me. She began by ignoring him, leaving him to stew alone in his bedroom while she helped around the house and with Bella. She even relieved Marc of milking duties. Just as I'd begun to think Paul wouldn't budge, he emerged from his bedroom. Not even a week had passed. His footsteps sounded on the stairs and a moment later he felt his way into the kitchen.

"Where is she?"

"Where's who?"

"You know who. Where's Suki?"

"I believe she's gone somewhere with Marc." I spooned more applesauce into Bella's waiting mouth. She was old enough to feed herself, but applesauce usually ended up all over her. I'd lost patience and taken over the job. "Marc said something about going into Jerome."

Paul frowned. "What's she doing with Marc? Isn't she supposed to be my nursemaid?"

"Nursemaid? What do you mean, Paul? Since when have you needed a nursemaid or has anyone acted as though you do?"

"You know what I mean—it's why you brought her here, isn't it?"

I wiped Bella's face and hands and took her out of her high chair. "No, being your nursemaid isn't why she's here. She's here because she has more patience to deal with your rotten temper than I do."

"Huh!" was all he said, but he didn't return to his bedroom.

April 12th, the country got the shocking news President Roosevelt was dead of a brain hemorrhage. Though I still disapproved of some of the things he did as president, namely the camps, I trembled to realize I'd never again hear his reassuring voice on the radio, the voice that guided the country through first the great depression, then the on-going war. How would a novice like Harry Truman, a former haberdasher for heaven's sake, handle the heavy burden President Roosevelt had passed to him?

The President's death not enough, thunder and lightning storms shook us, storms people claimed they hadn't seen the like of in years. Some claimed God was sending us a message. One evening we were all gathered in the living room listening to the nightly news broadcast—filled with static as lightning flashes came one after another in the mountains southwest of us.

At first the storm remained too far away to hear, but when it drew closer, thunder cracked and echoed all around, rattling dishes in the cupboards and the glass in the windows, reminding me of the day Marc blew up the dynamite. The lights dimmed then went out and the radio broadcast ended abruptly as the lightening lit up the roiling purple and gray sky. Rain crashed against the roof and beat against the windows. Bella cried and tried to cover her ears until I coaxed her into laughing with each boom and flash.

"I hope everyone is staying safe at Camp Minidoka," said Suki, huddled next to Paul on the couch.

Remembering the newspapers stuffed into the cracks around the window at the Ugawa apartment, something doubtlessly repeated in other apartments, I feared Suki right to worry.

Marc stood. "I need to go check the horses, make sure they aren't spooked."

"You're not going out in this, surely," Suki said as another boom shook us.

"Got to," Marc said. "Glad I put them in the barn, though."

Forty-five minutes later, he dashed back to the house. His jacket and hat dripped water as he took them off and hung them on one of several hooks by the door. "The colt was banging around in his stall. He scraped a hock, but otherwise he's okay—took me a while to settle him down."

The storm passed in the night and the clouds, once again docile as fluffy lambs, moved east. The power came back on around mid-morning and that afternoon, I drove into Jerome for supplies. On the way, I stopped to see how Keiko and Mr. Ugawa fared the storm. Little at the camp seemed to have changed other than I needed to pick my way through the mud puddles to their barracks.

Irene called and again asked me to come to Portland for a visit. Something in her voice told me I should go. Marc drove Bella and me to the bus station in Jerome. I was reminded of the day two-and-a-half years before when he'd picked me up in the same place. I thought of all the changes that had occurred in the short space of time since—Bella's birth, Paul's return from the war, blind, his arm and hand destroyed, me learning to be a mother, learning to be happy with myself, learning to like the farm and my family—even Dad, crazy as such a thing may seem. I thought about meeting Keiko and Suki and how much I'd miss them when the camp closed. I thought about John Sato and what he might one day mean to me—if he survived the war and if I allowed myself to have feelings for a man again.

Marc retrieved our cases from the back of the truck and carried them inside. He held Bella while I bought my ticket.

"Give Irene a hug for me," he said after the bus driver took my large suitcase and stowed it. I kept the smaller case with Bella's extra diapers, some toys, and snacks. "And be sure to get back before planting." Although he said it as a joke, he couldn't hide his concerns about summer, even though the sugar company men told him he could probably get help through something called the Bracero Program.

Looking forlorn, he stood on the sidewalk as the bus pulled away. Bella banged the window and I waved. After a bit, he waved back.

At least one bus occupied each of the four lanes in the large tunnel-like terminal in Portland. Some lanes held two and even three. Men and women, many in uniform, were boarding or getting off or collecting their luggage from storage compartments or down from roofs. Exhaust from idling buses filled the air. I got my suitcase. With the smaller one under my arm and Bella in hand, I went inside to look for Irene.

We waited nearly half-an-hour before she arrived, looking frazzled. "I couldn't get off work early. Sorry you had to wait." She barely looked at me before turning her attention to Bella. "She's beautiful, but of course she would be. Are these your things? Let's go, a friend is waiting outside to drive us home."

The friend, a man who worked in the same office as Irene, sat in his car, a faded coupe, smoking a cigarette and watching a policeman place a ticket on the windshield of a car parked next to a fire hydrant. I climbed into the cramped back seat with Bella. Irene introduced me to the man as we pulled away from the curb. "Pleased ta meetcha," he said around the cigarette still dangling between his lips.

He didn't come in, merely dropped us off at the curb.

Irene's apartment was on the third floor of an old house. "This place must have been a mansion," I said as Irene carried Bella and I carried our suitcases up the stairs. I was winded when we got to her door. She handed over Bella and fished her key out of her bag.

The apartment held a miniscule bedroom and a bathroom not much bigger than a closet. A tiny sink and a small, under-the-counter refrigerator with a hot plate on the counter above it made up the kitchen.

"It certainly is compact." I could think of nothing else to say.

"I'm lucky to have it," Irene said, her chin lifting. "You and Bella can sleep on the couch. It pulls out."

The next morning, after Irene left for work, Bella and I set off to explore the city. I needed to see where Keiko and her family once lived. She'd given me the address. I wanted to take her a report of what Japantown looked like now. I learned from the bus driver the area was no longer referred to as China and Japantown. "All the Japs are gone," he said. "Now it's just Chinatown. If we're lucky, it'll stay that way."

The small shops with foreign writing on the windows fascinated me. And the exotic smells made my stomach rumble, reminding me I'd only had coffee and a piece of toast for breakfast. On the sidewalks, people stared at us, but not in a sullen or disapproving way. Some gave Bella friendly nods. When we went into a small restaurant for lunch, the woman who waited on us seemed infatuated by our blonde hair. She patted first Bella's then mine. "Pretty little girl," she said, over and over. "Pretty mama, too."

"I'm sorry for the mess," I told Irene when she came home from work and needed to step over our opened suitcases. "The diapers shouldn't take long to dry." I'd washed them in the bathtub and hung them on the towel rack and over the side of the tub.

She assured me our disorder presented no problem and she loved having us. But underneath her assurances, I sensed she held something back. I didn't press it. She'd tell me soon enough.

In looks at least, Irene appeared much the same as I remembered. Tall and blonde, between Paul and me in age, she spent a lot of time on her own growing up, exploring, adopting strange critters, including a scorpion and a snake I thought to be poisonous, but which turned out to be a bull snake. She wore the thing around her neck like a feather boa—my skin crawled thinking of it.

In high school, she changed from tomboy to prom queen. She met Bob, who was two years ahead of her in school, and led him on a merry chase, flirting with other boys, even dating a few. But Bob, who worked in his father's shoe store after school and on weekends, was both smitten and undaunted. I thought my sister lucky to have a guy who obviously adored her, especially one as nice as Bob, and wasn't surprised to hear that they married almost as soon as Irene graduated high school.

For the next three days, Bella and I continued our exploration of Portland, including the neighborhood parks and the department stores, as big and grand as the ones in Phoenix. In the evenings, after I'd fed Bella and put her down for the night, Irene and I talked about a wide range of things, but mostly about growing up, before and after Mom died. Irene twisted a strand of her hair around her index finger, a habit I remembered from when she was a little girl.

"What do you suppose Marc is going to do after the war?"

"I asked him once what his dreams were as a kid, what he'd wanted to be when he grew up," I said. "Know what he told me? He said he always wanted to be a farmer—never thought of being or doing anything else. And when the war is over, he says he's going to buy up land. He plans to be the biggest, most successful farmer in Magic Valley."

Irene made a face and pretended to shudder. "Well, my hat's off to him, I guess. Personally, I can't think of anything more boring."

After Bella and I had been in Portland nearly a week, Irene took the day off—we planned to visit the zoo in Washington Park. As we put the final touches on the picnic we would eat in the park, church bells began to chime and sirens blared. A puzzled frown on her face, Irene turned the radio on. A deep baritone voice made the announcement. "Today, Tuesday, May 8th, 1945, the war in Europe is over."

At his words, Irene grabbed my hands and we jumped up and down like two ten-year-olds, hugging and repeatedly shouting "Thank God. Can you believe it? Can you actually believe it?" Bella looked bewildered at out antics. I grabbed her up and ran into the hall after Irene. We raced down the stairs and out of the building. People spilled from surrounding houses and apartment buildings as well, erupting with the news. I'd never seen people so deliriously happy.

With all thoughts of the zoo gone, I hugged Bella. "They'll be coming home soon, all of them. John Sato, Uncle Leo, Mako, Tommy! Everyone, Bella!" She put her chubby arms around my neck and squeezed me back, even though she probably thought her mama and everyone else had gone crazy.

Irene grabbed my arm. "Let's go downtown and celebrate." On Burnside, a couple of blocks from Irene's apartment, we waited for a bus. Several passed us, each one full, even the aisles—obviously, others shared our desire to be at the center of revelry. After yet another crammed to overflowing bus went by without stopping, Irene's patience ran out. "It's not that far. We can walk."

The sidewalk steadily filled with people, joyful and like us heading for the heart of Portland. Along with the crowded buses, cars streamed down Burnside, lights flashing, horns blaring. A few people threw streamers out their car windows. We passed several taverns, each noisy with laughter. A man came out of one and wanted Irene and me to go inside and have a drink with him. Bella clung to my neck, staring at the man. "You're scaring my daughter," I told him.

The man was undeterred. "Don't wanna do that. Hey, little girl. I'm not gonna hurt you."

Irene took my elbow. "Ignore him," she said and pulled me along the sidewalk. The man followed us for half a block, still pestering, but then lost interest and wove his way back to the bar. Irene and I looked at each other. Our hands covering our mouths, we sniggered.

Twenty minutes later we were in the middle of downtown. Confetti and streamers rained from the windows of office buildings, where people leaned out and yelled to the crowd below. The street so clogged with bodies, cars and buses were forced to a standstill, unable to move forward or backward. Most passengers got off the buses and joined the celebration. A few drivers abandoned their cars, or they stood on the cars' hoods, shouting, and waving their exuberance. Police officers on horseback couldn't get through, but instead of getting angry they laughed and joked with the crowd.

"I still can't believe it," I shouted to Irene.

"I know," she shouted back. "I thought this day would never come." Without warning, she sobered and a frown pushed away her previous joyful energy. "I wonder when they'll get home."

"Soon, don't you think?" I hiked Bella higher on my hip. My arms were growing weary from carrying her. No longer the nearly weightless little thing I'd been able to haul around on my hip for hours, she now weighed twenty-three pounds and at that moment felt closer to fifty. "Can we get out of this crowd and find somewhere to sit? Maybe get a Coke or something?"

Irene, still appearing subdued, agreed. "The fountain on the mezzanine in Lipmann's has great Green Rivers," she said, though her voice lacked enthusiasm.

After our cold drinks and another foray into the celebrating masses of people, we caught a bus heading back up Burnside. The boulevard was still thick with cars, their drivers pressing on horns, and we passed more than a few drunken pedestrians.

Night had fallen by the time we got back to Irene's apartment. The forgotten radio still played, relaying the news of Hitler's suicide and the end of the war in Europe, over and over until Irene turned it off. I fed Bella and put her down. The poor little thing was so exhausted, she very nearly fell asleep nursing on a piece of bread crust. Irene and

I collapsed as well, me on the sofa-bed next to Bella, Irene in the over-stuffed chair. Each of us sipped a gin-and-tonic, my first since leaving Phoenix. Outside, sirens screamed and church bells continued to toll the good news. I didn't know Portland contained so many churches, one on every block it seemed. Bella didn't stir.

Irene rose and slammed the window closed. "I've heard enough."

"What's troubling you, Sis? Something's been bothering you for ages—you should be over the moon right now with Bob coming home soon."

She buried her face in her hands and began to sob. "That's just it…I don't deserve him."

I couldn't get anything more from her for several minutes, but eventually she stopped crying and told me everything. A man, of course.

"He was so good-looking, and I missed Bob so much." She lifted her eyes from her lap and looked at me, her chin lifting a notch. "And I missed sex." She said this as though daring me to disapprove. I said nothing, simply waited for her to go on.

A lieutenant-commander in the Navy and working in the same office, he, too, was married, his wife in Pennsylvania. "We both tried to resist the attraction. For weeks, I made sure to stay with one of the other secretaries at lunchtime and on breaks." She sniffed and dabbed at her eyes. "But then one night I needed to work late. I thought I was alone. When Dan came out of his office we were both surprised. He asked me out for a drink after I finished a report my boss needed the next day. I shouldn't have gone with him. I knew the minute I agreed." She started crying again.  "He took me to his place. You can guess what happened."

Her hand clenched and unclenched. I reached across the gap separating us and took it. She grabbed on to me. "Was that the only time?" I asked.

She shook her head. "No. I went to his place two other times and once he came here. I don't know what I was thinking, other than I was so lonely. I know, you don't need to tell me. Loneliness is no excuse. Should I tell Bob? How can I not?" She clutched my hand tighter, tears streamed down her cheeks. "He'll hate me. What should I do?"

I smiled my sympathy, but shook my head. "I'm hardly the person to ask for moral guidance."

"Yes, but you know men. You've dated lots of them, some seriously, like Bella's father."

"We don't need to talk about him." Tucker was the last person I wanted to think about. I hoped I'd never need to think of him again—at least not until the day Bella asked who her father was. What would I tell her? I didn't want to think of that either.

"Still, you must have some idea."

"I don't, Irene. But if you decide you should tell him, you might want to write and explain before he gets home, give him a chance to accept what happened before he sees you."

Irene closed her eyes, her cheeks still wet with tears. "If I do, he might decide he doesn't want to come home at all."

"You're right—telling him would be a risk. Not telling him might be one, too."

Several times in the night I heard her quietly sobbing or moving around in her bedroom. Occasionally a car horn flared before fading away. The church bells at least were stilled. How odd the wonderful news of the end of the war in Europe had ended on a note of sorrow instead of jubilation.

The next morning, Irene came out of her bedroom with eyes red and swollen. "I need to go to work this morning—I know it's your last day and I was going to show you around the shipyards, but they'll be short-handed after all the celebrating last night." She filled her coffee cup and stirred in some milk and sugar then lit a cigarette. "I'm not going to tell him. I thought about it all night. I can't."

"Well, like I said, I'm hardly the person to give you advice, but I hope you've made the right decision." I took a sip of my coffee. "Is this fellow, this lieutenant-commander, is he still around?"

Irene stubbed out her cigarette. "He requested a transfer after I told him I wouldn't see him anymore. He shipped out last October."

"Good. When Bella wakes up, I think I'll take her back to the park where we ate dinner the other night."

Irene nodded, obviously distracted by her own thoughts. She soon put on her coat and left.

Everyone we met on the way to the park greeted Bella and me with a smile and "good morning.' Many drivers continued honking their horns and the church bells resumed tolling. As I pushed Bella in one of the swings, I wondered what John Sato was doing at that moment. I wondered if he even knew Hitler was dead and the war in Europe over. I brushed away a tear and gave Bella another push.

# 13
## KEIKO

The authorities announced Camp Minidoka would remain open until October for those wanting to stay. Many internees were grateful for the additional time. I was astonished to find I was one.

On another wry note, the Court announced its decisions on the Korematsu and Endo cases. With Korematsu, the judges once again confined themselves to the curfew violation. They ruled six to three in favor of the government. In the Endo case, they ruled unanimously in favor of Mitsuye Endo, declaring internment to be unconstitutional. That both decisions came from the same Court, on the same day, was so illogical it struck me as ludicrous. But not a surprise. Everything about our internment was illogical, and had been from the start.

The Court ruling aside, the rumor that we would not be welcome anywhere on the West Coast, including Portland, flew from barracks to barracks. My friends at *The Minidoka Irrigator* corroborated this. The editor handed me copies of the *Oregonian* and the *Seattle Times*. "Read the letters to the editor."

I took the papers to my old desk. My heart sank as I read. *"Our boys who are fighting them don't want to come home and see a bunch of Japs,"* one woman had written. A man wrote, *"Someone should be arrested for even thinking about letting Japs come back here. If they do, there'll be trouble."* And finally, *"Never trust a Jap. Send them all back to Japan."*

I carefully refolded both papers and put them on the desk. Closing my eyes, I reflected on the venomous words. Did everyone hate us so? Was it not enough that my father lost his job and my mother died a prisoner in this place? Did no one want us? What about Tommy and Mako and John? Will they return to America and find they aren't welcome after fighting for the very people condemning us?

The editor told me about a group in Seattle called the Japanese Exclusion Organization. "If they don't spread to Portland, I'll be surprised. They don't want us ever going back. In Washington, they've even proposed an amendment to the Constitution aimed at keeping us away."

Once home, I hung up my jacket and told Papa what I'd learned. "I'm beginning to wonder if we'll ever be able to return home."

He looked up from his writing. "Perhaps we should reconsider the suggestion of Mr. Ito's cousin."

Mr. Ito's cousin lived in a small town near the Oregon-Idaho border. He'd invited Mr. Ito to join him and his wife. He also wrote of a nearby house available for rent. Mr. Ito suggested we take it, at least temporarily.

"We wouldn't stay for long," Papa assured me. "I know the town has no university, but as soon as the war in the Pacific is over, people will be more reconciled. Then we can return home."

"But we won't know anyone except Mr. Ito. This place may be terrible, but at least we know it. Maybe we should wait." Thought pained to advocate staying at Camp Minidoka, there seemed no choice. "Japan may have surrendered by the time the camp closes in the fall." Mako and Tommy might be home, too. I didn't think either of them would be interested in living in Nyssa, Oregon.

In the end, Papa agreed to wait and I volunteered to help Virginia at the farm.

Happy to be together once again, one morning Virginia, Suki and I pulled weeds in the garden. Not for the first time, we talked about the English-speaking Italian, Niccolo.

"Such a flirt," Suki said. "But you always put him in his place, Virginia."

She laughed. "I may have done so, but I liked him, nonetheless. He was fun."

"I liked him too," I said. "I was sad when he and the other Italians were forced to leave."

Suki nodded. "Me, too. I hope they didn't get into too much trouble."

The laughter left Virginia's eyes. "Dad has a lot to answer for—Marc couldn't get help from Camp Rupert this summer, thanks to his shenanigans. The Bracero Program hasn't worked out either—they say they don't have enough workers—so Marc's talking to your friend at the *Irrigator*, Keiko. He wants to get a help-wanted notice in the next issue."

I shook my head, doubtful. "So many have already gone from the camp—I'm not sure there's anyone left wanting work."

Fortunately, three young boys answered Marc's notice, two were thirteen and one fifteen. Young as they were, Marc said they were hard workers. The three boys, along with two of the men from the previous summer, were enough to do most of the work. Often, Virginia, Suki or I helped. Sometimes, all three of us.

The sixth of August started out no different from any other August day. Hot. Virginia stood by the open kitchen window, fanning herself with a magazine. "My birthday is coming up in a couple of weeks. I can't believe I'll be twenty -eight." She shook her head, shrugged, and turned away from the window. "I know it's stifling, but I'm going to fry up these chickens. We can eat them cold tonight."

I wiped sweat from my forehead with the back of my arm. "Let's hope the temperature cools down, or people might not want to eat."

Virginia gave a short laugh. "You're kidding, of course. They don't care about the heat, they're always hungry."

I prepared lunch while Virginia fried the chicken. "Maybe I'll bake a cake for your birthday," I said, even though I'd never made one.

She smiled and dipped a chicken leg in milk before rolling it into seasoned flour. "It's too hot for baking, but thank you for the thought." Grease popped when she dropped the chicken leg into the cast iron skillet. "I think Bella's cutting another tooth. She didn't sleep well last night, poor thing."

"Is she with Suki?"

"I crushed half of an aspirin and gave it to her with some sugar. She finally went back to sleep."

After lunch, we took Bella outside and helped Suki in the garden. Not surprisingly, I found it cooler outside than in the house. Paul, as usual, sat nearby. Bella, sore gums forgotten, toddled after a butterfly. The old man had gone somewhere. We heard the horn before his truck turned into the lane. He drove even faster than normal.

Virginia stood and frowned. "What in the world has gotten into him?"

He climbed out of the truck and hurried toward the house. "We gotta turn on the radio."

The announcer's breathless voice filled the living room. "A bomb—the biggest the world has ever known—was dropped on Hiroshima, a city in Japan on the island of Honshu. An aide to President Truman predicts this will surely end the war."

Virginia stood. "I need to call them in from the fields." She went out and moments later, the bell clanged.

A short time later, Marc carried the radio to the porch and plugged it in.

"What do they mean this bomb is different from any other kind of bomb?" one of the young boys asked. "How?"

Paul sat in a wicker porch chair. "I can't imagine it doing more damage than they say the fire-bombing did in Tokyo, and yet that didn't generate talks of surrender."

Suki spoke for the first time. "My mother's family is from Osaka. I read in Pacific Citizen that it was badly bombed this spring, with thousands of people killed or injured. One has to wonder how many people must die for this to end."

Paul didn't say anything, but took Suki's hand in his own.

My head had gone light when the announcer said Hiroshima. What if Papa had stayed in Japan after his brother died? We could have been living there, gazing up at the airplane flying over, seeing the bomb falling…

Virginia's voice returned me from my thoughts. "Earlier they claimed an immense amount of the city was leveled," she said. "Does anyone know how big Hiroshima is? The announcer didn't say."

I hesitated before speaking. "My father grew up there. He told me Hiroshima is the same size as Portland, but most of the buildings are made of wood, not brick or stone. Wood couldn't withstand such a bomb." I pictured fires as well, terrible fires, people fleeing them. If they survived the bomb and the fires, where would they go? "Do you suppose this really will mean the end of the war?" We all stared at each other, but no one could answer my question.

After a while, Marc and the men returned to the fields.

Days went by and a second bomb fell, this one on Nagasaki, a city on the island of Kyushu. Still, despite what could only be unimaginable losses, no word came from the Emperor. On the nightly news, they speculated the Emperor's generals and admirals argued, offering him contradictory advice. Although this seemed plausible, I doubted the reporters knew.

Finally, on the fifteenth of August, the Emperor conceded Japan's defeat.

We heard people danced in the streets of every city, with confetti thrown down from windows above. Virginia had told me about the celebrations in Portland when Germany surrendered. I wished I'd seen it, could have join in. I'd like to be dancing in the streets now, too. But for Japanese-Americans, the Emperor's surrender seemed to call for a more subdued celebration. Perhaps we should simply be happy we would be allowed to walk freely and no longer be looked upon as the enemy.

How little I knew then of the way our lives were to be.

For days, it seemed nothing would change. A week went by, and another—hoeing, weeding and cooking keeping us all busy—until one day Virginia collected the mail and handed me a letter from Mako. I went outside and opened the envelope. First, he said it would still be several months before he came home. *When I see you again, I want to ask you something important.* My heart began a rapid beat. He planned to propose. My hands trembled. I read the words again. *I want to ask you something, something important.* He couldn't mean anything else. I drew a shaky breath. He was so handsome. I was sure I loved him.

I was only twenty, though. We were both only twenty. My parents had always expected me to go to college, earn a degree. I wanted that, too. I was sure his parents must have wanted the same for Mako.

My eyes returned to the flimsy paper between my hands. I reread the words until the lines blurred. My heart pounded harder. Finally, I folded the letter and returned it to its envelope. I slipped the envelope into my pocket.

That day held another surprise. Late in the afternoon, a strange car came down the lane. "Now who in the world could this be?" Virginia said, glancing out the living-room window.  A moment later, she rushed outside, the screen door slamming shut behind her. Bella wailed at the unexpected noise and her mother's sudden disappearance. I picked her up and followed Virginia.

"What are you doing here? Why didn't you call?" They hugged and laughed.

"I just decided," the other woman said. Irene—they looked too alike not to be sisters.

Virginia broke free and peered into the car. "And who is this?"

"A friend, Richard Small, he won't be staying." Irene pulled her suitcases from behind the seat.

Virginia frowned, but asked the man if he'd like something to eat or drink before he left. The man shook his head. Irene went around to the driver's side and spoke to him before the man put his car in gear and we all watched him drive down the lane and turn onto the highway.

Virginia gave a slight shake of her head before turning back to Irene. "How long will you be staying? Never mind. C'mon. Let's go in the house. Oh, but first, this is Keiko. Keiko, meet my sister, Irene."

I nodded and shifted Bella so I could extend my hand.

Irene took it. "I've heard lots about you," she said and held out her arms to Bella. "Come to Auntie Irene." Bella held back a moment, undecided, before lunging forward, into her aunt's embrace. Virginia and I carried the suitcases and followed Irene and Bella into the house. "Where are Dad and Paul?"

Virginia set Irene's suitcase next to the stairs. "I think Dad's in his room, probably painting or something. Hey

Dad—guess who's here. We've got company." She turned back to Irene. "I'm not sure where Paul is."

I put the other suitcase down. "He said he wanted to take a nap. Should I go up and wake him?"

"I'll get him," Virginia said.

Irene put Bella on the floor and she immediately started examining one of Irene's suitcases, flipping the handle back and forth. Irene patted her head. "Let him sleep. It's not like I'm going anywhere."

A bigger hint than we realized, we soon learned Irene had quit her job and sub-let her apartment. She planned to stay in Idaho until her husband returned from Europe. Like Mako, though, he wouldn't be returning for several more weeks.

Virginia fussed about where everyone would sleep. "All the bedrooms are full. To make room for Bella's crib and to give Suki someplace to sleep after Paul came home, we moved your old bed into Keiko's room—well, Leo's old one."

Irene brushed Virginia's concerns aside. "Don't worry about it. I'll sleep on the couch—same as you did in Portland."

I tried to reassure them both. "You won't need to sleep on the couch for long. As soon as the sugar beets are harvested, Suki and I will be leaving."

Irene wiped a fresh tomato on the front of her blouse. "Where to and why?" She took a bite of the tomato. Juice ran down her chin.

I handed her a napkin. "They're closing Camp Minidoka in October, so we'll have to go somewhere. Back to Portland for my father and me, where I hope people aren't as angry as the papers say." I studied her face, seeking reassurance, but got none.

It seemed strange leaving this place where I'd grown to feel safe and returning to Portland, where I'd once felt safe but which now filled me with foreboding.

At the dinner table that evening Paul gave us yet another surprise by announcing he and Suki planned to marry. "We're going to college. I'm going to use this new GI Bill law.  It will pay me to go to school and give us a place to live. Suki can come to my classes with me and take notes. That way we'll both get an education."

I hugged Suki, but scolded, too. "Why didn't you tell me?"

"We only decided, while you and Virginia were in the kitchen fixing dinner."

Virginia beamed.  "Perhaps some wine is called for. I have a bottle left over from Christmas."

Later that night, the old man, who'd remained silent when Paul made his announcement, threw a fit, his voice loud enough for everyone in the house to hear. "You're gonna marry a damn Jap? What in hell are you thinking about, boy? It's the stupidest damn thing I ever heard of. And you—you're blind. They'll laugh you out of whatever school you think you're gonna go to."

Paul's voice was quieter, but still easy to hear. "Shut up, Dad. Just shut up. You've caused me enough grief. I love Suki and I am going to school, whether you like it or not. And I'm going to be a writer. You may have kept me from my dreams before, when I was still a kid, but you can't stop me now. I'm going. We both are."

Suki and I were in our bedroom, directly above the living room where the old man and Paul argued, their words flowing up and through the baseboard register.

"Don't worry," I said. "He's just a hateful old man life has passed by. You and Paul will be fine."

She stared at the ceiling. "I know. I'm not worried about myself. I worry for Paul. It's not good to hate someone so much as he hates his father."

"Did something happen between them, something other than the old man's nasty mouth and sour disposition? I've always thought so."

Suki's voice held little emotion. "Paul earned excellent grades in high school. Just as now, he wanted to go to university and someday become a writer. In his senior year, his English teacher planned to take him to Sun Valley to meet Ernest Hemingway. Sun Valley is only a few hours from here and Hemingway was there visiting a friend. Paul's teacher and Hemingway knew each other from when they were both reporters in Spain. He told Paul he'd give Hemingway one of his short stories. When the old man heard about the intended trip, he went to Paul's school and accused the teacher of terrible things. The teacher was fired. Paul never forgave his father."

"I don't blame him." Even I knew the importance of Ernest Hemingway, had read some of his work. I reached across the small space that separated our beds and squeezed Suki's hand. "You're going to be so good for Paul."

The voices coming from below grew quiet for a while then suddenly escalated again. The old man's words roared up the register. "Enough—I don't want to hear about it again."

"Those people were innocent. They weren't causing harm to anyone."

"Weren't causing harm? Look what their people did to us."

"The only thing that family did wrong was have the misfortune of being Japanese and asking you and your cronies for help when their car broke down. I'm not even sure they were Japanese. They might have been Korean or Chinese, for all I know."

"Doesn't matter. I told you, what happened to them wasn't my fault."

"You were involved. And you dragged me, a fourteen-year-old kid, into it with you. I'll never forget what I saw that day. Never. I want to die sometimes, thinking about what happened and never telling anyone—to protect you."

Suki and I lay on our beds, neither of us able to utter a word.

★

Irene drove the farm truck and Virginia continued to drive the tractor and wagon. Marc hitched the horses to another wagon. And though it couldn't always be relied on, the old man drove his truck. Consequently, the beet harvest went faster than the year before. I returned to camp a few days earlier than expected, happy to leave the farm where everyone walked on eggs following Paul's and Suki's wedding announcement, plus I couldn't forget the conversation she and I overheard.

"A letter from Tommy arrived today," Papa told me soon after I arrived. "Unfortunately, spring might be here before your brother returns home."

"I got one from Mako saying the same thing." I didn't tell him what else Mako's letter contained.

"We need to make our plans," Papa said. "Tommy expects to find us in Portland."

"I know. But I'm still nervous."

"Hopefully the University Club will allow me to return to my old position."

My father was well-liked when he worked at the University Club. I hoped he wouldn't be disappointed. "Maybe they'll have something for me, too."

"You'll be in school."

"I can work part-time. We'll need the money."

Papa, although reluctant, agreed. We'd been careful, but what he and Mama saved over the years, and the little we'd gotten from the sale of our things when we were forced to leave Japantown, had steadily eroded. We'd need everything we could both earn to support ourselves in Portland and to pay for my schooling. At least Tommy's education was assured. Like Paul, he'd be eligible for the GI Bill of Rights, as would Mako. I wondered if Mako planned to go. We'd never really talked about each other's plans.

As people left, the camp grew more desolate and forlorn. Weeds popped up in the walkways, tumbleweed, papers, and other bits of flotsam gathered against the buildings. Gardens were neglected. One-by-one, barracks emptied and whatever could be carted away was taken by civilian workers and neighboring farmers, though I found it hard to imagine what anyone would want with most of the things.

With little fanfare, the afternoon before Papa and I were set to leave for Portland, Suki and Paul married in the

Methodist Church in Twin Falls. Reverend Greene, whom I remembered from my mother's funeral, officiated. His wife played the organ and sang *Again*, only a little off-key. Virginia and I stood at Suki's side and Marc stood next to Paul. To everyone's relief, the old man stayed home.

After the ceremony, Reverend Greene asked if we'd heard from John Sato. "We often talked when he worked on the stories about the No-No boys. John's a good man."

Virginia's face paled at his question. We'd heard nothing from John in months. Although she didn't say it, from the way she watched for the mailman every day, hurrying down the lane whenever he stopped, I knew she looked for a letter from him and was worried that none came.

"We're afraid he might be injured," I told Reverend Greene. "John has no family in the U.S., no one the authorities would notify. Could you find out something? You could let Virginia know and she'll pass the information on to the rest of us."

Reverend Greene frowned, appearing doubtful, but promised to do what he could.

After a few more minutes, we toasted the newlyweds with grape juice then Marc drove them to the farm and Virginia took Papa and me back to the camp.

I'd already boxed up the family photos and Mama's vase, Tommy's clothes, and the few other things we wanted to save, and sent them ahead to Portland. Our suitcases, too, were packed. I gazed around the room, bare except for the table and four chairs, the wobbly dressing table Tommy made for me, the bookcase, and the stripped cots. I couldn't believe we'd lived in this small space for nearly three years. I thought of all that happened in that time. Mama dying, Mako, Tommy and John Sato going off to war, Papa's friend being shot.  Besides the sadness, I also remembered the joy of Tommy's and my graduation from high school, new friendships made, little jokes and absurdities. I would never forget this place, but when Papa and I walked out and shut the door behind us, no sorrow at leaving followed us.

Virginia and Marc came to the station to see us off.

Virginia's eyes filled with tears. "I'll miss you so much."

"I'll miss you, too. All of you."

Virginia chuckled. "Even Dad?"

I ignored that.  "You'll have to take loads of pictures and send them to me, especially pictures of Bella so I can see her grow." She promised. "And please tell Irene good-bye for us." I'd been surprised Irene didn't come to Paul's and Suki's wedding.

"She's gone."

"Gone? She went back to Portland?"

Virginia's eyes darted to Marc. "We don't know where. The man she came here with, Robert or Richard something, picked her up. She left with him."

"But what about her husband? He'll be home soon. She planned to wait for him."

"Irene isn't much good at waiting," Marc said. "Never has been."

Virginia sighed. "Enough of Irene's dramas—we'll hear from her, when she gets around to it." She gave me another hug. "Promise to write as soon as you get settled."

"I will. You have the address of the hotel where we'll be for a while. I'll let you know when we find a permanent place."

Marc shook hands with Papa. He started to shake my hand, but instead grabbed me by the shoulders and hugged me. "I've never thanked you properly for coming to my rescue the night Bella was born. Keiko Ugawa, you were an angel. You *are* an angel. We'll miss you."

Tears sprang to my eyes once again. "I'll miss you, too."

Virginia and I hung on each other a few more minutes, until Papa told me we needed to board. Once we were settled in our seats, I stared out the window at the three on the platform. Virginia, with Marc standing by her side, showed Bella how to blow kisses. My hand clamped hard against my mouth to hold back the sobs. The train began to move, slowly at first. My eyes blurred with tears, I waved frantically. When no longer able to see them, I turned in my seat and faced forward, toward the west, to Portland and whatever lay ahead.

BOOK TWO

*2008*

# 1
# HELENA

The funny little *ba-bloop* of Bluetooth disconnecting, and Auntie Keiko was gone. In her usual autocratic mode, she had instructed me to contact Nori, her semi-estranged granddaughter, and insist she participate in preparations for Virginia's 90th birthday. The gathering would also commemorate another anniversary of the internment of over 100,000 Japanese-American citizens in the desert strongholds of California, Idaho, Arizona, Wyoming, and Colorado, plus the snake-filled swamps of Arkansas.

Grandma Suki called Auntie Keiko my 'spiritual' aunt. They met during World War Two at Camp Minidoka Internment Center in Idaho. With other internees, they worked on the Franconi farm. Both left Minidoka at the end of the war—Auntie Keiko for Portland, Oregon, and eventual law school. Grandma Suki and my grandfather, Paul Franconi, married and moved to California where my grandfather, using the GI Bill, entered Stanford University, my own alma mater. That was sixty-three years ago—another time, another age, another world.

Grandma Suki told me about all the trouble Auntie Kieko's family had when they first arrived in Portland. Although they found a rundown hotel that accepted them, when they tried to find an apartment, the signs in most of the windows said No Japs. They were met with hostility everywhere, it seemed—people on the sidewalks glared at them. Money was hard to come by, too. They even survived the historic Vanport Flood.

Auntie Keiko, her brother, and Mako Ito all attended a college in Vanport, a complex of apartments built by Henry Kaiser to house his shipyard workers during the war. After the war, nearly half of the forty thousand or so workers returned to the homes they'd left behind when Kaiser recruited them. The college was built to accommodate G.I.s returning from the war. Record heavy spring rains throughout the Northwest caused the Columbia River to breach the high, grass-covered berm separating it from the complex, where twenty-thousand people still lived. The flood wiped out everything. Auntie Keiko said cars bobbed in the water like toy boats.

She eventually received her law degree, but even then, success didn't immediately follow. The so-called hallowed halls of Portland's major law firms didn't welcome Asians in those days, particularly Asian women. So, like Californian Ruth Ochi, a friend, mentor, and another former internee, Auntie Keiko found work in the Japanese-American community. Slowly, case-by-case, she built a reputation reaching across the country, into the halls of Congress and even Ronald Reagan's White House. It earned her a Federal judgeship.

Long retired now, her connections still ran wide. They lay at the root of the problem between her and Nori.

"How is Suki," Keiko had asked after her brief and terse instructions regarding her granddaughter. "Still playing nursemaid to Paul? She once wanted to study medicine, you know."

I did know. Auntie Keiko never failed to mention it. My grandfather was blinded and lost nearly all the use of one hand and arm when an airplane crashed into his ship during the war. In the years since, including while they studied at Stanford, my devoted grandmother was Grandfather's eyes and his right hand.

"They're fine," I said. "In fact, I'm on my way down to Carmel for a visit."

"Tell them I'll see them in August at Virginia's. Don't forget to call Nori." With that she hung up.

I maneuvered past a Range Rover towing an Airstream trailer. The driver, a man in his sixties or seventies, was accompanied by a woman of equal years. They looked so much alike, they could have been twins. Two motorcyclists thundered past, sunlight glinting off their shiny black helmets. We all appeared to be headed to the coast.

I looked forward to a break from the city and my teaching job in Stanford's creative writing department. Breathing Carmel's clean salty air and feeling the sunny warmth of Carmel Valley, where my grandparents lived, would be a welcome treat. I'd grown up spending summers with them, when not at the farm in Idaho running wild with Nori, and with Lily, four years our junior. The three of us were cousins of some sort. Virginia Franconi Sato was my great-aunt, Nori's grandmother, and Lily's great-grandmother. But much more than cousins, of whatever degree, the three of us were friends.

Grandma Suki and her ancient Jack Russell terrier, Zelda, came out of the house to greet me. Zelda, in a brief return to her youth, yipped and bounced in circles around us. Grandma admonished her to stop being silly then turned to me. "Welcome, welcome. It's been too long since your last visit. Your grandfather has been growing impatient."

My grandparents' long, low house backed up against the side of the valley. Vines trailed up the posts of a broad, shaded porch facing a graveled, circular driveway. Behind the house were the pool, where I'd spent hours learning to swim and dive, a vine-covered loggia with brick terrace, and a large flower and vegetable garden. The place was as close to paradise as anyone could get. I grabbed my things from the trunk and followed my diminutive grandmother into the house.

"Paul is in the den."

Grandfather's six foot-three frame was folded into a wheelchair. Severe osteoarthritis, an unpleasant addition to his other physical trials, made the chair a necessity. "Grandpa, I'm here. How are you?"

"About time. Come over and say hello properly." I moved across the room, avoiding Zelda, who still pranced around my feet, and kissed his bald head. He grabbed my hand in his good left one. "Sit down now and tell me how you've been."

"Paul, let the girl wash up and catch her breath," Grandma said from the doorway.

"I need to put my things away, Grandpa. Give me a few minutes and I'll be right back."

"Rosie has lunch ready. We'll eat out on the terrace."

"Wonderful, Grandma, I'm starving. I'll be there in a sec. Keep Rosie with you. I want to say hello." Rosie, a fixture in my grandparents' house since before I could remember, was nearly as dear to me as my grandparents.

I quickly disposed of my suitcase and laptop then joined them outside. After hugging Rosie and in return getting a good scold about being too skinny, I sank into one of the comfortable chairs encircling the table, leaned back, and drew several deep breaths. The tension I'd been carrying around for weeks diminished, at least fractionally, with each breath.

"So," said my grandfather. "What have you been working on that's kept you so wrapped up you couldn't get down to see us in four whole months?"

Not prepared to divulge anything about my miserable love-life, I fobbed him off with a brief account of my busy schedule then changed the subject. "Auntie Keiko phoned."

My grandmother put down her glass of iced tea. "What did Keiko want—she wouldn't have called unless she had something on her mind."

"You're right—and authoritative as always about it."

A smile tugged at Grandma's lips. "She wasn't always bossy—intense, yes, but not bossy. That must have come from her years on the bench."

"Maybe so, but she drives Nori up the wall. Anyway, she's put Nori, Lily and me in charge of getting everyone to Idaho for Aunt Virginia's birthday in August and to commemorate another anniversary of Minidoka."

At the mention of Minidoka, the expression on my grandmother's face changed, as though a barricade just went up. "Best to forget those years."

"I can't agree with you, Grandma. People should know what happened in 1942 and how it happened—there are too many similarities to what American-born Muslims are going through today. Actually, that's one of the reasons I came down."

My grandfather interrupted. "I thought you said you came for a rest."

"I did. But I'm planning to write a book about Minidoka and I can't think of anyone better to talk with about the place and time than my own grandmother."

Grandma Suki was usually compliant—she liked to please people. But even as a teenager, when I first heard of the internment camps, no matter how I badgered her with my questions, she refused to discuss her experience at Minidoka.

"As I said, it's best to forget those years. Ah, here's Rosie with our salads."

Resigned, I leaned back so Rosie could deliver my plate of Salinas Valley greens topped by blackened mahi-mahi. "This looks delicious, Rosie."

She placed a basket of rolls on the table with a pot of butter. "We gotta fatten you up." When Rosie decided on something, she stayed committed. I knew she'd remain vigilant to my eating habits my entire visit. "Just because you got an important job at that school, doesn't mean you can't eat."

When Rosie returned to the house, my grandfather picked-up on one thread of her conversation. "So, what's the latest gossip in the writing department?"

"Nothing much—everyone's getting to know the new Fellows."

"Anyone special this year?"

"They're all special, Grandpa. They wouldn't be receiving Stegner Fellowships otherwise." I went on to tell him about some of the young men and women who'd received fellowships that year.

"Wallace would be proud of what he started."

"You and Grandma were part of that. You're still legend. I'm always asked if I'm related—as soon as people hear the name Franconi." My grandfather was one of Wallace Stegner's first students in 1946. Stegner had gone from teacher and mentor to lifelong friend.

I often envied my grandfather's literary past. He'd met and been friends with all the great western writers—Stegner, of course, but also John Steinbeck, William Saroyan and even the reclusive Robinson Jeffers, who'd lived in nearby Carmel. A decade or two younger than the others, my grandfather was the only one still living.

My comment about him and Grandma being legends at Stanford pleased Grandpa and he began reminiscing about their university days while Grandma and I finished our salads. I leaned back and let his words and the warm air wash over me. My anxiety about Bill Sheppard, his refusal to divorce his wife, and my own future slowly receded.

"It's time for your grandfather's and my afternoon nap and appears time for yours as well."

I opened my eyes. My grandmother was pulling Grandpa's chair away from the table. "Let me do that, Grandma."

I pushed the chair into the house and down the hall to their bedroom door where my grandmother said she'd take over. "We can manage from here. Why don't you go and lie down now?"

"I think I will. And maybe enjoy a dip in the pool later, if you don't mind."

As soon as I put my head on the pillow, my earlier anxieties returned, with vengeance.

I grew up in Palo Alto, literally and figuratively in the shadow of Stanford University. My parents were both busy and dedicated Silicon Valley players, but from an early age, I aspired to follow in my grandfather's footsteps. I set a course for myself, undergraduate studies then graduate work, all in Stanford's creative writing department.

Although as a student I'd sometimes seen Bill Sheppard in the halls or lounge—he was, a former Stegner Fellow in screenwriting and now a professor—I'd never taken a class from him. We officially met soon after I began teaching. Our attraction was immediate and mutual, but I think my name added some cachet—I was the granddaughter of the famous Paul Franconi, Noble prize-winning author of the definitive book on the War in the Pacific and several award-winning short story collections.

Ten years my senior, Bill already had a wife. He claimed the marriage was in name only, of course. It was selfish of me, but I didn't think about her or their two children much, not at first. Too young and full of myself, I guess. But as time went on, I decided I wanted more than an hour in bed a couple of afternoons a week, whenever Bill could work me into his schedule.

"You said you were going to ask her at the weekend."

Bill leaned over and stubbed out his cigarette in an ashtray on the floor next to the bed. "The timing wasn't right. You knew it was my birthday."

Naturally I knew—we'd celebrated the afternoon before.

"My parents flew out from Colorado. Sheila arranged their visit as a surprise for me."

"Well, what about next weekend?"

"I'm flying down to Los Angeles for the conference at UCLA. I told you. My agent will be there, too. We might have a deal with Warner's."

"And the next? What about the next weekend, Bill, or is that one going to be full, too?"

"Helena…you know I love you. I'll ask Sheila for a divorce. I told you I would and I will. I promise."

Six months passed and he didn't ask Sheila. He never would, and we both knew it.

Our final parting wasn't pretty. He'd left a few things in my apartment, a couple of shirts, a tie, a book of poetry. I put them in a garbage bag, along with his overflowing ashtray and handed it to him. I regretted the poetry book getting covered with ashes and cigarettes, but only for a moment.

After he left, I called Nori. "He didn't even have the grace to apologize for wasting nearly three years of my life."

"Bastard." Nori never wasted words. In that, she took after her grandmother.

"I know. The sex wasn't even that good."

"What will you do now?"

"I'm driving down to Carmel Valley next week and I plan to put everything out of my mind. Plus, I want to get Grandma Suki to tell me what she remembers about Minidoka."

"You're still working on that? You know how hard it's been to get any of them to talk—the *Issei* and *Nisei* internees. You'd think it was something they needed to feel ashamed of instead of their country."

"You're telling me. I've also come across something very interesting, but I'm kind of running into a stone wall. I'm hoping my grandfather can shed some light—something that happened before the war, near Twin Falls."

We talked on for a few minutes then Nori needed to take a phone call. "Tell Aunt Suki and Uncle Paul hello for me."

I'd be calling Nori again, perhaps tomorrow, to get her take on the family get-together in August. But now, time for a swim.

The alarm on my phone went off—six-thirty. With the jalousies in the window fully open and a breeze sweeping off the ocean, over Carmel's rooftops, into the Valley and my bedroom, I'd slept through the night for the first time in months. I pushed back the down-filled blanket, swung my feet out and sat on the edge of the bed for a few minutes. The ache behind my eyes was gone and the knot at the base of my skull, on the left, had eased. I took off my tee-shirt and panties and pulled on my swimsuit, still damp from the afternoon before. The house was dead quiet. I'd have the pool to myself. I tip-toed down the shadowed hall and opened the door leading to the terrace.

My grandmother was already engaged in her morning ritual. I watched for several minutes while she swam lap after lap, turning at the end of each in a smooth somersault flip before she pushed off toward the opposite end of the pool. After three more laps, she stopped and took off her cap, spotting me for the first time. "Good morning. Sleep well?" She wasn't even out of breath.

I eased into the semi-warm water next to her. "Perfect. And this is just what I need."

She nodded toward a thermos and cups on the table where we'd eaten both lunch and dinner the previous day. "Coffee's ready when you're done." She pulled herself out of the pool, stood and reached for a towel. Eighty-one and she could still do that.

After twenty minutes of vigorous exercise—how could I do anything less after my grandmother's sterling example—I hoisted myself out of the water and rubbed down with a towel. Struggling to control my ragged breathing and vowing to exercise more, I slipped into my terrycloth robe and strolled over to the table to join Grandma. My breathing was almost back to normal by the time I reached her.

She poured me a cup of coffee and moved the plate of croissants closer. "You haven't spoken of the man you've been seeing."

Her remark surprised me. I'd never told her about Bill. I'd never told my parents about him either. "What makes you think I've been seeing someone?"

"Because you're a lovely young woman—why wouldn't you be seeing someone?"

"Oh. Well, as it happens, I was, but I ended things."

"Which perhaps explains the timing of this visit?"

I tried to smile. "Nothing gets past you, Grandma."  I told her a bit about Bill and me, editing out the part of him being married, leaving in only his lack of commitment. "I think our relationship was becoming public knowledge. In the end, I began to feel humiliated."

"He's married, I expect?"

I nodded, my cheeks reddening.

"Then you made the right decision."

Neither of us spoke for several minutes. I sipped my coffee and watched two sparrows flit from tree branch to tree branch. The white wings of cabbage butterflies bobbed around the spears of lavender, tall yellow yarrow and the pink and coral roses blooming in the garden.

"Your grandfather should be waking soon. After he gets his swim shall we drive into Carmel?"

"Wonderful. Let's have lunch at Roscoe's and maybe we can drop by the bookstore."

By the end of the day, we still hadn't spoken about Minidoka. While enjoying a pre-dinner drink on the terrace, I brought it up again and got the same response from my grandmother—better to forget those years. I wondered if she would ever change her mind and talk about her experiences, as some former internees were beginning to do. Temporarily frustrated, I mentioned the other reason I'd come to visit.

"I've run across a disturbing puzzle I thought you might help me with, Grandpa. It's to do with an Asian family before the war."

My grandfather's mouth tightened and his cheek twitched, but he quickly turned his face in the direction of the house, saying nothing.

Grandma, facing me, didn't appear to notice. "What about them?"

"They were murdered, the entire family, brutally—I won't go into the details. It happened at a place called Lizard Butte. I can't locate it on a map, but it sounds close to Minidoka."

I took another sip of my drink, still puzzled by the expression I'd briefly seen on my grandfather's face. A breeze rippled through the vines shading the loggia, bringing the scent of the roses from the garden.

"I've had no luck finding out anything about the murder, other than that brief reference on the internet. It happened during all that pre-war, Anti-Asian League stuff when everyone was worried about Chinese and Japanese taking over the country—probably in the mid-to-late thirties." I looked hard at my grandfather, but could read nothing on his lined face. "It was obviously the work of more than one person, but apparently, no arrests were ever made. Did you hear about it, Grandpa?"

My grandfather picked up his half-filled glass and drained it before shaking his head.

"Well, do you know what and where this Lizard Butte is?

"A lava outcropping jutting up at an angle. From a distance, the thing looks like a lizard sunning itself. Irene and I used to hike out there."

"So not far from the farm."

"Five or six miles."

"But you never heard anything about the murders?"

"I said no." His voice was sharp and Grandma frowned. He apologized. "I'm sorry. My knee's bothering me."

Grandma covered Grandpa's hand with hers. "I think we need another drink."

"I'll get them," I said.

I frowned into the darkness above the bed. I hated the direction my imagination was taking me. My grandfather's reaction earlier had nothing to do with his knee—he hated anyone to know when his joints hurt. It must have been mention of what happened at Lizard Butte, a gory and brutal act that included rape and torture. But the murders occurred so long ago, when Grandpa was a kid. After all this time, why would he respond like that?

The band of storm clouds appearing earlier in the evening soon passed, revealing through my window the moon and a milky-white strip of stars above the pool and garden. The curtains fluttered in the breeze.

Heaviness formed in my chest the more I thought about the murdered family, and I determined to find out what happened to them—who they were, who killed them, and why.

Several hours passed before I found sleep, and it was nearly nine when I woke the next morning.

A light fog blew in during the night, filling the Valley like milk in a bottle. My grandparents' voices sounded from the kitchen. Occasionally Rosie's voice chimed in.

I'd packed my things the previous evening and planned to leave after breakfast. They argued, naturally, trying to encourage me to stay one more day. But I told them the truth, I needed to get back to town for a meeting the following morning. I also planned to stop in Salinas and see my mother's aunt.

The town of Salinas lay at the foot of the Santa Lucia Mountains, a mere eight miles from the Pacific Ocean, but a twisting and turning eight miles when coming over the pass from Carmel Valley. Salinas' restored downtown featured everything Steinbeck. Countless times I'd visited the library named for him. I loved the ornate old homes in the area, those still in existence and not supplanted by some modern McMansion. Salinas Valley, nicknamed the salad bowl of America, grew everything, from vegetables to flowers to grapes.

My mother's aunt, Millicent Tanabe, lived southeast of town. I found her mowing the huge lawn surrounding their old Victorian-style farmhouse. Nose to the ground, Buddy, her golden retriever, moved back and forth, fifteen or twenty feet in front of the John Deere riding mower. I watched the two for several minutes before walking out to get Aunt Millicent's attention. Buddy spotted me first and came running, the hair bristled on his neck until he got close enough his rheumy eyes could see me. Then his plume of a tail started to swing wildly.

Her cheeks round as the apricots she grew, Aunt Millicent pushed back her wide-brimmed straw hat, grinned and turned off the mower. "Helena, I wasn't expecting you. What a nice surprise."

"I just wanted to stop in and see how you and Uncle Henry are faring—it's been a while since I've seen either of you."

Born in Manzanar Internment Camp, Aunt Millicent had been too young when the war ended to remember the experience. Gunnery Sergeant Henry Tanabe, Aunt Millicent's husband and a fellow child internee, grew up to serve in Vietnam. A hero with several medals pinned to his chest, he came home a changed man.

As a child, Uncle Henry scared me the way he stared into the distance, like he saw something no one else saw. If he'd served in the First World War, he'd probably have been diagnosed as shell-shocked. Now they called it PTSD, Post-Traumatic Stress Disorder. By whatever name, Uncle Henry struggled with it, diabetes, too, and now vascular dementia. Sometimes, life simply wasn't fair.

Aunt Millicent took my arm. "Wonderful," she said. "C'mon in and say hello to Henry. I suspect he's bored with his own company and with watching the Military Channel on TV all day. My goodness, you'd think he'd seen enough of wars."

I cast a glance toward a small building about twenty or thirty feet from the house, surrounded by a charming flower garden. In my mind, the bathhouse and ofuro were the best parts of Aunt Millicent's place. She'd built the lean-to shed herself, around an old wine vat. About five feet in diameter, the vat was outfitted with a ladder on the outside and a bench inside. In the olden days, water was heated by a fire, built beneath whatever was used as a tub. But Aunt Millicent hired a plumber to put in a gas hot water tank and a recycle system so that the water in the tub remained the perfect temperature.

The bather soaped down, scrubbed, and rinsed on the wood-slat covered floor outside the tub and only climbed in when his or her body was squeaky clean and thoroughly rinsed. But, oh, to step into that steamy water and soak until your skin pruned-up…pure bliss.

"I detect a longing look in your eye. Want a soak?"

"I'd love one, Aunt Millicent. But I don't have much time. I need to stop at Mom and Dad's on the way home."

"How are they?" She said the words with care, knowing things didn't always go well between my parents and me.

"Same as always—too busy with their work to take much notice of what the rest of the world is doing."

She smiled her understanding and put a comforting hand on my shoulder. "Well, you surely have time for a glass of lemonade."

"I do. How is Uncle Henry?" I followed her into the living room and looked for a place to sit. The couch and every chair were piled with newspapers, magazines, and mail along with unfolded laundry. Housekeeping wasn't high on Aunt Millicent's list of things to do.

"He's okay," she said. "We're going to see a new doctor next week. Maybe he can help."

For years, Aunt Millicent had taken Uncle Henry to one doctor after another. So far, she'd only been disappointed. Who knows what Uncle Henry felt? I sometimes wondered if he simply liked the attention.

"I hope so."

"Henry, Helena is here." The only response was the television announcer's voice coming from another room, advertising a knife that would saw, cut, bore, open bottles and two or three other things I couldn't make out. Aunt Millicent tried again. "Henry, did you hear me? Helena is here to see you." When Uncle Henry still didn't answer, Aunt Millicent scurried out of the room. I was about to follow her when she came back and headed upstairs then quickly down. "He's not in the house. I need to find him."

No sign of Uncle Henry in the yard, Aunt Millicent went out to the road and stared both directions.

"I would have passed him if he'd been heading toward Salinas. I didn't see anyone."

"The bathhouse is locked. Maybe he's in one of the outbuildings." Aunt Millicent's voice frayed. She'd always been fearful Uncle Henry might harm himself. We both hurried in the direction of the barn, the chicken coop and the storage shed. No Uncle Henry. "I wasn't on the mower for long—maybe twenty minutes at the most. He can't have gone far."

Because we'd run out of places to look, we headed down the graveled path to the bathhouse. The padlock lay on the ground, the key in it. Aunt Millicent caught her breath. I pulled open the door, dreading what we might find.

Uncle Henry sat fully-clothed in the tub, a folded wet cloth across his forehead. He looked utterly content. Aunt Millicent let out her breath.

I kicked off my sneakers, pulled my blouse over my head and climbed out of my jeans. Skipping the usual cleansing routine, in bra and panties I climbed in beside him. "Hi, Uncle Henry."

Aunt Millicent hesitated only a moment then threw back her head and laughed. "Oh, what the Hell," she said and began stripping off her own clothes. Uncle Henry didn't say a word to either of us as she climbed into the tub and sat on his other side. Below the wet cloth, a smile slowly spread across his face.

I got back to my apartment and thumbed through the mail. Finding nothing needing immediate attention, I poured myself a glass of wine and went out on the balcony to watch the sun set and think about my visit to my parents that afternoon.

My mother greeted me with a harassed look. "What brings you here? Your grandparents are okay, aren't they?"

I'd texted her I was going down to Carmel for the weekend. She hadn't bothered to reply. "They're fine," I said. "Where's Dad?"

"He's in the library, in a meeting. Don't disturb him. I only came out to use the restroom."

"What's so important you're meeting on Sunday?" Not that important meetings, on Sunday or any other day, were uncommon in this household.

"We're getting ready to buy out another company. Your father is with the lawyers, putting the final touches on our offer."

"Oh, well I won't stay. Just wanted to tell you I stopped in at Aunt Millicent's."

"How is Henry? My God, why doesn't she put him in some kind of home and get on with her life?"

"Because she loves him?"

My mother chose to ignore my sarcasm. "I need to get back to the meeting."

She left the room without turning back. I was glad Aunt Millicent's daughter lived near her, someone to help when Uncle Henry became too much for her. Because she surely couldn't rely on her niece for help—my mother would never have time for anything except business.

I was well into my third glass of wine when the phone rang.

"Hey, Lily."

"Are you drunk?"

"Trying to get that way."

"Will you forget that jerk? He isn't worth a second of your time."

"I know."

"Well?"

"I have an appointment with the head of department tomorrow morning. I think I might be getting the boot."

"What? What the fuck for?"

"Bill is tenured, I'm not. He says seeing me around all the time is 'awkward.'"

"Awkward? I'd give him awkward. Tell them you'll file a sexual harassment suit if they even think of firing you. Nori will handle everything."

"Teaching was never my goal—I want to spend more time on my own work. My lease is up soon. I'm thinking of moving up your way."

Lily let out a whoop. "That would be fabulous! Have you told Nori? You know she hates her job in Portland. What if all three of us ended up here? Oh, my God. I won't be able to sleep tonight, just thinking about it."

"Calm down. I haven't decided anything yet." But I was becoming as excited as Lily.

"You know I have plenty of room here. I rattle around this place like a pebble in a tin can." Lily lived alone in the old farmhouse Virginia deeded to her on her twentieth birthday.

After Lily hung up, I went into the kitchen and poured out the remainder of my wine then fixed myself something to eat. The next morning, I handed in my resignation.

# 2
# NORI

I walked up Clay Street, toward Broadway, going over how to tell my boss, Danielle Lindstrom, I planned to leave Williams and Hachette, and start my own practice in Idaho. The chill in the wind off the Willamette River was nothing compared to the reception my news would likely receive.

Telling my grandmother, who got me the position at one of the Northwest's largest and most respected law firms in the first place, would be even harder. She considered my job in the product liability department at W & H the first step in her plans for me. I loved my grandmother, but I resented her efforts to turn me into her clone.

Old and beautifully kept, the University Club sat on the corner of Stark and S.W. Park, nearly kitty-corner from the art museum. Modeled after Yale's University Club, it had played an interesting role in Portland's history.

Danielle waited for me in the main dining room.

"Sorry I'm late. I needed to take a call from Mike Smith." Mike, in the top tier of the firm's many important clients, had been trying to get me to go out with him for several months. Danielle didn't know and I didn't plan to tell her. I didn't plan to accept his invitation either. For one thing, he was thirty years older than me and for another, I found women more appealing than men.

Danielle frowned. "He doesn't have another liability problem?"

"No. He just wanted to give me an update." I glanced at the menu and decided on the day's special, grilled salmon with rice pilaf. The waiter came and took our orders. I craned my neck to gaze at the room's high ceilings and rich appointments. Filled with businessmen and women, their glasses and cutlery clinking, voices droning, I suspected little had changed since the Club's founding all those years ago—except for the number of women, of course.

"My great-grandfather used to work here," I said.

"Oh?" Danielle's ears pricked, her eyes brightened. I rarely mentioned anything about my heritage.

I nodded. "My grandmother's father—Shigaro Ugawa. He worked here as a valet before World War Two, and again after returning from the internment camp in Idaho."

"Now you're a member." Danielle smiled and a warm look came into her eyes. She wasn't a bad person—ambitious, of course, but not in a dog-eat-dog way. I liked working for her. What I didn't like was product liability. Well, not product liability, exclusive product liability. I wanted diversity.

"Seems ironic, right? My mother says he was a lovely old man, devoted to birds and poetry. His poetry was published, but unfortunately not until after he died."

"I'd love to read some."

The book was long out of print. I didn't see Danielle as a poetry enthusiast, but I promised to loan her my copy.

After several minutes of desultory talk, she put down her iced tea. Her studied gaze made me uncomfortable. "So, what's up, Nori? You've seemed distracted lately. How can I help?"

With the moment arrived, all my prepared speech flew out of my head and I simply blurted, "I've decided to leave the firm."

Danielle's pale blue eyes immediately narrowed, her lips tightened. "What do you mean? Who's after you? I suppose you want more money, is that it? Is someone offering you partner?"

"No, that's not it at all." I shook my head and tried to explain. "Working for a big firm was my grandmother's dream for me, not mine. Back when she graduated from law school, Asian women weren't welcome in Portland's legal circles. She always resented it. I'm her…well vindication I guess is the right word."

"Asian women weren't alone, women in general were excluded."

"I know. But after the war, Asians, particularly Japanese -Americans, found entering any profession outside of their own community nearly impossible. Vicariously, I suppose, my grandmother encouraged me to find a position in one of Portland's big firm's—even pulled strings to get me this job. I appreciate all she's done. You, too, Danielle—I've enjoyed working for you. But I'm going back to Idaho. My roots are there."

"Your grandparents live here."

"True. I went to college here, too, but I have another grandmother in Idaho, older than Grandmother Keiko. My parents are there along with a myriad aunts, uncles and cousins." I rubbed the back of my neck. "Besides missing my relatives, I find a steady diet of corporate law doesn't satisfy me. I need more diversity—family law, estate-planning, patents. Consumer rights even."

The iciness began to leave Danielle's eyes. "I don't want to lose you from my department, but I could talk to Mark, see if he's willing to transfer you to one with a bit more variety."

"I appreciate the offer, Danielle. I do. Like I said, I like working for you. The firm, too." I drew a deep breath and tried to sound assured. "Much as I hate the thought of leaving Portland, it's time for me to go home."

An hour later, back in our building near Naito Parkway, we rode up in the elevator together. Danielle got off on seventeen and I went on up to Human Resources, two floors above.My conversation with Danielle, followed by my visit to HR, brought home the finality of my decision.

I wished I could avoid telling my grandmother—the thought of such a conversation made my stomach knot—but I had no choice. At six-thirty, I gave up trying to get any work done. I collected my car from the parking garage and drove up Broadway then headed south, toward Lake Oswego, or Lake Ego, as some called it.

A large, complicated, and colorful Dale Chihuly work, each gorgeous and richly colored piece of glass entwined with another, dangled from the ceiling in my grandparents' living room. One of Lily's paintings hung above the mantle; an African woman with a child on her back. I never tired of the exquisite calmness in the expression on the woman's face. Her eyes seemed to acknowledge life in all its variations of adversity and joy. I felt sure Lily had captured her perfectly.

Outside, visible through the windows and French doors, a forty-foot wide deck and terraced, landscaped lawns led down to the lake, where sailboats and motorboats plied the water.

I perched on a suede-covered sofa across from my grandparents, seated on an identical sofa. Together, they weighed about one-hundred and sixty pounds. But what they lacked in size, they made up for in presence and energy. At least Grandmother Keiko did. My grandfather generally deferred to her. I expected this evening to be no exception.

A young man I hadn't met brought us drinks. Grandmother waited until he'd returned to the kitchen before grilling me. "So, what do we owe the pleasure of this visit?"

Her hair, pulled back in a smooth chignon, still gleamed shiny black thanks to her hairdresser. She wore a red St. John's knit pantsuit with black patent-leather heels. I glanced around for a briefcase—all she needed to make her outfit complete.

Before I could answer her question, she told me she'd gotten a call from Mark Olsen, my firm's managing partner. "I can't believe you're throwing away this opportunity. Honestly, Nori. What are you thinking? You want to go back to Twin Falls and start your own practice? You can't be serious."

I tried to explain my reasons for leaving, but she countered every argument I offered with an outline of what she believed I would be giving up. The litany ran on and on. I gave up trying to interject, simply clutched my drink and waited for her to run out of steam.

To my surprise, Grandfather Mako stood and faced her. "Stop browbeating her, Keiko. She's a grown woman and has a right to make up her own mind. If she wants to move back to Idaho and be near Neil and our Amy-chan, you need to let her go. Stop this infernal meddling and badgering."

My grandmother started to speak then bit her lower lip. I was nearly struck dumb myself. I'd never heard my grandfather speak so to my grandmother, though I'm certain there'd been many times he'd been sorely tempted. My grandmother raised her glass to her lips and lowered it. Again, she opened her mouth to speak before closing it.

My grandfather watched her closely. When she remained silent, he nodded, lowered himself onto the couch once again and turned his attention to me. "When will you be leaving us, Nori?"

"I need to finish a case I'm working on—I've given a month's notice."

I must have appeared a fool driving back to John's Landing. I couldn't stop grinning. In one month, I'd be heading home. My parents, Lily, and Helena—they all knew how much I missed home and disliked product liability—but I'd managed to keep to myself the plans I'd been making, including sneaking over to Twin Falls the month before to search for office space.

I found an ideal place in a mixed-use building on the outskirts of town. It held enough room for a single desk and a couple of chairs out front and a small office for me. Restrooms and a break room were on each floor and shared by other tenants. First thing in the morning, I'd call the realtor.

The marmalade cat I'd found digging through the dumpster behind my condo, waited for me inside the door. I scooped him up. "You're going to like Idaho, Cat."

Lily lounged on the red leather couch I'd brought from Portland. "This is heaven compared to my old one."

"You can thank Grandmother Keiko. She got it for me, the chairs, too. She said I needed decent furniture if I planned to *entertain*."

Lily lovingly patted the firm leather on the couch's arm. "I will definitely thank her—they'll be over in August, right?" I nodded. "How did she take you quitting your grand job in Portland and moving over here to Podunk, Idaho?"

"Things were brewing up for world war three, but Grandfather Mako spiked her guns. I didn't think such a thing possible."

Lily took a sip of her wine and chuckled. "I bet. She is one strong-willed woman. Your mom still hops, at least a little, when your grandma says jump."

"Have you seen Momma recently? She said she and Daddy will be over in the morning."

"On Sunday, at our weekly lunches at the big house. I run into your dad more often. He comes out to check on the men in the field. Virginia may be getting old, but Franconi & Sato Farms is still going strong."

Even though Lily owned the old farmhouse, the land stayed with the company formed years before by my great-uncle, Marc Franconi, and my grandfather, John Sato. Both men were gone now and Virginia Franconi Sato, my grandmother and Lily's great-grandmother, had long ago turned over the whole operation to my father to run, all thirty-five hundred irrigated acres of potatoes, corn, wheat, and sugar beets.

"My grandfather may have made Grandmother Keiko stop badgering me, but I'm afraid she's been giving Momma a bad time—she always does. Just because Momma didn't become a world-famous pianist like Grandmother planned, she's probably now blaming Momma for me blowing my chances to become a world-famous lawyer."

"Forget it. Your mom's a grown woman and she knows how to deal with Keiko. She moved to Idaho and married your dad, didn't she? Now you've broken out of Dragon Lady's clutches, too. God, she must be slipping."

I laughed with Lily. "Well, she is eighty-something—even if she still has enough ambition for ten women. I don't think she had any objections to Momma marrying Daddy, though. It was the music thing."

"And maybe Idaho. Anyway, enough talk about what was. We need to start you on the path of what is to be. First, though, I want some dinner. The frozen lasagna I stuck in the oven a while ago smells about done."

I got up early the next morning to finish unpacking before my parents stopped by. I wondered who this bedroom belonged to all those years ago—Leo, Marc, or Paul? Virginia and Irene?  I searched for signs, but found none. No ghosts. No initials scratched into the windowsill. The window overlooked the front lawn and the ancient rose bushes bordering it, the graveled lane leading out to the highway, and a large tree. I'd parked my car beneath it, next to Lily's white Toyota pickup.

Which of the Franconi kids once stood at this window and saw men and women working in fields that seemed to stretch forever? Fewer laborers were needed now. Big and cumbersome-looking equipment did the job of plowing, thinning, topping, spraying, and harvesting. I'd met more than one such behemoth on the highway, both here and in Oregon, lumbering along, swaying from side-to-side, impossible to pass.

My meandering thoughts were interrupted when I spotted Momma's car turn into the lane. I ran downstairs and rushed outside to greet them. My heart nearly exploded when my parents got out of Momma's car and each enveloped me in a hug. Momma's black eyes sparkled, smiling her pleasure. "Home at last," we said together.

Momma looked exactly like pictures of Grandmother Keiko when she'd been the same age, slender and elegant, her black hair showing only a little gray at the temples. Even with Idaho's dry weather, her complexion was smooth and nearly unlined.

Daddy called himself *hapa-haoli*, Hawaiian for half-native and half-white. His face was shaped like Virginia's, but his almond-shaped eyes were the color of amber, his skin golden. His hair, completely gray now, once reminded me of desert sand. Even nearing sixty, my father was a handsome man.

He echoed Momma's and my sentiments. "About damned time, too."

I hooked an arm through the elbow of each and we went into the house where we spent the next hour catching up on family news.

"You know Mandy and Opal are grandmothers now," Momma said, referring to Daddy's two sisters. She spoke with only a hint of reproach at my unmarried and childless state. I smiled in resignation. I'd come out to them at sixteen. They took it hard, in part, I suppose, because I was their only child. For days, we moved around the house barely speaking to one another. I hated the pain I'd brought them, pain that shone from their eyes whenever they looked at me. Eventually, though, their love for me triumphed and they came to accept what I couldn't change, even had I wanted to.

"I brought baby gifts—I'll see them Sunday?"

Momma nodded. "Of course—everyone will want to welcome you home."

Daddy said they needed to go. "Some things require my attention before the day's over. It's halfway gone already." I glanced at my watch. Nine-thirty. Daddy chuckled. "You're on farm time now—our days start early."

"You go ahead, Neil," Momma said. "I want to talk to Nori a minute." After he left, Momma took my hand, her eyes filled with sympathy. "Your grandmother called last night. She might be sending you another one of her 'prospects.'"

Although I'd come out to my parents and to Lily and Helena, I hadn't to my grandparents. I rolled my eyes. "Thanks for the warning. I'll be on the lookout." I walked out to the car with her. Daddy, always content to let my mother drive, already sat in the passenger seat.

After they left, I rinsed our coffee cups. Eager to get to Twin Falls and start organizing my new office, I scribbled a note for Lily, who never got up before noon, telling her I'd be back later.

Helena took us both by surprise. "I would have been here sooner, but with Grandpa getting the flu, I didn't want to leave Grandma Suki to care for him on her own—he's kind of a lousy patient." She dropped onto the couch, leaned back, and spread her arms. "Wow, this is great. Anyway, Grandma made me leave—she said she has Rosie to help and Mom and Dad nearby—like there's time for anything but the latest buy-out or take-over with them. At least he's better now and Grandma said they wouldn't miss Aunt Virginia's birthday for anything. Oh, my God," she said, leaning forward, her elbows on her knees. "I can't believe we're all here together! It will be like endless summer—only with no parents or aunts and uncles spying on us, ready to foil our plans." With a laugh, she threw herself against the back of the couch again.

Lily shook her head. "Endless summer it won't be. Wait until you experience an Idaho winter."

Helena protested. "I've been here for Christmas. Several times."

Lily shook her head again and laughed at her naivety. "Sure, you have—for a week. Talk about endless—that's what winter is here. At least it won't be so bad with all three of us together."

We raised our glasses. "Here's to here! And here's to us!"

My joy at seeing Helena and with being once again with my best friends, was dampened somewhat by the fact my law practice appeared to be going nowhere. I'd joined Rotary and Lions and a couple other networking groups, but so far, the only time the phone rang it was either a wrong number or Lily asking me to pick up something for dinner or my mother, querying me on how my day went. My nest egg would be nothing but an empty shell if I didn't find some clients soon.

With so little to do, the days passed slowly. I turned my energies to preparing for the birthday party in August, not all that far off. Momma helped when she could, but her schedule was generally filled with taking care of the books for Franconi & Sato or running errands for Daddy. Lily spent her days in her studio, the old prove-up shack, and Helena spent hers researching or writing, so it was left to me to put into action the plans we hashed over each evening.

At the sound of the door opening and closing, I sprang up from my desk.

"Hello? Anyone here?" I didn't recognize the deep and masculine voice.

I brushed crumbs from my top and straightened my skirt. "I'll be right there," I called before grimacing in the mirror to make sure I didn't have the remains of my lunch between my teeth. I hurried out to the reception area to introduce myself.

Even I could appreciate Will Davis's good looks—black hair, crystal blue eyes, and a body most women would drool over. Besides being gorgeous, he was also in a lot of trouble—his former partner left him holding a rather stinky bag of unpaid taxes, unfulfilled promises and maybe some patent infringement.

"My grandfather is friends with your grandmother," he said, enlightening me as to Grandmother's latest 'prospect.'

To my surprise and consternation, the phone rang almost the moment he and I began talking, not once, but several times. Not Lily or my mother, either. My networking paying off, I needed to jot down the numbers of two callers and promise to call back.

"Where's your receptionist?"

I glanced up from my notes, tempted to lie, tell him my receptionist was at lunch. I decided to tell the truth. "Well, as you probably heard via your grandfather, I'm just getting started here in town. I haven't the funds to hire a receptionist yet and no one has volunteered to work for free." With the possibility of three new clients, though, I figured I needed to think about getting someone part time.

First, I needed to concentrate on the one in front of me and turn him into an actual client. "What kind of business did you and your partner own?"

"We build, well, built ag equipment. I designed a new kind of sugar beet harvester." He went on to explain how this piece of machinery worked and how his design differed from all the other sugar beet harvesters. "After WWII, farm equipment got revolutionized," he said. "But around 1970, the changes slowed down and then stopped."

"You changed that, though."

He smiled and nodded while trying to appear modest. "A bit, yes."

"So, who was your patent attorney?"

He gave a rueful sigh. "I didn't have one, which is part of the problem. My partner was supposed to take care of everything. He said he'd done so." Will's brows drew together and a nerve at the corner of his mouth twitched. "Now, another firm claims my design infringes on their harvester."

My cell phone rang. I turned it off and let it go to voicemail. Will said his partner took care of all the company's finances, including taxes, both state and federal.

"I should have paid closer attention," he said. "I was busy with the operations side of things—too busy, I guess. I got a call from the bank saying some of our checks were going to be returned and we lacked enough funds in our payroll account to cover payroll taxes. I became alarmed, but Ron assured me he'd take care of things. An oversight he said, he forgot to make a deposit." Will shook his head. His voice filled with self-disgust. "A week later, the bank called again—then I really got concerned."

I put down the pen I'd been taking notes with. "I think you need a couple of things, the first being a good account-ant, someone who can also deal with the IRS—not the firm your former partner dealt with. I'll refer you to someone if you'd like. I can help you with the patent infringement problem."

"What about my ex-partner? He embezzled at least half -a-million from the company."

"Well, we don't know that for sure," I said. "We can't be certain until the accountant sorts through everything. Do you know where he is, the ex-partner?"

Will snorted. "Right here in Twin Falls, running his other business—a pharmaceutical supply company."

We talked about my fee and what I'd need from him to get started. He wrote me a check, which I hoped wouldn't bounce, and left.  I returned the calls I'd gotten earlier. One turned out to be a sales pitch but the other call came from a real client, or at least a real potential one. We set an appointment for the following day.

The voicemail, from my grandmother, sang the praises of Will Davis. This time I didn't resent her meddling. I needed his business.

I stopped at the store on the way home and bought fresh salmon for dinner. A big slab of it. Whatever Lily, Helena and I didn't eat, Cat would enjoy. I was tired of frozen lasagna, Lily's go-to meal.

We grilled the salmon and afterwards talked more about Virginia's birthday celebration.

True to her nature, Helena was in a reflective mood. "Think about all that's happened in the world during her lifetime—both world wars, the cold war, Korea, Vietnam, and now Iraq and Afghanistan."

"I got a new client today."  Helena and Lily clapped. I smiled my thanks. "He said farming, especially the equipment used in farming, was revolutionized after World War Two. She witnessed those changes as well."

Helena chuckled. "Remember the hay derrick—the thing that looks like a guillotine or something equally deadly? You've seen it Lily, I'm sure. I'll bet it's still out behind the barn."

We sat on the screened porch to avoid the mosquitoes. Lily stared into the distance as though she hadn't heard a word Helena said, her mind still clearly on Virginia. "The woman defines revolutionary. Just think—she bore an illegitimate child in 1943—Bella, my grandmother. Marrying a Japanese-American man in 1946 couldn't have made her popular with her neighbors, either. After Bella died, she raised Grace, and then, after Grace ran off, got stuck raising her great-granddaughter, me. Not to mention being part of building the farm into a showcase that draws people from all over the state."

A flush of pride spread over me at Lily's words. "You're right—you, too, Helena. She's seen and done a lot. We have every right to be proud of her—which is why we're going to throw her one heck of a birthday bash."

I thought of what Lily said about Virginia as I crawled into bed that night. My grandmother told me John Sato loved Virginia from the moment he first set eyes on her. "I remember the two of them, three actually," she said. "Bella on her blanket, kicking and cooing, while we all ate lunch. John and Virginia couldn't hide their attraction. I found it amusing."

When the war ended, no one heard from John. A local minister tracked him down. Certain Virginia would spurn his advances, following his discharge from the Army John went to Seattle in search of work. The minister gave Virginia his address and she and Bella set out to find him and bring him home.

I lay on my back and smiled into the darkness.

What had my grandfather thought when he saw Virginia standing at the door of his room in a rundown boarding house off Jackson Street, holding Bella by the hand? What did they say to one another in that moment?

Whatever it was, John came back to Idaho, where he and Virginia married and had three children together, including my father. All three adored their big sister, Bella.

Bella died before I was born. I did know her daughter. Grace was impossible to control. Even though I'd been only four or five then, some of the raging arguments between her and Virginia were etched into my memory. At fourteen and little more than a child herself, I doubt it surprised anyone when Grace ran off and left two-week old Lily behind. She occasionally drifted back into Virginia's and Lily's life, but never for long. I wondered if she'd make it to Virginia's birthday.

I rolled over in bed. The night was warm, and humid with all the irrigation canals around. The sound of an owl came through the open window. I stared at the moon and the star-filled sky. Nowhere was the sky as big and expansive as in Idaho.

# 3

# *LILY*

The hoot of a great-horned owl came through my open bedroom window. During the day, the bird often perched in the cottonwood tree next to my studio, twisting his head nearly backwards to preen his feathers.

I'd kicked the covers off, and lay naked on my bed. A breeze, warm as bathwater, trickled over my bare skin. The muggy air smelled of ripening corn.

From the direction of Twin Falls came the lonely wail of a train whistle. Who said time is like a train running through your mind and at night the heart listens? Shadows tore away from the wall to dance in the moonlight. They twirled, pirouetted, and swayed around my bed, a young Virginia, Bella, even teenaged Grace, no longer angry. I rose from the bed to join them and soon all four of us danced and whirled, swaying to the night music. The breeze picked up, tugged on the leaves of the cottonwood. The window curtains billowed, rippled. The owl called again. My heart listened.

I came downstairs the next morning to find Nori already gone to her office in Twin Falls and Helena getting ready for her daily trek to the county historical museum in Jerome. She claimed the museum held a treasure trove of information about Minidoka, Magic Valley, and the Northside Canal Company. Even though I'd grown up here, I hadn't known Magic Valley got its name from the transformation brought by all the dams on the Snake River and the irrigation system that turned the desert into an agricultural bonanza. My mouth turned down—too much thinking for so early in the morning. "Any coffee left?"

Helena nodded. "Probably mud by now, though."

Sunshine poured through the kitchen window. My eyes automatically closed against the glare. "I don't know what you and Nori see in getting up at dawn."

Helena gave her low chuckle. "Most of the world gets up with us. You'd be surprised what happens while you're still sleeping."

I shuddered. "Don't even want to know—probably more shootings and plane crashes." I groped my way to the coffee pot and got a cup down from the shelf. "Any cream left?"

"In the fridge."

I grunted. "I hate mornings."

Helena showed no sympathy. She laughed. "See you later, Princess."

I cut myself a generous wedge of the coconut cream pie Nori bought to go with the salmon the night before, and took it into the living room with my coffee. I sank down on the new couch and nearly purred my contentment. Cat slinked across the room and hopped up next to me. He showed no interest in coffee, even with cream, but we shared the pie.

One July day, heading to my studio, a low engine growl made me look up. A vintage, canary-yellow Corvette, driven by a shirtless young stud about my age, drove toward me down the lane.  He had a great body, I saw that right off. Grace was draped over his shoulder.

I'd sworn a hundred times I wouldn't let her get under my skin, but my resolution flew out the window—it seemed all I needed to do was look at her to get pissed off. My feet planted wide, I faced her. "What are you doing here?"

"Is that any way to talk to your mother?"

"What are you doing here, Grace. I'm busy. You said you'd come for Virginia's birthday. That's still two weeks away."

"I wanted to see my girl, of course. This is Henri, by the way. Henri, say something to Lily in French." When he obliged, Grace grinned. "Isn't that just the sexiest thing you've ever heard?"

It took everything I had not to shout at her to get lost. "I suppose you want to come in." A muscle in my jaw twitched.

She pretended not to notice my annoyance. "Henri, get our things out of the trunk."

"Our things? You're both staying?"

"Didn't I mention Henri when you called?"

I scowled at her. It was a good bet she hadn't even met Henri when she called. "Nori and Helena are living here now."

"No problem. Henri and I will take the downstairs bedroom. " She made a big play of needing Henri's help getting out of the Corvette. Once on her feet, she turned and grabbed a large red handbag from behind the car seat. The leather on the seat was cracked and worn. The Corvette needed body work, too. Grace spurted ahead of me, her butt sashaying in her tight jeans. "This way, Lover," she called to Henri.

Henri hoisted the bags, which appeared suspiciously heavy for a few days stay, and set off after her like a love-starved bull.

"Shit," I muttered and followed them inside.

Grace turned up her nose at left-over lasagna, but Henri polished it off—fortifying, no doubt. After lunch, they headed to the bedroom for a siesta, but the noise soon coming from the room didn't sound like resting. I snorted and slammed out of the house to go spend the afternoon painting, which is what I'd planned to do in the first place.

How well I'd succeeded in turning the prove-up shack into a real studio gave me pleasure every time I stepped inside the door. Built around 1912, the place had been the first home of the first Franconi to lay claim to the property, Virginia's father.

Lighting had been my first issue. The prove-up's few windows were cracked or so grimed they were beyond repair. I found two large windows in a salvage yard and borrowed two of Neil's workmen to get them installed across one side of the building. A friend put me in touch with an electrician who moonlighted. He rewired everything and replaced the two bare bulbs hanging from the ceiling with a double row of lights. From the salvage yard, again, I unearthed cupboards that I installed myself and topped with a long sheet of laminate. The laminate was the only thing I paid full price for. Well, that and the gas stove installed at one end of the room and the window air conditioner at the other, two items that made the building bearable in the summer and winter.

I stood back to study the panel mounted on my easel. After a few minutes of contemplation, I collected my brushes from the utility sink near the door, where I'd left them after cleaning them the day before. I may have been careless about some things, okay, many things, but taking care of my brushes was not one of them.

Once I put brush to canvas, I didn't tear my eyes away until another car rumbled down the drive. Nori. I called to her from the door of the studio. "I'll be with you in a minute—just need to clean up."

"Whose car?"

"Grace is here, with a boyfriend."

I didn't need to say any more. Nori understood. Helena, too. They'd been around Grace. Nori gave me a reassuring smile. "Want me to threaten to sue? I'm sure I could find something to scare the bejesus out of her, get her to leave."

I laughed, but without much humor. "Let me think about it."

Grace and Henri emerged from the downstairs bedroom, rumpled and without shame, in time for drinks before dinner. I introduced Henri to Helena and Nori, both of whom gave him a cool hello. He tried to flirt with Helena, but ignored Nori, who came to stand by me like a mother hen with her chick. Grace's dilated eyes told me she'd been smoking or popping something. I didn't bother to ask her what—she'd lie anyway.

Helena extracted herself from Henri and strolled over to join Nori, now setting the table while I finished mixing the salad.

At dinner, Henri made a couple more attempts to engage Helena, but each time she gave him a brief answer then turned away and addressed Nori or me. Once she asked Grace a question, but Grace was too far gone by then to know she'd been spoken to.

After finishing the remains of a second bottle of wine, Henri stood, swaying slightly, and bowed. He almost fell over, but managed to right himself. "I will retire now."

"Aren't you going to take Grace?" Nori asked.

Henri looped his arm through Grace's and half-dragged, half-supported her to the bedroom.

I sighed. "Sorry, guys. I had no idea she planned to bring someone. She did call me, but I didn't think she'd show up until Virginia's birthday—if she came at all, which I doubted."

Nori opened another bottle of wine and after refilling our glasses, suggested we go out on the porch. "I don't know which is worse," she said. "A mother who embarrasses you all your life or a grandmother-on-steroids who tries to dictate your every move."

We each took one of the rickety wicker chairs that had resided on the porch since I was a little girl.

Helena gazed at a moth attracted by the porch light and darting at the screen. "Or parents too busy with their precious business to even notice when you're thirteen and you get your period the first time, you fall in love and the boy breaks your heart, you get into the school you always dreamed of, get your first job, sell your first article."

I studied the faces of my cousins, who were also my best friends and, for the first time, realized I might be the lucky one.

The rest of the evening we chatted or enjoyed a companionable silence. Nori talked about her two cases, the guy with the messed-up business affairs and a mother fighting for custody of her two children.

Helena told us about her research. "I read something today that blew my mind. During World War Two, about nine-hundred young fathers from Seattle and Tacoma suggested they be exempted from the draft and replaced by nine-hundred men from Camp Minidoka, many of whom were most likely also fathers, some several times over. How dared they suggest such a thing? And can you believe the newspapers actually supported them?"

"I wonder if Suki and Keiko will ever tell what Camp Minidoka was really like," I said. "I've seen pictures of the place—grim is all I can say. I don't suppose life was a picnic here on the farm, either."

Nori smothered a yawn. "Driving over from Portland, I recalled Grandmother Keiko telling me of coming to Minidoka on the train, traveling through the Columbia Gorge for the first time, and how splendid she thought it, even though she was terrified of what lay ahead. It's the only time she ever said anything to me about the entire experience. And for sure, the only time she ever used the word terrified in connection to herself, at least in my hearing."

Nori got in her red BMW and put the car top down. Helena slipped into the passenger seat while I climbed into the back. Everyone settled, we headed to the 'big house' for the traditional Sunday lunch.

Grace and Henri hadn't appeared before we left, but moaning, grunting, and shouting along with the sound of squealing bedsprings, came from the downstairs bedroom all morning.

My face stayed red with embarrassment. Helena commiserated with me, but Nori joked. "Despite all the drugs and stuff Grace does to her body, you can't deny the woman has stamina." I knew she was trying to make me feel better and normally I would have laughed along with her. Today, for some reason, I wasn't in the mood.

We pulled onto the highway and I spread my arms across the seat back and lifted my face to the sun. My hair hung loose except for a narrow hair band. It whipped around in the wind, stinging my cheeks as the car picked up speed. Helena and Nori chatted in the front seat, but I ignored them and let my thoughts drift to the day I first realized Virginia wasn't my mother.

Even though she was in her late sixties by then, she didn't act like it. She didn't look like it, either. Hard work kept her naturally slim figure lithe and trim. Her navy-blue eyes, the same color as mine, remained alert and unclouded. I called her Tutu. She was part of my life and the only maternal figure I knew.

My first memory of Grace was her standing at the front door and staring at Virginia, defiance in the lift of her chin, the set of her mouth.  She would have been about twenty-one then, just a few years younger than I was now. "I've come to get the kid."

Immediately, I knew she meant me. I stepped back and edged my way around until I stood behind Virginia.

Virginia didn't answer her. She turned, took my hand, and led me out of the room. "Go see Papa John. He's out by the barn."

"Make her go away, Tutu."

"I will, Lily. Don't worry."

I suspect Virginia paid Grace to leave. I suspect extorting money from her grandmother was the reason Grace came.

That evening, Virginia sat on the side of my bed. She took my hand and held it for several moments, stroking my fingers one-by-one before she spoke. "Grace is your mother, Lily."

I stared at her, confused. "But you're my mama, Tutu."

"Yes. But Grace gave birth to you, Lily. She was too young to be a mama to you, though. That's why Papa John and I became your parents."

I tried to understand, but I couldn't. Not then. Maybe not even now.

As I grew older, Virginia told me about her daughter Bella, Grace's mother.

"Bill's work as an engineer specializing in dams took them all over the world. I cried when she left, but she and Bill were so happy together, I had to let her go, I had to let her fly away from me. Grace's birth, three years later, added to their joy in one another."

She smiled and took my hand as we sat together on the screened porch. I remember the soft *ka-kock* of a pheasant somewhere nearby.

"She and Bill brought Grace to us when she was seven. They thought she should go to a regular school." The smile went out of Virginia's eyes. "She resented being left behind and no matter how hard I tried, I couldn't seem to console her. Bella's and Bill's deaths a few months later, shattered us both. Losing a child is not to be borne, nor is losing a mother. Poor Grace. Wrapped up in my own grief, too often I ignored her, let her drift when she needed me."

Her eyes filled with tears and I squeezed her hand, trying to give her comfort.

"That's why I blame myself, Lily. I blame myself."

I was twelve or thirteen before I thought to wonder who my father was. Virginia couldn't tell me. She didn't know. Neither, apparently, did Grace.

Grace showed up every few years. Sometimes, when she was clean, Virginia let her stay. But after a few days, she always disappeared, leaving nothing but a lipstick or a gum wrapper behind. She never threatened to take me away again, probably because Virginia paid her not to. Whenever she came to the house, though, I'd watch her, looking for something, some connection. I never found one.

"Hey, wake up, sleepy-head." Nori smiled at me in the rearview mirror. "We're here."

We turned into the long, tree-bordered driveway leading to the large and rambling house surrounded by about twenty acres of fenced pasture. I was in sixth grade when Virginia and Papa John built the house on property they'd bought years before. Situated in a bend on the Snake River, the well-irrigated pasture never held more than a few head of grazing cattle. Lush and green no matter the season.

The whole place could be an advertisement for something—the good life, I guess. Outbuildings matched the main house in design. Neil and Amy, Nori's parents, now lived in one wing, Virginia in the other. My bedroom had been upstairs, along with several other bedrooms where guests and visiting dignitaries often stayed. Grand as it was to live there, I always missed the farm house. I couldn't believe it when Virginia told me she'd deeded the old place over to me.

The entire family gathered for lunch: Neil and Amy, Neil's two sisters, Maddy and Opal, their husbands, children, and the two new grandbabies. Maddy's husband was Hispanic, Opal's German or Austrian, I forget which, and one of Opal's boys married a girl from Brazil.

"We need someone from Australia—we've got South America, North America, Asia and Europe represented. If someone would marry an Australian, we'd have all the major continents covered."

Maddy grinned at me. "Guess that's your job, 'Mate.'"

Her back still ramrod straight, Virginia entered the room and went to her accustomed place at the head of the table. Neal stood and held out her chair. "Mom, you're looking chipper today."

Virginia sat and sent her gaze around the table. I wondered how she could remembered us all, but she nodded and smiled, easy recognition in her navy-blue eyes.

Plates were passed, grilled trout, probably caught that morning by Neil, rolls, fresh-baked and crusty, a green  salad with olives, capers and croutons, and a choice of fresh melon to top it off.

Virginia put a little of everything on her plate, but ate only a few bites before putting down her fork. "Lily, why are you and Nori and Helena down there at the end of the table? Come up here and sit by me. Neil, you and Javier take their places—you're only going to talk farm business anyway. You go too, Evan. Amy, scoot down a place and give the girls room here next to me."

Helena, Nori, and I obediently picked up our plates and glasses and the men did likewise. Amy moved down one chair to make room for Nori, her only child. Once everyone was seated to Virginia's satisfaction, she began querying the three of us.

"First, how are the plans coming for my birthday party?"

Nori told her of the arrangements she'd made for the Mariachi band and portable dance floor. My idea—I love Mariachi music. Besides, many of the farm laborers were Hispanic, and they'd be taking part in the celebration. "Among other things, we'll have planked salmon, done in a fire pit lined with cedar boughs. And I've arranged for a barbeque wagon to be brought in. We'll have games for all the kids, too."

"Your grandparents, Keiko and Mako, they'll be here?"

"They wouldn't miss it."

"Helena, how are Suki and Paul?"

"Both well now that Grandpa Paul is recovered from the flu bug. Grandma and Rosie were busy spoiling him rotten, last I saw. They're looking forward to being here, too."

"I hope they plan to stay for a while and not rush back to Carmel Valley as they usually do. How are your parents?"

"Busy as always—something to do with a merger or buy -out last I heard."

"And your work?"

Helena told about her research at the Jerome museum. I was surprised when she mentioned something she hadn't spoken of before, at least not to me. "I'm trying to find out about something that happened in the mid- or late-thirties at a place called Lizard Butte. Do you know it?"

Virginia nodded. "Oh yes. We used to have picnics out there. Lily, you know Lizard Butte. Why don't you take Helena?"

I couldn't imagine picnicking at Lizard Butte, or wanting to. The butte eerily resembled a lizard, but not a cute little iguana—more like something from a Japanese horror movie. Reluctantly, I agreed.

"How is the painting coming?"

Virginia knew I was working on something special to commemorate her birthday, but even to her, I hadn't explained. "I'm pretty pleased with things so far."

Apparently content we were all on track she rose and said she was ready to go back to her rooms. Helena, Nori, and I stood and kissed her cheek before she left. While she'd been talking to us, the rest of the group kept their voices down. Once Virginia rose and took her leave, the noise quickly escalated.

"I forgot to tell her Grace is here."

Nori chuckled. "She probably already knows—she seems to know everything else going on."

"I wonder what she'd make of Henri." Helena emphasized 'Hon-ree' making it sound tres French. Nori and I giggled.

Amy asked to be let in on the joke.

"A couple of days ago, Grace showed up with one of her boy-toys in tow. He's French. His name is Henri."

Amy reached across the table and laid her fingers on my hand, her eyes filled with compassion. "I'm sorry, Lily. I know she's a trial to you."

I shrugged and assured her I was fine. "Nori and Helena are with me now. They won't let her get under my skin too much."

"Please tell me if Neil or I can do anything."

Grace being Bella's daughter made her Neil's niece. Step-niece, I guess. But he, like everyone else, was stymied when it came to dealing with her. Nori told me Grace tried to seduce him once. I should have been shocked—Grace had been twelve or thirteen and Neil in his mid-twenties when it allegedly happened. But nothing Grace did or didn't do shocked me anymore. Instead, I felt sorry for Neil.

I smiled at Amy and promised I'd call if I needed their help.

★

Nori and Helena took off Monday morning, Nori to her office in Twin Falls, Helena to Jerome and the museum again. I returned to my studio. Grace and Henri, who'd gone out somewhere the previous night and not returned until three or four o'clock in the morning, noisy as hell, were still in bed. I shook my head. "They're acting like a couple of randy teen-agers," I muttered, then realized I was acting like an out-of-touch parent. I determined not to think of them or the whole, ridiculous situation.

Still, as I gathered my clean brushes and painting material, carrying everything to the paint-smeared table next to my equally paint-smeared easel, the image of bronzed and muscular Henri making love to my sensuous thirty-eight-year-old mother, her long blonde hair entwined around them both, her drugged eyes, half-closed and vacant, inserted itself into my mind and wouldn't leave.

"Goddamn it," I shouted at the ceiling. "Will you please stop fucking with my head?" Cheeks burning, I threw down my brush. I should kick them both out, but I knew I wouldn't. They'd stay until they got enough money from Virginia to go somewhere else. Or Henri got bored with my drugged-out mother and moved on.

Revolted by my errant imagination and my lack of fortitude, I slammed out of the studio and took a walk. I passed the cottonwood tree, and the great-horned owl peered at me with sleepy eyes. I returned an hour later, calmed and ready to paint, not stopping until both Nori and Helena returned home.

After a hastily thrown-together dinner of cold cuts and leftovers, the three of us gathered on the porch. Grace and Henri were nowhere to be seen, the yellow Corvette gone. I'd been too engrossed in my work to hear the noise of its engine when they left.

"My client was right," Nori said when Helena asked how her case was going. "The accountant says the ex-partner did make off with close to half-million dollars. I've advised my client to bring charges. His former partner has another business in Twin Falls that at least appears to be solvent. Hopefully he can get some of his money back."

"What about the patent infringement?" Helena asked.

"I'm still working on that, but I think the other company will come to some sort of agreement."

It all sounded boring to me, but I tried to show an interest in Nori's work. "What about the mother trying to keep her kids?"

"That may be a problem, but shouldn't be. The husband claims she's having an affair with the teacher of one of their kids. He says her actions prove she's an unfit mother. While I don't usually approve of affairs, I don't think the teacher being a woman automatically makes my client an unfit mother. The problem is the husband carries a lot of clout in the community."

"Wow," I said, forgetting my earlier boredom with law. "What are you going to do?" The comparison of my own mother abandoning her child, to this woman who was fighting to keep hers, didn't escape me.

"I'll have to argue on the merits, show she is a good mother, her sexual orientation nothing to do with her ability to care for her children."

I knew Nori wanted kids eventually, but hoped she wouldn't marry some man, maybe one of those her grandmother kept pushing at her, to achieve that dream. I didn't think she would, she was too smart.

Helena and I made plans to drive out to Lizard Butte the next day. "But I don't want to eat our lunch there—it's too creepy. We can drive to Thousand Springs State Park and maybe stop off at the winery in Hagerman after. We're running low." I held up my near-empty glass to illustrate.

Helena took the hint and refilled it. "If you don't mind, I'd like to stop at the National Park Service office in Hagerman. I understand they have a Minidoka display."

"Speaking of Minidoka," Nori said. "We need to plan a tour while my grandparents and Suki are here."

Helena took a sip of her wine and nodded. "I'll take care of that. I can make the arrangements tomorrow. Since Minidoka is a national historic site, the Park Service runs it."

We drove down a gravel road to where someone had moved an old Minidoka barracks. After the war, the government auctioned off much of Minidoka's irrigated land and the buildings, the first choice given to returning GIs. This building might have belonged to one of those men. The old barrack stood empty now, piles of tumbleweed blown up against the foundation. The land surrounding it was empty, too, with no sign of irrigation.

Helena wanted to stop. "Someone lived here once. Probably had a wife—see the ratty curtains still hanging from the windows."

We got out of the truck and started prowling. A door swung inward on one rusted hinge. I peered inside. "This end is full of junk." Bails of rusted wire, a broken pick-ax and shovel, a couple of barrels, the writing on their sides obliterated by time. I saw nothing of value in the place. "I wonder what happened to whoever lived here—poor guy must have been following some kind of dream."

"Think of who lived in this building before they moved it from Minidoka. Four or five families—all of them crammed together in this space—maybe Grandma Suki, or Auntie Keiko and her family."

I gazed around me, trying to see the place with Helena's eyes, as it once would have been. I pulled out my cell phone and took several pictures.

Back in the truck, we turned and drove south for a couple of miles. We came to a cleared spot where I parked the truck. "We walk the rest of the way, but it's not far."

The path led past an arroyo and several small granite outcroppings. We rounded a sagebrush-covered hill and saw the jutting lava outcropping shaped like a lizard sunning itself on a sandy expanse of desert.

Helena stopped, a troubled expression on her flushed face.

"Why did you want to come here?"

She hesitated for a moment. "Because, years ago, an entire family was murdered here." Her voice was barely above a whisper. "Right here, Lily. These days, they'd call it a hate crime. Back then they brushed it under a rug, or at least tried to."

"I always knew this was a bad place. It gives me the creeps—even when I was a little kid. Who were they?"

"A man and wife and their two sons—most likely Japanese," Helena said. "I'm not sure when it happened, probably in the late thirties, maybe a bit earlier. All sorts of hateful rumors were going around back then about the Japanese and Chinese." Her face and voice grew grim. Her eyes filled with tears, angry or sad, I couldn't tell. "It was a terrible, dreadful thing and not one soul ever arrested."

I stared at the jutting black rock and surrounding wind-scoured terrain and understood why, even as a child, I'd sensed evil here. I shivered. "Let's go."

Helena hesitated. "If you don't mind, I'd like to explore a bit. You go back to the truck. I'll be with you before long."

I didn't want to leave her, but she insisted. "Okay, I'll go. But if you're not back in thirty minutes, I'm calling in the Air National Guard from Mountain Home."

She managed to make it with a minute to spare. "Okay, on to Hagerman and Thousand Springs Park."

I pulled out of the cleared space, pleased to see the plume of dust roiling up behind the truck, blurring the image of Lizard Butte in the rearview mirror.

We were half-way to Hagerman before either of us spoke. "Why do you suppose no one was arrested?" I asked. "There must have been more than one person involved. Someone would have talked, maybe even bragged about it."

"I know," Helena said and sighed. "I've searched every-where though—on the internet, in books and old news-papers. I haven't been able to find anything more about what happened. Whenever I ask someone I think might have information, I get nothing but blank looks. Well, all but from Grandpa Paul. His reaction seemed odd to me. Then he changed the subject. I haven't had the opportunity to talk to him about it again." We drove on for a few miles, both of us silent, until Helena pointed upward. "Look, a Bald Eagle. We must be getting close to the river." The eagles liked to fish from the rocks.

We ate our sandwiches in a patch of shade and enjoyed the power and beauty of the falls spilling over the cliffs, a comforting contrast to Lizard Butte. The sound of the rushing water lulled me into a brief nap. Helena, too. We stopped at the winery on the way out of Hagerman, after Helena visited the folks at the Park Service office, and headed home with two cases of wine in the back of the truck.

# HELENA

At the Jerome museum, I poured over several copies of old issues of *The Minidoka Irrigator*. My silenced phone vibrated on the table next to me. Grandma Suki. They'd missed their connecting flight in Salt Lake City and could I meet them at the Boise airport instead of Twin Falls. I assured her I'd be there.

I put away my notes and returned the copies of *The Irrigator* to the volunteer in charge of the museum that day. Once outside, I called Nori to let her know I needed to head to Boise. "Their plane gets in at 3:10. I'll bring them directly to Virginia's. We'll be in time for Happy Hour. What about your grandparents?"

"They get in around two," Nori said. "I'll let Lily know not to expect you at the house."

"Good. I'd call her, but you know how she is when she's in her studio. She won't pick up."

"Exactly," I said, heading toward my car, hoping it was still in the shade. "I wish she'd tell us what she's working on."

"Must be something special. She says it's for all three of them—Virginia, Keiko and Suki." Nori's voice started to crackle.

"I'm losing you," I said before the connection broke entirely. "See you this evening."

The trip into Boise took about two hours. I got to the airport with only minutes to spare. After telling the woman at the check-in counter I'd come to pick up my elderly grandparents, she gave me a boarding pass so I could meet them at the gate.

I thanked her, breezed through the short line at security, and reached the gate in time to spot my grandparents crossing the tarmac toward the breezeway leading to the terminal, a flight attendant pushing grandpa's chair. When they came through the door, I greeted them and smiled my thanks to the young flight attendant. "I'll take my grandfather's chair now."

"Their bags will be on the carousel in a few minutes," he said. "Thanks for flying with us Mr. and Mrs. Franconi. Perhaps I'll be lucky enough to serve you on your return flight."

Out in the parking lot, we got Grandpa settled in the passenger seat and I put their bags in the trunk. "His chair will need to go next to you in the back, Grandma. I hope that's okay."

She scooted over. "My, but it's hot. I always forget the weather here."

I hurried around and started the car. "The air-conditioning will cool us off in a few minutes."

"Oh, I don't mind, dear. The heat feels good, especially after the frigid air in the plane—I had to ask for an additional blanket. How about you, Paul? Are you too warm?" My grandfather said he was fine. I turned the air-conditioner to low, directed the vents toward me, and hoped I wouldn't melt.

In minutes, we were out on the freeway and heading east, toward Twin Falls. A triple-trailer truck roared past in a flurry of wind and tiny bits of the hay it carried.

"How are you settling in?" my grandmother asked.

"Great. You know I've always loved the old farmhouse. It's wonderful of Lily to share it with Nori and me."

Grandma reached forward and rested her hand on Grandpa's shoulder. "I love that house, too. I met your grandfather there."

"Tell me what the farm was like back then. I try to imagine, but things have changed so much, it's hard to picture."

"You need to ask Virginia and Paul, or even Keiko. I worked only two summers at the farm before Paul and I married and moved to California. Marc ran everything. He had a passion for farming and didn't suffer fools or sluggards in the fields. I admired that in him."

I glanced over at Grandpa, but he didn't add anything—I wondered if he and his brother had gotten along.

"He must have been glad when Virginia brought John Sato back to Idaho," I said. "There was so much work to do. With the internees gone from Minidoka, he must have been terribly short-handed."

My grandmother didn't rise to the bait. "You're right. And his brother, Leo, was no help—he was a broken man. Not physically, but mentally." Although I'd been told Leo's story before, I let her go on. "What he'd experienced in the war, and what he'd witnessed at the labor camps hidden away in the forests of southern Germany, where he and his unit discovered them, must have nearly destroyed his mind."

Having seen pictures of those camps and some of the people who'd survived them—like walking dead—I could well imagine.

"He tried to help Marc and John, but mostly he drank. Then one night he went out to the barn and shot himself."

Still, my grandfather said nothing.

"Poor Virginia was in such a state. We were students then—your grandfather, I should say—and money almost non-existent. Still, there was no question we'd come." She leaned forward again and patted Grandpa's shoulder. "We told people Leo's death was an accidental shooting, but everyone was aware of the truth. That damned war wouldn't stop taking lives."

"You had another sister, didn't you Grandpa?"

He nodded. "Irene. She'd gone back to living in Portland by then and was between husbands, as I recall."

Grandma leaned back in her seat. "She was full of life, that one."

"Full of something," Grandpa said.

All of us were quiet for a while, lost in our own thoughts. I took the Mountain Home off-ramp and stopped at the first gas station. "Anyone want a drink or to use the restroom?" Both declined and we were soon on the road again. I glanced in the rearview mirror. Grandma had fallen asleep, her head cocked to one side. I expected my grandfather might fall asleep, but he didn't. After a while, we passed the turn off to Twin Falls. "We're almost there, Grandpa."

"I can smell it," he said.

I laughed. "Can you? Me, too."

"Suki, wake up," Grandpa said. "We'll be at Virginia's in a few minutes."

We turned down the tree-lined driveway. Grandma, as though she'd been awake for the entire drive, leaned over the back of the seat. "This place always makes me think of some southern mansion. The white paint enhances that, don't you think, Helena?"

"Oh yeah," I said. "Not to mention the acres of green pasture surrounding it. Tara personified. I expect we'll find Uncle Mako already out back fly-fishing. We might have fresh trout for dinner."

"And maybe Scarlett O'Hara will be on the terrace with mint Juleps," Grandpa said. The three of us chuckled as we alighted from the car.

Not Scarlett, but Amy. She greeted us with hugs. "How was your trip? Too bad you missed your connections and had to make that long drive from Boise."

I got Grandpa's chair out of the back seat and brought it around for him.

"The drive was fine," he said. "Very relaxing, actually. Suki slept most of the way."

"I most certainly did not."

I wondered how Grandpa knew she'd been asleep, then realized when people were married so long as the two of them, they were aware of everything about the other person, including when that person slept. That she'd quit talking might have been a clue, too.

Neil carried their bags into the house. I pushed Grandpa to a small elevator near the back of the entrance hallway while Amy and the others took the stairs. Their bedroom, located next to the elevator, overlooked the back terrace and the river. I spotted three figures along the riverbank and grinned. Just as I thought, Uncle Mako had a fly rod in hand.

Neil set down the bags and excused himself, saying he needed to make a phone call. Amy asked if we wanted something to drink. "Tea, coffee, wine? Dinner won't be for another couple of hours—around seven."

"I think Grandma and Grandpa will want to rest for a bit," I told Amy. "I'm assuming Auntie Keiko and Uncle Mako are here. I think I spotted Uncle Mako out the window."

Amy nodded. "Mother is napping and yes, Papa is already trying his luck. Nori and Lily are giving him instructions."

I laughed. "I'll go join them. Unless you want me to help you unpack now, Grandma?"

My grandmother was already preparing to stretch out on the bed and Amy assured me she'd give her a hand later.

The carpet covering the stairs was whisper-soft. I all but skipped down them. My footsteps echoed on the marble floor but were quickly softened by the oriental carpet running the length of the hall leading to the kitchen and a huge great room that overlooked the back yard and the river. The place was so different from Lily's old farmhouse. Air-conditioning made the rooms cooler, carpets and rugs made them more comfortable. Still, I liked the farmhouse. I wondered if Virginia missed it.

I said hello to Uncle Mako, who gave me an absent-minded hug then quickly returned his attention to his rod, reel, and the river that rippled over rocks, heading to Shoshone Falls. Some called the Falls the Niagara of the

West. The canyon wall across from us was a soft rose and yellow in the late afternoon sun. I sat on the grass next to Nori and Lily. After a while, Amy called for us to come and join them.

Everyone had gathered on the terrace. Neil acted as bartender. Virginia, Grandma Suki, and Auntie Keiko sat near the covered fire-pit. I nudged Nori when Auntie Keiko giggled at something Grandma Suki said, something about an Italian with dimples and liquid eyes.

Grandma asked Nori about her new practice. I almost wished she hadn't mentioned it in front of Auntie Keiko, but Nori didn't hesitate to tell my grandmother things were moving along nicely. Auntie Keiko narrowed her eyes, but managed not to respond.

Behind her intensity, which Nori shared though she probably wasn't aware of it, Auntie Keiko was a kind woman. She was not used to being thwarted, however, and Nori had done just that when she left the big law firm in Portland and moved to Idaho to set up her own practice.

For Nori, it was a step in the right direction, but not far enough. She needed to stop looking over her shoulder, stop worrying about what her grandmother thought. Only when she realized she didn't need her grandmother's approval would she be truly independent. Auntie Keiko needed to let go. Perhaps her refusal to be drawn into an argument with Nori was an indication she was learning to do that. I sighed. They had so much in common. If only they could see that.

Amy came out to tell us dinner was on the table. "Neil's sisters will be over with their families tomorrow, but tonight it's just us."

Once seated around the dinner table, the talk was non-stop. Reminiscing about previous visits and more about the old days on the farm, including a story about Virginia's and Grandpa's father helping some Italian POW fieldworkers escape. One POW, the one with the dimples and the liquid eyes, they apparently all fancied.

About half-way through the meal, the dogs outside set up an uproar, and a few minutes later, Grace and Henri strolled into the dining room. Grace wore a pair of shorts so short and tight, I wondered how they didn't cut off the circulation to her legs.

"Looks like we're late," she said. Her eyes, gazing around the table, held a malicious glitter. "This is Henri. Henri, meet the Franconi family."

My eyes flew to Lily, whose face was drained of color. Virginia said nothing, but her hand shook when she set her fork down on the edge of her plate. Grace and Henri weren't late—they hadn't been asked. How typical of Bella's still-angry daughter to show up without invitation. I wanted to shake her, and I wanted to comfort poor Lily.

Grandma Suki managed to put everyone at least somewhat at ease. She stood and embraced Grace. "It's so good of you to come, dear. It's been much too long. Paul, say hello to your grand-niece. And this young man is Henri? Helena, why don't you and Lily round up a couple of extra chairs?"

Amy came to life as well. "I'll get plates and silverware." She turned to Lily and me. "I have some folding chairs in a closet near the pantry. Come, I'll show you."

Lily took my hand in a death grip. "How could she bring that creature, that gigolo here?" she whispered as we left the room. "I hate her, Helena. I really, really do."

I tried to calm her. "We all know what she's like, Lily. No one holds her actions against you, so stop worrying."

"Easy for you to say—I'm the one with her genes floating around inside me."

When we got to the kitchen, Amy showed us where she kept the extra chairs while she got out two more place settings.

When we returned to the dining room, Grandma Suki stood with one arm through Virginia's, also standing now, and the other arm through Grace's. Neither Virginia nor Grace appeared comfortable. My dear grandmother would always play peacemaker. Auntie Keiko rolled her eyes at me. I had to smile.

When everyone was settled and dishes were passed to Grace and Henri, the conversation, though a trifle stilted, resumed.

"Nori and I are taking Auntie Keiko, Uncle Mako and Grandma Suki to Minidoka tomorrow," I announced. "Does anyone else want to come?"

"A few days ago, I went there with The Friends of Minidoka," Amy said. "We're planning to rebuild a watchtower. But I'd be happy to go again. How about you, Lily?"

Lily shook her head. "I can't. I'm on a deadline—only three more days until Virginia's birthday."

"Paul and I will stay here and enjoy a nice chat," Virginia said. "I need to gather my strength for the big celebration you girls are planning."

"What is this Minidoka everyone talks about," Henri asked.

Grace stared at the food on her plate; she'd barely eaten a bite. "It's an old concentration camp from World War

Two. Like the Germans rounded up the Jews, good old Uncle Sam rounded up Japanese-Americans." She finally lifted her eyes. They darted from person to person, daring anyone to contradict. "What's left of it, which isn't much, is a few miles from here. That's how the Franconi family and most of the farmers around here survived, got rich even— the 'internees' worked in the fields, planted and harvested the crops." She shifted her glittering eyes from Virginia to Grandma. "How much did you and Keiko earn, Suki, working your asses off for the Franconi's? Not even a dollar a day, I bet." She drained what remained of the wine in her glass and reached for the bottle in the middle of the table.

Neither Grandma Suki nor Keiko responded. Henri went on eating, as though unaware of the tension in the air. Virginia finally interrupted the heavy silence. "Amy, will you bring dessert in now?" She gazed around the table. "Would anyone like coffee?"

"Not I," Grandpa Paul said. "And no dessert, thanks. I couldn't eat another bite."

I stood. "I think I'll skip dessert tonight as well. I'm a bit tired. Goodnight, Aunt Virginia. Don't get up." I leaned over and kissed her on the cheek. "Amy, dinner was delicious, as always." Amy tried to smile, but looked uneasily from her mother to my grandmother. "Nori and I will be here around noon," I said. "Will that be too early?"

"Of course not," my grandmother said. "We'll be ready, won't we Keiko?"

Lily stood. "I'm going home, too. I'll see you all tomorrow." She all but fled out of the room. I followed her.

Behind me, chair legs scraped across the floor. Grace had succeeded in bringing the party to an uneasy and rapid close.

The next morning, Amy decided to stay home while the rest of us managed to fit into Nori's car. Auntie Keiko fastened her seat belt. "The problem with these little cars is the lack of legroom in the back seat."

Grandma Suki, between us, tried to squeeze closer to me. "You're fine," I whispered to her.

Uncle Mako, up front in the passenger seat, wanted Nori to put the top down.

"Mako, hush. Don't even think about it, Nori. We'd get blown apart back here." As usual, Auntie Keiko was dressed in designer-fashioned elegance—linen pants and jacket, strappy high-heeled sandals. She was the only eighty-plus-year-old woman I'd ever met who never wore sensible shoes.

Grandma Suki may have been ready physically, in loose -fitting slacks and top and sturdy-looking walking shoes, but she still wasn't mentally prepared to visit Minidoka. Grandpa had insisted.

I wished he'd come, too, but he said he and Virginia needed to talk, that he had something to tell her. I wondered what.

"Nori, I need you to pick someone up at the airport tonight," Auntie Keiko said.

Nori glanced in the rearview mirror. "Oh? Who and what time?"

"Mako's great-nephew from Japan—Hayoto Abi. He comes in at four-thirty. He's a potter—quite a well-known one. He's been in the States teaching and doing demonstrations for several weeks—including at Lewis and Clark, your alma mater, Nori. I thought it would be good for him to come and meet the family."

Nori continued to study her grandmother in the rearview mirror. It was easy to read what went through her mind—here was yet another man her grandmother insisted on pushing at her. "I'll go with you," I said, hoping to reassure her.

Grandma Suki seemed to be shrinking further into my side as we drew closer to the Minidoka site. "I really don't want to do this," she whispered to me. "I wish Paul hadn't pressed for me to come."

I wanted to reassure her, but there was nothing I could say. This was her memory and she'd always refused to share it. Instead, I took her frail hand in my own, stroking the papery skin.

Nori turned into the graveled parking lot. "Here we are."

The first thing that struck me about the site was its peacefulness and except for a few birds singing, the utter quiet. "Seems impossible nearly ten thousand people once lived here," I whispered to Nori.

Grandma Suki, Uncle Mako and Auntie Keiko walked ahead of us. Their silent gazes went from the Northside Canal and the fields bordering the site to the overgrown field within the fence. A graveled path meandered through the high, golden grass.

We followed the path, Auntie Keiko sometimes struggling in her high-heeled sandals and needing to lean on Uncle Mako's arm, until we came to a large sign indicating where a swimming hole had been. *"The parched ground in front of you was once a swimming hole built and used by the internees to escape the heat, dust and boredom of camp life,"* the sign read. The accompanying picture showed men, women, and children swimming and playing in a large, muddy-looking hole or sunbathing on its banks.

Suddenly, Grandma Suki, Auntie Keiko, and Uncle Mako were all talking at once.

"I think that's Myoko, Suki."

Grandma nodded. "Mako, isn't that you and Tommy on the left?"

The picture was so grainy, I didn't know how they could make out faces well enough to recognize anyone, but Uncle Mako agreed the two figures were he and Tommy. He said he remembered the picture being taken.

"To prove to the public that we were all happy and content, no doubt," said Auntie Keiko, before Uncle Mako went on to identify five or six others in the photo.

Despite Auntie Keiko's sarcastic comment, which my research corroborated—photographs at the various internment camps were taken for public relations purposes—the picture of the swimming hole served to relax everyone, even Grandma Suki. Eventually, we walked on until we came to a cluster of buildings. Auntie Keiko pointed to one. "They made furniture in that building. I remember Papa being so pleased when they brought us a small table and chair where he could sit and write his poetry, along with a bookcase for his books. But he liked the table and chair best. They weren't pretty, any of it, but they served a function."

Grandma Suki pointed west. "The poultry and the pig farms were over by the vegetable gardens. Remember the awful smell of pigs and chickens when the wind blew from that direction?"

"The wind always blew," Auntie Keiko said. "Why it isn't right now, I have no idea. Remember my coat?" Grandma Suki and Uncle Mako laughed. "A man's uniform coat from WWI," she said to Nori and me. "It came down to my ankles, but kept me warm in the winter."

"The administration buildings and the hospital were that way," Uncle Mako said, pointing to the east.

"And the *Irrigator* office was over there," Auntie Keiko said. "I worked at the newspaper, you know. John Sato, too. I remember how we used to talk—I'm still surprised he didn't become a No-No Boy. But too many people were against it, I guess. Now, of course, he'd be a hero."

Auntie Keiko's words surprised me. I'd never heard that about John Sato. I took Uncle Mako's arm, squeezing it. He'd frowned at Auntie Keiko's lightly spoken words about No-No Boys now being heroes. Only rarely did he speak of his experiences with the 442nd, mostly confining his remarks to the humorous things he'd witnessed, never the horrors. Nori smiled her thanks to me.

That night, as we drove to the airport to pick up the mysterious Hayoto Abi, Nori and I discussed our morning at Minidoka. She glanced over at me. "I think the visit went well, don't you?"

"Grandma Suki was nervous about going, but once everyone started talking and remembering, she relaxed."

"The swimming-hole sign did it."

"Who do you suppose this Hayoto guy is?" I asked.

"You probably know the story about Grand-father's sister getting caught in Japan by the war—how she'd actually been on her way home when Pearl Harbor happened."

Grandma Suki had told me about it. "Yes, and how no one knew whether her ship got sunk or turned around and went back to Japan, didn't find out until after the war ended."

Nori nodded. "Her parents, my great-grandparents, were frantic—they didn't know what happened to her." Nori stopped talking for a minute as she turned the car onto the road leading to the airport. We drove on for a few minutes in silence before she continued. "At first Nobuko tried to come back to America, but was denied the right of return—apparently, the government decided she'd renounced her citizenship when she applied for rice rations in her father's old village." She shook her head with disgust and I had a fleeting mental picture of what Auntie Keiko must have looked like at her age. "After learning both her parents were dead—her mother died while still at Camp Minidoka and her father shortly after the end of the war—she quit trying to come back. She made a life for herself in Japan, got married, and had a daughter. Hayoto is her grandson."

I felt callouses on his palms when we shook hands. He was quite tall. He'd tied his hair, long, straight, and unruly, in a ponytail. Nori elbowed me on our way back to the car. "Are you smitten?" she whispered, grinning at me. I had to admit he was handsome. Very handsome, in fact.

Once in the car, Nori and Hayoto chatted. His English was exceptional. He told us he and his mother always spoke English with his grandmother. He leaned forward. "I stayed at your grandparents' house in Lake Oswego," he told Nori. "A beautiful place and very convenient to the school."

I felt his warm breath on my ear and cheek as he spoke.

# 5

## NORI

Although my grandmother hadn't said as much, I knew she'd intended Hayoto Abi for me, and I was fed up with her pushing men in my face. I'd met someone I thought might be the one.

Cat had gotten out one evening—a surprise, since he normally showed no inclination to leave the safety of the house, apparently finding being inside, fed and cared for, preferable to living by his wits. Nonetheless, he'd scooted out the door when someone came in. I called and called, but to no avail. The next morning, I found him huddled against the door, his ear torn, part of his tail missing and one paw bleeding profusely.

Lily didn't know any vets, but I'd met one at one of my many networking meetings. Susan Wilson. She had strawberry-blonde hair, freckles all over her face and arms, and sparkling blue-green eyes. Everyone liked her. Her contagious laugh entranced me—a gurgle at first, coming right up from her belly, before bursting into laughter. I found her phone number and called. She told me to bring Cat in right away.

"We can't do anything about his tail—he's lucky whatever got hold of him, a coyote maybe, didn't hurt him worse. Probably found a hole to hide in—an irrigation pipe, maybe. I'm concerned about infection. Do you mind if I keep him here a couple of days?"

I didn't. Cat had become my mascot.

I knew the attraction between Susan and me was mutual. All the signs were there—the quick glances, the accidental touches, the shared smiles. I hadn't asked her out, though. I wasn't ready to declare my 'sexual orientation' in Twin Falls, Idaho. No surprise. I didn't even have the courage to tell my own grandparents.

I dragged my thoughts away from Cat's misadventures and Susan-the-vet. The Twin Falls airport receding in my rearview mirror, I returned my attention to Helena and Hayoto.  By the quick glances thrown over her shoulder and her slightly flushed cheeks, I could tell that Helena was taking note of our passenger's good looks. It made me smile. Since her disastrous affair with Bill what's-his-name, the jerk, she'd refused to date or show any interest in men or sex.  It wasn't natural.

I looked at Hayoto in the rearview mirror. "So, will you be with us long? Where do you go next?"

He leaned forward again and I grinned to see Helena give a slight shiver.

"I've finished my demonstrations and lectures in Portland and Seattle. I'm supposed to be in San Francisco in a week. In the meantime, I thought I might take a few days to explore this area, since my great-grandparents once lived here."

I nodded at Helena. "Here's someone who can be your tour guide. Helena has been traveling all over this area. She's writing a book about Minidoka, the camp where your grandparents lived. She also knows San Francisco well since she grew up in Palo Alto, practically next door to the city."

"Really, that is excellent." He smiled and sank back in his seat. Helena flashed me a look I didn't quite understand. Panic?

When we got to the house, we found everyone once again gathered on the shaded terrace. Virginia greeted Hayoto with delight. "I always admired your grandmother. Her story enthralled me. Such a tragedy for her parents and for Mako, but I'm so glad she eventually had a happy life. Tell me how you came to be a potter."

Hayoto held everyone's attention as he told us about being taught by a master potter in the factory he inherited from his father's family. The factory was in a mountain village not far from Hiroshima.

"John's family came from that area," Virginia said.

Hayoto nodded. "That's not surprising. A lot of the Japanese who came to this country back in the early 1900s, and even before, were from the area around Hiroshima. There is a history of draughts in southern Honshu."

"That's what John said."

At dinner, the talk about Japanese immigrants and their descendants continued. Helena brought up how most had settled around the West Coast before the war, but now lived all over the country. Grandmother Keiko said that was in good part because of how young, Japanese-American women were encouraged to attend East Coast and Midwest colleges and universities during the war.

Lily remained surprisingly quiet. I was sure she worried about a repeat performance from Grace. I told her I thought

Grace, whom I could never think of as Lily's mother, was unlikely to show up again.

When a brief lull in the conversation occurred, Paul spoke. "Nori, Helena, Lily—can you girls come over after breakfast tomorrow? There's something I need to discuss with you."

I looked at Helena and Lily, my eyebrows raised in question.

"Of course, Grandpa," Helena said.

Lily nodded. "I won't be able to stay long, though. The paintings need a few final touches."

"You are a painter?" Hayoto asked. "I'd like to see your work."

"Several of Lily's pieces are here," Virginia said. "One is hanging over the fireplace in the great room."

Hayoto turned back to Lily. "The African man? I'm impressed. You captured his essence well." The picture was the mate to the African woman hanging above my grandparents' mantle.

Lily had always been intrigued with Africa. Because of Bella dying there, I suppose. Growing up, she'd been fascinated by Bella's story, just as Helena and I were.

She blushed. "Thank you. I'll be bringing the pieces I'm working on over here in a couple of days. They're to celebrate Virginia's birthday."

The next morning, we drove separately to Virginia's. I had an appointment, another new client, and Lily needed to get back to her studio. Helena had agreed to take Hayoto around that afternoon. When we got to the house, we found my grandparents, Virginia and Suki already gathered in the den. Coffee and rolls were on the low table in front of the couch, where Virginia, Suki and Grandmother Keiko were seated. Grandfather Mako sat in an over-stuffed chair next to one end of the couch. Three chairs were lined up for Lily, Helena, and me. Paul sat in his wheelchair, facing us. I wondered if everyone else was as curious and puzzled as me. After a few words of greeting, coffee poured and rolls at hand, we looked to Paul to begin.

"Last spring Helena came down to Carmel Valley to visit with Suki and me for a few days. While with us, she asked me about an event that happened at a place called Lizard Butte—it's not far from here. I told her I knew nothing about it." He stopped and cleared his throat before going on. "I lied. A heinous crime happened at Lizard Butte in 1936. A heinous crime I've tried hard to forget—a heinous crime involving this family."

Lily's hand flew to her mouth. I darted a look at Helena, who stared at her grandfather. With a sinking feeling, I returned my attention to Paul.

"I'd just turned fourteen that summer. One hot July day, I went into Eden with my father—Keiko and Suki can attest to what a miserable man he was. Anyway, he wanted to visit some of his cronies, most as mean and suspicious as him. As usual, they sat out front of the barber shop, smoking, drinking beer and complaining about one thing or another. I was about to leave and find a friend when these people suddenly appeared on the road in front of the barber shop. A man and woman, each carrying a child—one a toddler and the other a bit older. Four or five, I'd guess. They were foreign-looking to me. Japanese or Chinese, I figured."

The room remained utterly quiet except for Paul's voice. Suki watched Paul closely. Virginia stared at her hands, clasped together in her lap. My grandmother, head cocked to one side, looked strangely perplexed.

"There'd been a lot of bad talk about Asians back then," Paul said, his voice low, but firm. "Farmers especially didn't like them—I think because the Chinese and Japanese, who'd come here to work the mines and build the railroads, turned out to be good at farming. The local farmers didn't like the competition."

I briefly thought of Grandfather Mako's landscaping and nursery business and remembered hearing how white nursery owners had tried to sabotage him.

"These folks didn't speak English well, but the husband finally made clear their car had broken down about a mile or so out of Eden. Don't ask me what they were doing in such an out-of-the-way place—probably made a wrong turn somewhere. They looked beat. Their shoes were dusty, the kids whining and tired, The man made the mistake of asking my father and his pals for help."

Paul broke off talking and asked for a drink of water. Suki brought him one from the kitchen. He drank a third of the water then Suki helped him set the glass on the table next to his chair so that he could help himself when he wanted more. He took a deep breath and began speaking again.

"Dad and his cronies did a little quiet back and forthing among themselves, then one of them said they'd take the family to find a mechanic to fix their car. Everyone piled into a couple of trucks, the Asian family in the back of one.

Dad and another man climbed in with them. Dad hollered to me to follow. As they started to head out, the wife gave the husband an uneasy look—I suppose she had a feeling things weren't right."

Paul stopped and took another drink of water. His hand shook so badly, he almost dropped the glass when he set it back on the table.

"Like most farm kids, I'd been driving since I was ten or so. I got in Dad's truck and took off after them. Ahead of me, the Asian man pointed in a different direction to the one we were taking. He managed to get to his feet in the back of the truck and banged on the roof of the cab, trying to get the attention of whoever drove. Dad pulled him back down. The man gathered his wife and children in his arms. She was crying by then, both kids, too."

Once again, he had to stop and take a deep breath before he could continue.

"They drove out on the desert, all the way to Lizard Butte. I guess roads lead out that way now. Not back then, and it was a pretty rough ride. When they got to Lizard Butte, the men pulled the couple and the kids out of the back of the truck and dragged them to the outcropping. Part of me wanted to drive back to town as fast as I could, the other part of me felt compelled to stay. That's what I did. I got out of the truck and stayed."

Suki rose and went to stand behind Paul, her hand on his shoulder. He swallowed hard.

"I've thought about what happened a thousand times, trying to figure out how they could do what they did. They weren't evil men, no meaner than Dad anyway, but on that day, evil possessed them. They beat the man. My father helped hold him while one of the other men did the punching. Then they made the man watch while they started in on his wife. The same man who'd done the beating ripped her dress down the front. She'd been screaming when they beat her husband and at first, she screamed when they turned on her. The older boy cried and tried to drag the men away from his mother. She'd gone silent by then. One of the men cuffed the boy, knocked him backwards into the side of the rock. He sank to the ground and didn't move. I can still picture his small body sprawled at the base of that giant outcropping."

He stopped and closed his eyes for a few seconds then took another sip of water. Not a sound came from anyone else. When he began to speak again, there was a tremor in his voice.

"I'd been unable to move or make a sound up to then, but when the boy fell to the ground, I ran into the middle of them, yelling for them to stop. I grabbed my father's arm, trying to pull him away. He shook me off. He and the others were staring at the man on top of the woman. Their tongues were all but hanging out as they waited their turns with her."

Oh God, I thought, please make him stop. He didn't, even though tears had begun to roll from his sightless eyes down his thin cheeks, filling the lines and crevices, dripping from his chin onto his crisp white shirt.

"I ran into the desert. I ran for what seemed like hours, until I fell and couldn't get up. I stayed out there all night. In the morning, I went back. The men and the trucks, including my father's, had gone. What remained were four burned and mutilated bodies. They'd even killed the toddler."

Suki put her arms around his shoulders, rested her cheek on his head.

"No one talked. Dad tried to act like nothing had happened. Something did happen though, something evil and horribly wrong. My father was part of it. Since I did nothing to stop them, I didn't even tell the sheriff afterwards, I was part of the evil, too."

My stomach roiled. I swallowed hard. Everything I'd ever known about my family needed to be re-examined. Lily's face had turned white as her tee-shirt and Helena, tears on her cheeks, appeared equally stunned. Grandmother Keiko stared at Paul as though she'd never seen him before.

Grandfather Mako regained his voice first. "What happened to the bodies?"

"I don't know. I went out there one more time. I couldn't stay away. But everything had disappeared. There was no trace."

"Weren't the people missed? Did no one come asking for them?"

Paul answered. "They must have been missed by someone—parents, brothers and sisters—but no one came looking for them and no one was ever arrested, much less tried for their murders."

"Remarkable," Grandfather Mako said.

Helena spoke. "If no one ever told, who posted that bit on the internet?"

Suki's quiet voice answered. "I did."

Helena stared. "You did? Why, Grandma?"

"Paul told me all this before we married. He said I shouldn't marry him without knowing what kind of family I was getting into." She patted Grandpa's shoulder. "After he told me, he refused to discuss it again. He couldn't forget, though. He had such terrible nightmares. Still has them. And the hatred he held for his father wouldn't go away, even after the old man died. The only way to help was to get it out in the open. He couldn't go on keeping it buried." She smiled at Helena. "I knew you'd find what I posted. I wanted you to and I wanted you to push for an answer. You didn't let me down."

Helena went to Paul and knelt at his feet. She took both his hands in her own. "That poor family, Grandpa— what happened to them was horrible, a nightmare. I feel terrible for them, but sad, too, for the fourteen-year-old boy who witnessed it, witnessed his own father take part."

Paul face held no color. Despite all the physical ailments he suffered, he generally appeared fit and healthy. Now, for the first time, he looked every minute of his age.

"Dad swore he didn't take part in it, that he was a by-stander, like me. But he did take part. I saw him. I told Leo. He believed me—I think that's part of why he killed himself. I blamed myself for that, too."

"What about Marc?" Helena said. "Did he know?"

I didn't look at Virginia. I didn't want to think she, too, had known about this and never told.

"I didn't tell him," Paul said. "But I think he overheard Dad and me arguing one day. Irene was twelve and in her own world back then. Virginia had already left home. I told her everything yesterday, Amy and Neil, too, while the rest of you went to Minidoka."

We all remained silent for several minutes. Then almost as one, we suddenly began to move. Virginia said she needed to lie down. Suki took Paul out to the terrace for some fresh air. My grandparents disappeared, probably upstairs to their room, leaving Lily, Helena, and me on our own.

Lily stood and began to pace. "I always knew Lizard Butte was an evil place. Remember, Helena. I told you. But I never dreamed Paul had anything to do with it. He's so gentle."

"You're right," I said. "Think of all he's written in praise of men like Gandhi and the Dali Lama, the money he's donated from the sale of his books. He's a man with good intent. Perhaps what he's done has been to atone somehow for what he didn't do then—and for what his father did do."

Helena sighed. "He didn't really have anything to do with what happened—except at first, maybe, when he was chasing after them in the truck. To a fourteen-year-old the chase would have been exciting. He may even have pictured himself as a hero, about to save lives. But then, of course, he became an unwilling witness, unable to do anything to help those poor people." She stared into space for a minute. "What a nightmare. God his father must have been a miserable S.O.B."

"Not only him," I said. "There were other men involved, too."

"That one was ours," Lily said. "Those poor kids—Paul, Virginia, Marc and the other two, Irene and Leo—no wonder Leo killed himself. The old man might be the reason Irene kept going through husbands—he may have sexually abused her when she was a kid. From everything people have said, I wouldn't put anything past him." She pushed her blonde hair back from her forehead, her brows drawn together over her navy-blue eyes, so like Virginia's. "I'm always feeling sorry for myself, getting saddled with Grace, but imagine what it must have been like growing up with a bastard like that for a father."

I shook my head. "I can't even begin to imagine. No one ever says much about their mother, though…poor woman. On the other hand, she may have been as bad as him."

"Grandpa Paul said he didn't remember her very well—she died when he was young," Helena said. "He only remembers special times—like when they helped make taffy and string popcorn and cranberries for the Christmas tree. And on Christmas Eve she always prepared some special Swedish and Italian dishes—her parents were Swedish. Anyway, he said all the kids had fun at Christmastime."

I pictured five kids pulling taffy in the farmhouse kitchen or sitting on the floor stringing popcorn. Paul and Virginia were lucky to have been part of that, even if the rest of their memories of childhood weren't so great. Lily, Helena, and I never experienced siblings. Maybe the lack of a brother or sister is what made us so close over the years.

Lily stopped pacing. "I've got to go. There's something I need to do."

I nodded. "I'll be by the house to take a shower and get cleaned up after work. How about you, Helena? What are your plans for the day?"

"I'm not sure. After what we heard this morning, my mind is still whirling. I guess it depends on what Hayoto wants to do. We talked about Shoshone Falls and the park at Hagerman. Tomorrow we're going back to Minidoka. I've arranged for a guided tour this time. Grandma Suki wants to go again, too. Can you believe it?"

I wondered if my grandmother would go with them. Our recent trip to the site had broken their resistance to talking about their experiences. Helena might get their help with her book after all, because all the way back to the house they'd talked about what Camp Minidoka had been like, what they'd done, what had happened to some of their friends.

Lily grabbed a couple of rolls. I took one, too, before Helena added them to the tray with the empty coffee pot and dirty cups. She headed for the kitchen with the filled tray as Lily and I said good-bye and left the house.

Once at my office, I couldn't concentrate and accomplished little other than shuffling some papers around. I was too frazzled by Paul's revelations. Too late to charge anyone—they were all dead except for Paul—but I wondered about the family, wondered if there were any relatives we could find. We needed to atone in some way, if we could find them. How to go about that, I didn't know. I'd ask Helena. She moved easily around the internet, where I felt sure we'd need to go to begin our search. Locating them, giving them closure, would surely help Paul's peace of mind, too.

I also thought more about the expression on Grandmother Keiko's face. She'd looked as though an ancient puzzle had been solved. I'd eventually get an explanation, but only what she was prepared to divulge.

I sighed and leaned back in my chair. When Lily said that my mother had no trouble standing up to Grandmother Keiko, she'd been right. Since my grandparents' arrival, several times I'd watched my mother listen patiently to my grandmother, and then do precisely as she'd intended in the first place. Suki and Virginia teased my grandmother about her intensity, but they weren't in the least frightened by her. And Lily was mostly joking when she called her Dragon Lady. Why did I alone allow myself to be intimidated? Quitting my job in Portland and coming back home to start my own practice had been my first act of independence. It was about time for another.

I didn't need to look up Susan's number. Her receptionist put me through right away. "Would you be interested in coming to dinner tonight?" I said. "I'd like you to meet my family."

# 6

## *LILY*

I followed Nori's red BMW down the long, shaded drive leading away from the big house and all its inhabitants. At the highway, she turned left, toward Twin Falls, and I went to the right. I was barely aware of the landscape I passed, the leafy foliage of sugar beets and potatoes, the golden fields of wheat, the tall stands of corn. I didn't even notice crossing over the Northside Canal and several other canals. Trance-like, I thought about Lizard Butte and what Paul told us in Virginia's quiet den. His tale of horror boggled my mind, and yet confirmed everything I'd always sensed about the place.

I've never claimed to be clairvoyant or anything, but I do get feelings about places. Like Lizard Butte, which had always creeped me out. I get mixed vibes in the farmhouse. Some are good, especially the newer ones, but I've always sensed sadness and anger lurking like ghosts in the corners. Perhaps the sadness came from Paul's and Virginia's mother, poor woman. The anger must belong to Paul and his father. I wondered if what Paul's father told him could be true. Maybe he hadn't taken part in the brutality of that day. He could have driven off after Paul ran into the desert. But in that case, he should have gone to the sheriff.

I sensed things about people I met, too. A sort of aura glowed around most. Hayoto, for instance. I saw he was a good man, but his aura had a dark blue edge that showed he struggled with an incredible sadness. I wondered what it was.

For years, I thought everyone saw the auras, had the perceptions, but eventually I learned that wasn't so. I still thought everyone capable, if only they'd open their minds. Not that seeing auras or getting vibes made a person happier—sometimes just the opposite. I took a bite of one of the rolls I'd brought from Virginia's and wished I'd thought to butter it before I'd left.

I slowed the truck and turned into the lane, eager to get into the studio. I pulled up under the cottonwood tree and was about to jump out of the truck. Then I spotted the studio door ajar. "Shit." I scrambled out of the truck and rushed to the studio, visions of some critter getting in and wreaking havoc tumbling through my mind.

Grace stood in front of the three panels as if mesmerized. I came to an abrupt halt. "What are you doing in here?"

"Just looking around. You're good."

"Thanks, but I really don't like for people to be in here, especially when I'm not." She looked tired, her eyes showed strain. Probably up all night carrying on with Henri. She wasn't wearing the layers of make-up she generally applied before appearing in public. I guess I didn't qualify as 'public' this morning. "Where's Henri?"

"Gone."

Intent on the open studio door, I hadn't noticed the yellow Corvette wasn't in its usual spot. "Gone where?"

"Just gone. He won't be back."

"Oh…well, sorry Grace. I'm sure you'll miss him."

She shrugged and wandered over to the Formica-topped cabinets where she picked up a carving of a small blue and white bird sitting on a piece of twisted greasewood. Its head was cocked to one side. "This was my mother's," she said.

I nodded, remembering when Virginia had given the little bird to me. She'd said her father carved him for Bella when Bella was still a baby. How was it possible to reconcile a man capable of carving and painting that exquisite little bird, so inquisitive in the way his head was posed—like he was about to ask a question—with the brutality of Lizard Butte? I couldn't.

Grace returned to studying the three panels. "I assume these are for Virginia's birthday."

"Yes, and I really need to get to work on them."

"They look finished to me."

"They mostly are finished, but I realized I need to add something to two of them before I seal them."

"I suppose you want me out of here."

"I'd prefer it, yes." For some reason, I felt kind of sorry for her.

"Okay."

"What are you going to do?"

"I don't know. Maybe read a book. I can fix you something for lunch if you want."

I frowned. "What's this about—you suddenly getting all motherly and domestic?"

"Never mind if you're not hungry."

"I'm not."

"Then I'll see you later."

She left, leaving me to wonder why I'd been so rude. It struck me that I didn't see an aura around Grace. I never had. I shrugged and got to work finishing my project. Tomorrow, I'd put them in the back of the truck and take them to Virginia's.

Around five o'clock, feeling very self-satisfied as I cleaned my brushes, I heard a car coming down the drive. I opened the door and spotted not one car, but two, Nori's bright red BMW followed by Helena's not so bright red Nissan. A woman I didn't recognize sat next to Nori. In the Nissan, with Hayoto seated beside her, Helena's face was lit in a way I hadn't seen for a long time. My eyebrows went up. Romance might be blooming on two fronts. I grinned, delighted for all of them. After I finished cleaning my brushes, I went in the house to say hello.

I'd forgotten about Grace. As soon as I walked in the door, I saw how she'd spent the day. The dishes piled in the kitchen sink were gone. No crumbs remained on the counters, either. And I smelled furniture polish. What was she trying to prove? In the living room, she sat discreetly in a chair, wearing a skirt that looked suspiciously like one of mine, black, gathered and long, with a white tee-shirt I also recognized. I stared at her from the doorway for a minute before Nori called me over to introduce me to her friend, Susan Wilson.

Susan's hair was a kind of orange-blonde and she had what looked like a million freckles. Her aura was great. I loved her laugh. I decided to paint her, if she'd let me.

"Where are Helena and Hayoto?" I asked.

"She's showing him the barn." Nori's eyes had a knowing gleam when she told me. "Now you and Susan have met, I'm going to run upstairs and change into something cooler. I'll be down in a few."

Grace remained in her chair, sipping iced tea, while Susan and I got acquainted. After a few minutes, Helena and Hayoto came in, chattering away like life-long friends. I had no idea Helena spoke fluent Japanese. They switched to English as soon as they joined us.

Nori came downstairs and declared she was ready to go. From the worried expression now on her face, I guessed she was mentally bracing to face her grandmother. I smiled at her, hoping she knew Helena and I would be right beside her. Her parents would be, too, along with Suki and Paul and the rest of the family.

"Let the others go ahead, Grace. You can ride with me in the truck." I kind of surprised myself with that. I generally avoided being anywhere in Grace's proximity if I could help it. She looked surprised as well. "What happened with Henri," I asked after we'd buckled and were following Nori's car down the lane.

"Nothing special, I just decided the time had come for him to go."

"Really? As simple as that? He must have had something to say."

"He knew it was time."

Her hands were shaking and her voice had a brittle edge. I suspected she was beginning to miss her drug of choice. Whether the sex drug or the pharmaceutical drug, I didn't know—she was addicted to both.

I drew a deep breath. "Keiko and Suki are looking good these days."

She nodded.

"Virginia, too," I said.

"She won't be around much longer."

I looked at Grace and scowled. "Why do you say that? She's in good health. Lots of ninety-year-olds live another ten years or even longer."

Grace shrugged. "I don't know. It struck me when I saw her the other night."

Was it possible Grace got vibes about people, saw auras too? I didn't want to think of Virginia dying. She took up so much room in my heart. What would I do without her? We drove the rest of the way in silence. I tried to put missing Virginia out of my mind and mostly succeeded.

At the big house, we got out of our separate vehicles. Nori's expression had grown from worried to panicked. Helena took her hand and whispered something to her. Nori gave a nervous giggle. Susan, talking with Hayoto, seemed oblivious to the tension. We found them all on the terrace, Opal, Maddy, and their families included. Drinks in hand, they were all gabbing. A person would think they didn't run into one another or talk on the phone nearly every day. I wondered if Paul's story had reached everyone's ears. Not Grace's. I needed to tell her.

Amy spotted us first. She'd been talking to Suki, but when she saw Nori with Susan, a look of concern flitted across her face. She put down her wine glass and hurried over to greet us.

"Mother, this is my friend, Susan Wilson. Susan, my mother, Amy Sato."

Amy's smile was genuine as she held out her hand. "That's Dr. Susan Wilson, isn't it? Welcome."

Susan took Amy's hand and nodded. "Thank you. It's a pleasure to meet you, Mrs. Sato."

"Call me Amy, please."

"Okay, it's a pleasure to meet you, Amy. I love this house. It's wonderful, situated right here on the river. I'll bet it's a great spot for fishing."

"My father has been trying his hand every morning and evening since he and my mother arrived. Do you fish?"

"What true Idahoan doesn't?"

Nori stood between the two, her eyes going from her mother to Susan. Helena and Hayoto had already wandered off. Grace stood beside Paul's chair, silently pleating the black material of her borrowed skirt between her white fingers.

"Let me introduce you to my father," Nori told Susan. Arm-in-arm they strolled across the terrace toward Neal. Keiko, sitting between Suki and Virginia, stared after them, a line forming between her eyebrows.

I positioned myself near the three, my eye on Nori and Susan's progress as they stopped to talk with various family members, Susan's robust laugh occasionally ringing out.

Helena was on guard, as well. Though talking with Hayoto, her eyes constantly flicked toward Nori and Susan as the two made their way around the terrace, eventually arriving to stand in front of Virginia, Suki, and Keiko.

Nori spoke first. "Susan, I'd like you to meet my grandmothers, Virginia Sato and Keiko Ito, and my great-aunt Suki Franconi. This is my friend, Susan Wilson."

While Virginia and Suki welcomed Susan and murmured pleasantries, Keiko stared, her black eyes glittering. When she spoke, it was to Nori, not Susan. "I suppose this is the reason you've shown no interest in Will Davis or any of the other men I've sent your way."

Nori raised her chin, defiant as she nodded.

"Hunh," said Keiko. "You might have told me. I wouldn't have gone wasting my time."

I blinked. That was it?

Nori gawked at her grandmother, as dumbfounded as me. Susan extended her hand to Keiko. Keiko smiled and took it between both of hers. "Welcome, dear, it's a pleasure to meet you," she said.

I exchanged a look of wonder with Nori and Helena. We began to laugh, softly at first then the laughter spilled out and we laughed so hard tears started from our eyes. Probably because of all the emotion of the day, we couldn't stop, not even when Amy called that dinner was ready. Susan looked from one to the other of us, before smiling and looping her arm through Nori's. We followed everyone into the house.

Virginia's birthday dawned clear and bright, the mountains sharply visible on the horizon. I surprised myself by getting up early enough to catch the sunrise, beating Nori and Helena downstairs. When the coffee pot hissed that it was finished perking, I filled my cup.

Passing Grace's door on my way out to the porch with my coffee, I heard a moan. I stopped and listened. The sound came again. I knocked on the door. "Grace, are you okay?"

Another moan answered.

I opened the door and went in. Grace lay on the bed, covered in sweat. The twisted sheets were on the floor. "Grace?" I rushed across the room to her side. "Grace, what's wrong? Can I get you something?" I knew what was wrong, of course. I'd suspected the night before. She was coming down and her body was reacting to the absence of whatever she normally fed it.

"Go 'way. Le' me 'lone," she muttered.

I went to get her a cold cloth. Maybe coffee would help.

When Nori and Helena came down, we decided to call the hospital.

"They should be able to refer us somewhere," Nori said. "She needs to be monitored while her system dries out."

The place we were referred to was the same sanitarium Virginia had sent Grace in years past, and had her records in hand. She was still covered in sweat. Puke, too; the coffee had come up almost as soon as it went down.

"We'll take care of her," the admitting doctor said. "But you know, even after she's dried out, the likelihood of a relapse is high."

"I know. But for now, please get her as well as you can."

He nodded.

I said goodbye to Grace and told her I'd come back later and tell her all about Virginia's party.

She moaned and threw up again.

Back at the house, I discovered Helena and Nori were already gone. Nori had said she needed to meet the man with the barbeque wagon and check how the fire was coming for the planked salmon. They'd dug the pit by the river and would be burning branches of alder and cedar all day to build the coals to the right temperature. Helena planned to help set up. The party would be on the expanse of lawn between the house and the river.

I headed to my studio so I could cover the panels with brown wrapping-paper before loading them in the back of the truck. My thoughts, however, were on Grace. In her room that morning, I'd seen her aura for the first time—faint, but definite.

Tables, apparatus of various sorts and people were everywhere. Sand-filled paper bags with candles in them, to be lit when darkness fell, lined the terrace. Colorful flags flew from wherever they could be attached. Helena and Hayoto were hanging a large piñata from a tree branch. The Mariachi band was setting up by the river. A generator and a big fan filled a 'bouncy' house with air. A waist-high plastic fence formed a good-sized corral for toddlers, filled with toys, a sandbox, and a shallow wading pool. Food stands, the barbeque wagon and long tables occupied one entire side of the lawn. Fabulous aromas reminded me I hadn't eaten. I grabbed a hot dog from one of the stands and went to find out from Nori what she wanted me to do, though everything looked well in hand.

I found her sitting at a small table under a canvas pavilion, a cup of coffee on the table in front of her. A notepad lay open next to it, but she gazed off into the stratosphere, a tiny smile tugging at the corner of her lips. I sat across from her. "Nori, this is fantastic. I never dreamed all the things we talked about would come together like this."

She blinked and came back to earth. "They probably wouldn't have," she said with a laugh. "But when things got dicey, I got hold of a party planner. She's in one of my networking groups. She took me in hand and, voilà, behold a miracle." She held up both hands to express her surprise at the magic her contact had produced. "I hope you and Helena don't mind."

"Mind? Are you kidding? This is fabulous!"

Late in the afternoon, people began to arrive, farmworkers and their families, the children slicked and dressed in their best Sunday outfits, along with neighbors and longtime friends. I shook hands with people from Twin Falls, Jerome, and Eden, some of whom I hadn't run into since before I went away to school. Susan showed up. I thought again how much I'd like to paint her, maybe at her clinic, examining one of her patients. I waved to her. Later, I saw her and Nori together, walking through the crowd, holding hands.

Virginia sat on the terrace holding court, meeting and greeting old friends, all of whom wished her a happy 90th birthday. Like court attendants serving royalty, Keiko and Suki were seated on either side of her. Paul sat in his chair next to Suki's. I'd earlier explained about Grace, so didn't need to say anything more.

"Where's Mako?" I asked. "I haven't seen him for at least an hour."

"He's getting me another piece of that wonderful salmon," Keiko said. "Have you tried it?"

"I don't think there's anything I haven't tried—the salmon, the barbeque, the roast chicken, the tacos. I'm afraid if I had a bite of anything more I'd be sick."

Virginia scoffed. "You never get sick. I think your stomach is cast iron."

With Neal's help, I'd earlier brought the panels in from the truck and set them up in the den, still hidden behind their brown paper wrapping. "I have something inside to show the three of you."

Virginia clapped her hands. "You finished the project."

"Yes."

"This is likely to go on for several more hours. Let's go see—we won't even be missed." Virginia sounded as eager to view the paintings as I was to show them.

"I'd like Helena and Nori with us, too. And Hayoto." I wanted his professional opinion.

"Don't take too long rounding them up," Virginia said.

Easily said, not so easy to accomplish. Eventually we all trooped inside, me in the lead. Amy, Neil, and Susan joined us, too. "Wait here. I need to do something first." I darted into the den and tore the paper off the panels, wadded it up and threw it in a corner. "Okay, Virginia, Suki and Keiko—you first then everyone else can follow."

I stood proudly by my tribute.

Using pictures from when they were young women, a portrait dominated each panel. Virginia's showed her gazing down at the infant Bella cradled in her arms. Surrounding her were vignettes of the farmhouse, baby Bella with John

Sato kneeling beside her on the lawn, laborers in the field, the hay derrick being dragged to the fields by six horses, Marc at the reins, Neal, Maddy, and Opal sitting on the front steps of the farmhouse, an adult Bella and Bill McKnight holding hands, a bridge in Africa, Grace, me, and a painted tin soldier with a trumpet held to his upturned mouth.

The portrait of Keiko showed her standing in the sugar beet field, leaning on a hoe, a slight smile on her face, gazing at the distant mountains. Surrounding her were parts of old Japan-Chinatown and the Portland skyline, including its many bridges, Mako in front of his first garden shop, a courthouse, sailboats on the lake, Amy as a toddler and at the piano, as a young woman, and again with Neil, holding Nori, Nori in cap and gown.

Suki's panel showed her in the garden at the farmhouse with Paul sitting nearby in a chair under a sunshade, the house in Carmel Valley and the swimming pool behind, where Nori, Helena and I swam and played as kids, splashing water onto the surrounding garden and lawn, Paul's award-winning books, a bit of Stanford University, Rosie, Helena's parents, Helena in front of a computer and Helena at Thousand Springs Park, napping by the waterfalls.

Prominent, but not dominating each of Suki's and Keiko's panels were a watchtower and strands of barbed wire. In one corner of both Virginia's and Suki's panels was Lizard Butte.

The bad with the good—the lives they'd lived.

I stood silent, waiting for their comments, but no one said anything. I swallowed and my stomach suddenly felt like a stone had lodged in it. Did they hate them? Then I looked at their faces and realized they didn't need speech to express what they felt. Tears pooled in Suki's eyes as she gazed at all three panels. Virginia's eyes and Keiko's glittered as well.

Helena hugged me. "They're wonderful, Lily—your best work, I think."

Nori simply smiled and hugged me. Then she hugged me again.

Suki, voice soft, leaned over Paul in his chair, explaining the panels. As she spoke, Paul ran his fingers over the swirls of paint. Keiko and Mako examined each one in detail.

Helena tried to tell Hayoto what the things in the panels meant. She wouldn't be able to in one night. Explaining all that would take a lifetime.

Virginia came to stand beside me. "Lily, you couldn't have given us a finer gift. These are wonderful. Thank you."

I blinked back my own tears. "I'm glad you like them." I paused then said, "I'm going to take care of Grace."

Virginia closed her eyes and a long sigh escaped her. Her normally rigid posture slumped slightly as she took my arm and leaned against me. Her voice was husky with emotion when she spoke. "Thank you."

# Author's Note

Nishimi, Japan

I was privileged to know Virginia, Suki, and Keiko, and happy to share their stories, as they finally told them to me. They're gone now, as are Mako and Paul and John Sato before them.

Nori has a busy practice in Twin Falls. Amy and Neal are the besotted grandparents of Nori's and Susan's two-year -old twins, a boy and a girl. Both Nori and Susan are inexhaustible in the fight for gay rights and marriage equality.

Lily's panels are often on tour along with her other work, including a wonderful portrait of Susan and Cat, minus most of his tail. Grace fights to stay clean. When she fails, Lily is there to pick her mother up once again.

After an exhaustive search on the internet, neither Nori nor I could find anything about the missing Asian family. We searched through newspaper archives from all over the West Coast, where most Asians had lived at the time, but found nothing. It was as though the family never existed. At times, I wondered if they'd been a figment of my grandfather's imagination.

As for me, Hayoto and I and our four-year-old daughter have been enjoying a month-long visit with Lily, Nori and Susan. As usual, though, it is good to be home. Hayoto is in his studio near the factory, happily working on another marvelous creation, while I stay busy gathering stories and knowledge about this place I've grown to love.

Helena Franconi Abi
August, 2014
Nishimi, Japan

# About the Author
# TONI MORGAN

Toni came home to Oregon from a summer as an exchange student in Denmark knowing two things: she loved history, and she loved traveling and meeting new people. Her parents collected early-American antiques. By their measure, anything over 75 years of age qualified. The house of Toni's host family in Denmark was 400-years-old, and the church where her host-father preached was 800-years-old. She saw where battles had been fought and where Danes had lived ten centuries before she was born. It was a revelation. Her writing career began with that trip, keeping the editor of her hometown paper apprised of all she saw. A former NYT editor, he convinced her that she should continue writing. Although a west-coaster by birth, marriage, and preference, Toni has lived in many places, including nearly four years in Japan. That rich experience led her to write *Echoes from a Falling Bridge*, *Harvest the Wind* and *Lotus Blossom Unfurling*.
(http://authortonimorgan.com)